THE
NO
VARIATIONS

Originally published in Spanish as *Peripecias del no: Diario de una novela inconclusa* by Interzona, Buenos Aires, 2007.

First edition, 2013

Library of Congress Cataloging-in-Publication Data

Chitarroni, Luis, 1958-
[Peripecias del no. Spanish]
The no variations : journal of an unfinished novel / Luis Chitarroni ; translated by Darren Koolman. -- First edition.
pages cm
ISBN 978-1-56478-729-3 (pbk. : alk. paper)
1. Authorship--Fiction. I. Koolman, Darren, 1982- translator. II. Title.
PQ7798.13.H52P4413 2013
863'.64--dc23
2013001670

Partially funded by a grant from the Illinois Arts Council,
a state agency

This work was published within the framework of the "Sur" Translation Support Program of the Ministry of Foreign Affairs, International Trade and Worship of the Argentine Republic.

www.dalkeyarchive.com

Cover: design and composition by Mikhail Iliatov
Printed on permanent/durable acid-free paper and bound in the United States of America

THE
NO
VARIATIONS:
JOURNAL OF AN UNFINISHED NOVEL

Luis Chitarroni

Translated and with a preface by Darren Koolman

DALKEY ARCHIVE PRESS
CHAMPAIGN / LONDON / DUBLIN

Translator's Preface

"The writer doesn't really want to write, he wants to be; and in order to truly be, he must face up to the difficult challenge of not writing at all . . ."

Nicasio Urlihrt, the first name we encounter in *The No Variations*, and the writer to whom the quotation above is attributed, can never truly *be*, at least in the legal or corporeal sense, unless, that is, he rearranges the letters of his name and starts calling himself Luis Chitarroni. But Urlihrt is only one among a multitude of fictive entities the author of this so-called diary has created to do his scribbling for him, so that he can face up to the truly difficult challenge of *being* Luis Chitarroni.

Although largely unknown in the English-speaking world, in South America he's long been recognized as a prominent editor, literary critic, and author of exceptionally weird books. The first of these, *Siluetas* (Silhouettes), published in 1992, is a collection of satirical biographies of writers, both real and fictitious, that had previously appeared in the aptly named Argentine literary journal *Babel*. More ambitious in scope, his 1997 follow-up, *El Carapálida* (The Paleface), is perhaps the only book he's yet written that can properly be described as a "novel." Set in an elementary school in Argentina in the early seventies, it is in fact a pasquinade on the bourgeois pretentions and puerile rivalries among Buenos Aires writers and intellectuals at that time. For his next work, Chitarroni planned to write a hybrid of the preceding two. This "novel" would feature many of the "characters" from *Siluetas*, portraying them as members of a high-minded literary circle calling itself *Agraphia* and producing a journal of the same name to which its pompously erudite contributors would be required to submit their stories and poems pseudonymously. Chitarroni would of course be the "sole actual contributor" to this journal, all the pseudonyms being his own, for he wanted to lampoon the literary preciosity and cliqueism he observed first-hand among the self-applauding Argentine literati, and parody their common tendency of concealing a lack of originality beneath a veil of impenetrable difficulty. In order to do this, his "novel" would therefore itself be impenetrably difficult, the difference being that it would mock itself in its own making, laugh at itself, and encourage the reader to laugh along with it.

Of course, this novel was never written. Instead, in 2007, after ten years of planning, Chitarroni presented for publication a book entitled *Peripecias del no*, subtitled "Diary of an Unfinished Novel"— an *omnium gatherum* of obscure references, cryptic anagrams, parenthetical remarks, indecipherable aide-mémoire, overblown critical extracts, imperfectly-wrought poems, bewildering drafts of unfinished stories, characters with unpronounceable names . . . everything, in other words, a reader might expect to find in the diary of an impenetrably difficult unfinished novel, the result being a book that seems to resist all acts of interpretation—be it reading or translating—a book that, according to one Spanish reviewer, reads like a roman à clef that's been passed through a shredder.

As the translator of these shreddings, I was of course confronted with more difficulties than I'd have space to outline in a preface. The trouble it took to translate the title, for example, certainly augured what I was to encounter on every page of the text. The literal meaning of *Peripecias del no* is "Peripeties of No," but while the title works great in Spanish, in English, it is inkhorn. Next, I considered "The Adventures of No," which was definitely an improvement, but "pulpy" qualities aside, this seemed a little offhand, and didn't fully capture the several senses of the Spanish word *peripecias*. So, after deliberating on many other less satisfactory options, everyone concerned finally agreed on "The No Variations": "variations" is hardly an adequate rendering of *peripecias*, admittedly, but this did seem the best English language title for what was, in essence, a self-negating book—a book in which stories, poems, snatches of incomplete dialogue, critical extracts, biographical sketches, etc. are variously written and then rejected with a curt and peremptory "NO." Translating the subheading, "Diary of an Unfinished Novel," was less troublesome, except that, initially, it made me suspect Chitarroni was playing a kind of literary prank, especially on those readers and critics who love a difficult book. It was as if he were inviting serious readings of what was only a series of haphazard notes for a novel he had neither the time nor talent to complete, and, being unwilling to face up to the loss of time and effort, he'd submitted this aborted embryo for the scrutiny of demented anatomists, cryptographers, and cruciverbalists. This is, of course, decidedly not the case, as the reader will discover, although in an interview with *La voz*, Chitarroni did candidly and unabashedly admit that *Peripecias* was "the diary of someone who's probably lost his ability to ever again write clearly and coherently." This confession proved more than a little disconcerting to me, as it seemed to require that I ignore the editor inside me and purposely translate the book in the spirit of this diarist.

Besides the difficult prose, the many obscure allusions and references made me seriously consider including annotations on every page. But once I'd translated the first ten pages, I figured that even a partially annotated edition would triple the length of the book. Moreover, since the Spanish edition is bereft of a single merciful gloss for the reader, I was happy to disburden myself of the task, adducing the convenient excuse that readers shouldn't be deprived of the pleasure of uncovering for themselves the innumerable "buried keys" in the text. After all, readers today are lucky they live in an age when technology allows them to carry a million libraries in their pockets—a million electronic Virgils to guide them out of darkness into light. And, besides, I didn't want to encroach on Chitarroni's plans for a possible "sequel" to *Peripecias*, which he envisions will consist entirely of annotations to *Peripecias*, then another of annotations to these annotations, and so on, ad infinitum. Of the writing of books there is no end.

Despite frequently availing myself of my electronic Virgil, however, there were other challenges not even an Internet search engine could help me resolve, such as how to translate Chitarroni's Spanish imitations of great English language writers such as Henry James and Sir Thomas Browne. Of course, Chitarroni wasn't imitating James or Browne directly, but only their Spanish-language translators. The equivalent task would be if someone were to write an imitation in English of an English translation of Cervantes and submit it to a magazine or journal as an imitation of Cervantes himself. But, being only the English-language translator of Chitarroni, I had the unfortunate task of having, as it were, to back-translate an imitation of a translation—an exercise not unlike something a contributor to *Agraphia* might attempt. So, in both diction and syntax, I had to find the balance between outright parody and plausible imitation.

The greatest difficulty I faced, however, is one that plagues every literary translator: how to render seemingly untranslatable elements like slang, wordplay, etc. For example, when I asked Chitarroni to explain his use of the name "Falduto," he said it was supposed to suggest a henpecked man, or a man dominated by women. It is derived from the River Plate slang word *pollerudo*, but incorporates the more familiar Spanish word *falda* instead of the colloquial *rioplatense* term, *pollera*. Furthermore, "Falduto" was meant to suggest a similar word, *falluto*, which means a "discreditable, hypocritical man." After scouring every available lexicon, I finally thought it best to simply keep the original "Falduto" and explain its inclusion *here*, instead of providing an inadequate rendering of so peculiar a word. In general, though, I always strived to capture in English the various ambiguities of style and substance of the original, and avoid lazily settling on prosaic or banal compromises.

All in all, as strange as *The No Variations* will seem to readers, it's not a book without precedent: in Spanish, for example, Mario Levrero's *La novella luminosa* (The Luminous Novel), also makes use of the personal diary form to address the failure to write a novel; and in English, Cyril Connolly's *The Unquiet Grave*—written under the pseudonym "Palinurus"—is another fragmentary hodgepodge of quotation, allusion, personal reflection, and so forth. Although, admittedly, neither of these two books is as challenging as *The No Variations*, I nonetheless resolved not to condescend to the reader by providing too many explanations or oversimplifications—to lead her as a toddler by the hand, as it were—for I believe it is an error peculiar to many writers today that they often underestimate the diligence and perspicacity with which readers will endeavor to unlock a challenging text. Moreover, I think the continued popularity of so-called "difficult" novels attests that while the aesthetic of difficulty is often an end in itself among affected writers, discerning readers know that not every difficult book should be dismissed as affected simply for being difficult. Having now read *The No Variations* several times in the course of translating and editing, I was continually amused by its author's mock affectations, moved by his corybantic delight in language, and, despite the difficulty, I believe it has that quality proper to all fine literature, which Tertullian first noted of scripture: *semper habet aliquid relegentibus*, however frequently we read it, we shall always meet with something new.

I express my sincere gratitude to the author, Luis Chitarroni, for providing answers to my many "prayers" during the course of the translation, and for being so kind as to compliment the final result for its occasional "improvements" upon the original: he is a subtle god, but certainly not malicious. I also thank Jeremy M. Davies and the editorial staff at Dalkey Archive Press for their extraordinary insight in helping me to render faithfully into English this difficult though deeply rewarding text.

Darren Koolman, 2013

THE
NO
VARIATIONS

THE NAMES are the same ones that were around back in 1986, or possibly earlier (I can even recall an embarrassing note in some publication—I can't remember which—referring to them as "The Shanghai Group"). Nicasio Urlihrt, Hilarión Curtis—anagrams. Oliverio Lester. Inés Maspero. Cora Estrugamou.

Strong names, weighty even, although admittedly less so than the ones I used in my novel *El Carápalida* (The Paleface). Calvino notwithstanding, there won't be any lightness here.

Weighty, yes, grave even: like the leaden spirit of Enrique Luis Revol (I once defended him in a note on contemporary writers—although it was with little conviction, and only for the sake of argument). Must retrieve the book. Didn't lend it to anyone. Probably moldering away on the back-shelf of some library.

Revol *against the Crepuscular Spirit in Modern Poetry* (Pound)

An anthology collecting work published in *Agraphia* (Unwritten) [or *Alusiva* (Allusive)?], a journal exactly as old as me—since the first issue was published the day I was born—and to which, under various assumed names (pseudonyms, not heteronyms) I will of course be the sole actual contributor.

The anthology is edited by one Víctor Eiralis (a character I created for my book *Siluetas*—a collection of miniature biographies of authors both real and imagined—to introduce me to the works of his "shadow," W. Gerhardie) at the behest of Antonio Arguimbau, proprietor of a publishing house that's on the verge of being sold, and a compulsive womanizer to boot, who only agreed to publish it after he was seduced by Urlihrt's second widow. Eiralis writes the preface. There'll be an exchange of letters between editor and publisher inserted "by accident" at the back, as though to fill up space. Over the years, the original contributors will have become more or less famous, but at the time of their collaboration, none of the stories were signed. So Eiralis—a disgruntled drifter, typical among editors who've realized too late they've chosen the wrong profession—will have the invidious task of matching each story with its author. He happens to be the least suitable for the job, because he despises all of them.

Clausás. Julio Clausás

Lame: a lame anthology

Exergue: "Being familiar with many styles / he imitated all."
??? Aldecoa Inauda, presumed ancestor (of Eiralis or Urlihrt?)
Kleptolalia / Cryptodermia

Chronology of *Agraphia*: 1958–1999
Ages [as of circa 1974]:
Nicasio 49
Elena 46
Oliverio 34
Luini 22
Portrait by Fantin-Latour, *Coin de table*?

It's likely that people of such disparate ages wouldn't get along. Let the combination of disloyalties within the group provide insight into the secret/key to *Agraphia*: vengeance through anonymity, with a little help from plagiarism.

Aubrey

N. Urlihrt is short and stocky, but with a paradoxical softness; in fact, he's very gentle, glib (in every sense of the word), full of nervous energy, but soft as a cotton ball on the outside. Avoid emphasizing this last aspect. Avoid making him look like an ass.

He writes in longhand. Born in 1913 or 1914? Make it 1913, like Dad. A year older than Cortázar and Bioy.

Eiralis isn't tall. Need to make this clear from the outset. Is underfed, has all the hallmarks of undernourishment. Affects elegance to conceal indigence. Clothing: raincoat, checkered shirt, corduroy pants. Drinks Cubano Sello Verde. Campari. Bols gin. Domestic whiskey. Born in 1941?

Sabatani is tall. One of those lanky Italian types. He writes a short story called "Sircular Cymmetry" [not sure whether this text should actually appear in the novel], dramatizing the night *Agraphia/Alusiva* held its first meeting—without Urlihrt—as though this were as momentous as the night when, during a meeting of the Rosicrucians at Whitehall Palace, John Florio stood in front of an assembly that included the poet Philip Sydney, and translated some works by their honored guest, Giordano Bruno, about the possible existence of life on other planets, etc. (Details in Frances Yates, though sparse.)

Basilio Ugarte is very short. A sort of Juan-Jacobo Bajarlía. He has unusual eyes: pale blue, vacant—indicating (appropriately enough) both candor and malice. Fashion conscious. Small, insignificant, almost invisible: see the Bartlebyian short story "Janóvice" by Denevi . . . Does Beerbohm ever mention Enoch Soames's height?

Oliverio Lester is taller than everyone except Sabatani, behind whom he likes to lurk, and in whose shadow he's content to hide. As a clerk, or a beadle, or a beadle's clerk (did I get the word "beadle" from *Moby-Dick*?)—a bureaucrat through and through, in other words—he's the pet pencil pusher at *Agraphia/Alusiva*—that bordello of letters. He shuffles along with his briefcase pressed close to his chest, arms crossed, in the same solemn attitude as a Native American

(Iroquois?) carrying a peace pipe. Or were the Iroquois not a peaceful tribe? Let's say the Sioux then.

Crossword bordello.

Edition/Sedition. Sounds like a stupid hippy slogan from the seventies.

According to Benito (a mutual friend of mine and Abelardo Castillo's), one of them is a *ufologist*, like Borges, William Empson, and Benito himself. The first time I heard the word, I thought "ufologist" meant someone who played the euphonium in an orchestra. Ah, those good old hippy crackpots.

Good old Julian Cope!

The land where everything is possible (especially if it isn't true), because there's no such thing as criticism there. THD's (Toribio Hesker Dubbio's) niggling praise of Quaglia's novel (*Existential Resignation?*) is an obvious example: like one of those old Unitarian matrons, a grande dame who, having read her first novel, commends the author's diligence and intelligence for having brought its historical setting to life . . . and not merely a historical setting but a geographical one to boot—although lacking an appendix of fold-out maps, sadly. The kind of mordant observation the resentful Eiralis would make.

Beneath the sign of the capital [S]: sibilant, sinuous—more than deserving of those protective parentheses: brackets guarding against all the excess, malice, and falsehood in the world.

Luini isn't tall. Neither is he short. In fact, no one quite knows his height [see Kenner on Pound]. He's cynical, he's droll. And he lives in an age when this conjunction of qualities boils down to the single abominable adjective: intriguing. He edits, corrects— usually what's already been corrected. He practices the art of supererogatory copyediting.

Luini, a disciple of Leonardo. Opacity.

Dos is homosexual (*smart, camp, bitchy*). He's the first to extol the genius and glamor of the women in the group, their absent muses: Elena, Eloísa, Irena, Inés.

The painting is from the early seventies, based on the original photograph showing them all seated together at a table in Estrambote, a restaurant belonging to Dos (double, Charlie). Nicasio's prominent place in the picture is intended to highlight ["underscore," perhaps?] the position of Inés (Eloísa), who's attempting to imitate Rimbaud's pose in the F-L original, despite there being no *coin* in the frame. Nicasio sits with his barracan jacket slightly open, his hand reaching—in plenipotentiary gesture—for his wallet ("ample as a library," according to Dos) so he can pay the bill. To his left, Elena—slouched forward like a haystack—has a puzzled expression, her hand seeming to tug at a piece of thread, as if to unravel the solution to some cryptic name game; and seated next to her, the Dostoyevsky of the group,

Lalo (Sabatani), seems to be searching for a way out of the shot. Above left, in the top hat, Luini stands next to the leisurely Dos, who has a "silk scarf draped in modest abandon" around his neck, standing in stark contrast to the shy and bespectacled Prosan. Ah, and I almost forgot about the cadaverous figure of Belisario Tregua (or Basilio Ugarte?), seated bottom left. The photo was taken by Remo Scacchi, but the barely conspicuous watercolor hanging on the wall (deep down he liked to imagine that it was his own portrait of Elena hanging there, sketched in sanguine chalk) was actually painted by his brother. In the early stages of his painting, he took care to capture her likeness accurately, but in the end he succumbed, as he always did, to his annoying proclivity for disfiguring his work with brash and gaudy brushstrokes. Reckless Expressionism, I call it.

Eiralis describing either the first group meeting or the first group photo.

People like B[] P[] who, in his strict observance of Q's exercises in obedience, has become impervious to the teachings of Borges.

Another one smuggling in Glenn Gould under his shirt.

Who, because of his droning inanity, and making use of one of his own awkward metaphorical niceties, was given the nickname: "Luminous puree."

Lunar puree. Woolen puree.

Add after A.P. on the women who

Intersection of adulteries / collaborative writing

Some bit of idiocy, as in Guattari?

Analysis of the variations provided by only two options (remember, two wasn't even a number before Socrates [see the pre-Socratics, Barnes, Watts]): two bloodlines: two illnesses:

Aldecoa Inauda / Hilarión Curtis

Kleptolalia / Cryptodermia

And vice-versa: kleptodermia—cryptolalia

Oliverio's story about the Venus who repeatedly swaps her true form for human "furs" . . . Nicasio's instance of cryptolalia: the mute little brothers in his short story, "The Imitation of an Ounce."

Collaborative writing. Comprised of two varieties:
Analysis of all possible combinations
Plagiarism

Laurence Sterne / Lautréamont

Stewart Home / Bajarlía

Basilio Tregua / Belisario Ugarte

Incoherency / Contradiction. Postpone dealing with this for the time being.

Title of the first story: "Early"

Or else rename it "Too Late"? It's quite an old story (from back in '86, or earlier) about the wanton world of plagiarism, a two-dimensional world existing in a two-dimensional space, populated by ferociously competitive inhabitants with two-dimensional outlooks. It appeared in an anthology published by Monte Ávila of Venezuela, edited by Héctor Libertella.

Unease: there are always extenuating circumstances.

Strategic reassurance and remorse. Would like to include the sestinas on departure and return (formalist nonsense!)—and the short poems in English from *The B(achelor) in B(edlam)* that Charlie was so fond of.

I wrote "Early" for a meeting of *The Cause*—which was either a writer's group none of us founded or a magazine none of us launched, in order to fulfill the mandate to start such organizations that was issued by (cacophony of resentment) the magazine *El periodista de Buenos Aires* (ah, that brings me back!). And before that?

I think I was the only one who did his homework that time. The meeting was held in Charlie's flat on Independence Street (the one from Ignatieff's *The Lesser Evil*). Charlie, Alan, Chefec, Guebel, Bizzio, and myself. I remember them all going over the pages I typed on my mechanical Hermes while I waited, having nothing better to do. The Pole was the first to finish reading, or the only one who didn't give up. "I like it," he said, "I think it's very sentimental."

The capriciousness of memory. I can't imagine even Sergio or Danny being able to follow all this.

Speaking of Sergio, in *Trichinopoli* (a novel I was writing in jest while others were working on theirs in deadly earnest), the basic unit of currency was the "chefec" (derived, supposedly, from the phrase *check feckless coin*). Sergio B[izzio], who was always prissy and pedantic, told me he could never read a book with such a title. It's the name of a city in southern India, I puffed affectedly (being even more prissy and pedantic than he). There's also a brand of breadsticks called *Grissinopoli*.

Now let life obscure the difference between life and art.
—J.C.

Another reminder re: "Early": The Répide Stupía book the narrator plagiarizes is a collection of poems, not short stories. Same title, however: *Accents.*

The beginning [#5]

I won a literary competition with a story actually written by Francisco Répide Stupía. Every page of the story is basically a word-pimp's larding-on of obscurities and contradictions, the better to obfuscate the plagiarism—and written in a light tone to sugar over the gravity of the crime.

Although I'm not really a writer, I've had many things published in my name. I knew others who did the same: Marina Ipousteguy, for example, who spent the summer writing, living with a man who wrote. As soon as she stopped living with the man who wrote, she published a book of poems; the man who wrote is still writing, but now Marina lives with an architect who reads. The whys and wherefores of all this escape me, as they would anyone. But I'm not writing this to resolve them.

We'd been friends for quite a while, so, at Marina's request, I happily agreed to write the foreword to her book. Due to my interest in encyclopedic trivia, the more esoteric the better, I made reference to a seventh-century monk by the name of Cosmas, and his having written a book inspired by scripture, entitled *Christian Topography*, in which he denies the sphericity and oblateness of the earth, describing this heresy as a pagan superstition, and proposes instead a world shaped like a parallelogram, having one side twice the length of the other. Who knows where I find my factoids. I compared Cosmas's opus, which I'd never seen, to Marina's unavoidable [all-too-urgent, all-too-assertive] book . . . its exhausting pursuit of so much as a single idea. I wrote that Marina's book, entitled *The Estate of Heaven*—in which there wasn't a word that couldn't have been dispensed with—was a groundbreaking work, for it described on the verso and recto of each page a twofold world, a contingent rather than a necessary world: a cosmogony very like the one described in the *Topography*; that for Argentinian writers (having no choice but to implicate myself, since I'm a member of that tribe) *Heaven* would become an unavoidable point of reference. I also replied, in passing, to a comment made by Insúa Alvizur to the effect that our generation (the observation was a general one, but I took personal umbrage) would be condemned to merely aping our predecessors, to producing crude imitations of what others had done before us, if better . . . To making faces, as Insúa Alvizur put it: to putting on masks, not the least bit unsettling, because everyone's seen them before. I used as many quotations as could reasonably be included in a foreword (for, as we used to say, in order to shed light, we have no option but to cite). Whatever space I had left was devoted to the ever-shrinking world of Argentinian literary criticism, into which I take credit for introducing, in this piece, a vastly important term: "vestigial."

As soon as I sent in my contribution, I waited . . . waited, having sacrificed any last inclination toward fairness or sincerity, for Marina to call and say thanks. But she never did, so things went on as before.

All the characters from R.E.'s stories gather together in the end for the naming (of the story). What about the poems? A dilemma.

The stories of Francisco Eugenio Répide Stupía were written by a literary virtuoso in a style that betrays the recklessness of an apathetic plagiarist. Marina's betray the same quality of listless intensity, the better to conceal all evidence of her poems having been written in a shitty apartment complex in a city she liked to call "a principality of proles." Marina's primary preoccupation seems to have been with choosing words that sounded *nice* (and she had no trouble finding them—how acoustics betray us!), without regard for their definitions or the context in which they were to be used. If anything redeems them—their only saving grace—it is a certain stubborn elegance, what Charles Tomlinson called the *principle of gentility*, a certain exaggerated sophistication that persists despite all the solecisms. In the eighties, or anyway the early eighties, Marina started out—like so many of us—translating the poems of John Ashbery for this or that poetry journal. And, you know, it's still going on: for at least fifteen years now, no journal or review can call itself literary without printing at least one translation of a John Ashbery poem. Funny.

Marina's English, fortified by her years in East Anglia, Urbana, and Ann Arbor, where the various jobs she'd held had only helped fortify her ennui, proved a useful tool in translating all that imprecision, suspicion, and vagueness into an even vaguer Spanish, worthy of the local literary magazines, who are wont to applaud these qualities, mistaking them for ambiguity and semantic richness. Luckily, I got to know her while she was still free of those parasites of prestige, while she was still a perfect, irresistible ape of idleness, the sort of person Shakespeare (on whom, like so many others, Marina thought herself an expert) warned us about. If pleonasm is the soul of offense, at least I know when to shut up. For dignity's sake, if nothing else, I won't bother to spell out what anyone can imagine. Today, early became too late.

Répide Stupía's stories in *Accents* deal mainly with quotidian matters, trivialities, and yet no one seems to have noticed this. Peculiar: neither too French nor too Anglo-Saxon, neither too lyrical nor too narrative. The intention seems by and large to be the invocation—or evocation?—of an epic of dissimulation, a paean to the unheroic. Stupía's aesthetic: a parsimonious late Baroque, like Faulkner's Dixie Gongorism. There's a sequence in his book entitled "Surnames," among which is this mysterious poem: "The fewer words you seed by *your* design, / the more I'll cede, distort to fit my own. / I clothe my thoughts in lies, but halt, recede / each time I think our thinking coincides. // I've sealed our pact without your worn insignia . . ." etc.

Kilgore Trout, the Abe Lincoln of fictional characters. Vonnegut.

Basilio Ugarte / Belisario Tregua

Répide Stupía: called *Répide* simply because it's a name that's stuck with me since my days at the National Conservatory of Music, and *Stupía* after the artist Eduardo, of course. Basilio reports someone once called him "Rápido escupía!" ("swiftly spat")! Onomastic autonomy.

(Titles)

Accents

The Estate of Heaven

The name of Elena Siesta's (Cora Estrugamou's) father's company: *Ziggurat*.

The book is called *Accents* because Répide is preoccupied with the idea of "dramatic meter."

Other related organizations: Blamires, Haedo and Haynes (Hayms). Memi & Memi. Memi & Wuhl. Arrowsmith & Babbage. Babbage & Arrowsmith?

The law firm on Viamonte Street—Memi & Memi—employs someone's little sister: a scribbler of bucolic poems in her schoolgirl penmanship, which, to the law firm's embarrassment, have actually been published.

Marina Ipousteguy.

Friends: Judith, Honorata. Clarissa. The Death of Clarissa and Hudson.

At one of their homes, a touch-me-not, which bristled about you, *feeling* your presence, hemming you in. The first overtures of a carnivorous plant.

Perhaps a pitcher plant.

Marina. The way she speaks on the telephone. The way she laughs.

[Morecambe & Wise: their way of walking: like Robert Mitchum, John Wayne. Ladies' day: every Wednesday at the National Palace with my mom and sister. The Puig-like gayness or queerness I should try to include—because . . . etc, and then we'll have more culture (cf. Gerardo Deniz). A narrative. Norman Wisdom.]

Ways of looking at a blackbird. Ways of smoking in a literary salon.

What made me think of the day Inés died? I'd been up to her little roost many times, as had Dos, although I didn't exactly approve of her work. I liked her, or I liked that she didn't care as much about Nurlihrt as he liked to boast. No one (not even me in my foreword) ever mentions that she had a little mascot. In his diary, Nurlihrt wrote (with a nod to Chekhov) that it was a "paranoid Pomeranian." As if he could tell the difference between a dachshund and a mastiff, the old hypocrite! My sister said it was actually a Chihuahua, and she's known Inés a long time, having befriended her back in the old days of discotheques and pool halls. I myself think it was a Pekinese. Besides, Luini and I are the only contributors to the journal who know anything about dog breeds. The thing's name, though, escapes me.

Still, how could people neglect to mention the dog—be it a Pomeranian, Chihuahua, Pekinese, or even a Yorkshire terrier, for that matter—when her apartment was just a single room? There's nothing so indecent—as Pepe Bianco never tired of repeating—as rhetorical questions.

I'll never forget it. The first people the police allowed to enter were Dos and me—along with Nelly of course, her mother. Wilson, the doorman, let us in; he stayed on the threshold. The place was a temple to narcissism. There was a series of photographs taken by Richard and Charlie at Villa Gesell in which Inés is shown playing the coquette with everyone present—not only the two photographers, but also D.H., who just happened to be visiting the seaside village with a "friend," and then another of her in a Citroën, posing with the dog. The best photo in the apartment didn't feature Inés, however: it was a snapshot of Christopher Niaris, taken in motion, capturing the glowing snake trail of the cigarette perched greedily between his lips, evoking the beauty and cupidity of a man who couldn't be more different from Nurlihrt. Christopher Niaras was also featured in the largest picture we found, enshrined in a vanity cupboard—a black and white shot, *masterwork* of Calixto Mazzeloth—showing Niaras in his characteristic pose, pouting like a dandy Don Juan, though he was never interested in women; after which we were treated to a photo of a man who looked to be in his late fifties, with a profusion of white hair, wearing very thick glasses, behind which his farsighted eyes seemed full of his then-recent if premature diagnosis of cancer [colon]. *Meanwhile Sofía was sleeping with Scacchi, Eloy was sleeping with Niaras. Oh, God.*

The dog was running around with its tongue hanging out, moaning and groaning; Eloísa called such behavior—when Nurlihrt was out of earshot—*convulsions of canine delight. Entre nous,* her exuberant flaunting, her canorous bays, are they not in fact . . . symphonies? All of us are prone to exaggeration. Soon, Schnabelzon, her psychiatrist, arrived. We'd met on a number of occasions, because he was something of a bohemian, or anyway liked to seem like one, if only until, like Cinderella, the clock struck twelve. Dos was fawning all over him.

a) It was summer. She waited until midnight, as for [adultery, ennui, self-denial?], before taking a non-prescribed dose of Tryptizol, and smoking a joint, or as she used to say, "killing her daemon": the servile attitude she used to have as a writer, the ignorance she once flaunted; her anxiety as to how future generations might view her works—the links of her life as irregular as the beats of a headless dactylic line. "Dreaming with Tears in My Eyes" (Jimmy Rodgers). Bags packed, opaque. She went to bed thinking something would interrupt it, this filthy business; that Nurlihrt would call and wake her. The noise of the phone, the next link in the chain, the dream that would in fact go on without her.

The certainty of being disturbed:

[*That the sound of the telephone would still be heard through death's muffling hands. That something would eventually wake her from her sleep. Nurlihrt, the telephone, whatever. That there would be another link in the chain. That the sound of the phone would be louder even than death. Yes, louder than the sudden, if expected, vertiginous, deafening hands of death.*]

b) She'd fallen asleep listening to a song by Laura Nyro: "And When I Die" . . . How obvious! If the so-called experts had paid attention, or at least understood a little English, they'd have realized it wasn't just the note that indicated Inés's intention to die.

The dog was running around. On the nightstand, some books: Dickson Carr's *He Who Whispers*, Marguerite Duras's *La Vie tranquille*—in a Spanish translation by her Avellaneda school friend—Henry Miller's *The Colossus of Maroussi*. . .

[*The Woman Who Rode Away*, by D. H. Lawrence. A Corso or Ferlinghetti anthology. *L'âme romantique et le rêve*, by Albert Béguin. *Pale Fire*, the poorly bound South American edition, with an inscription furiously scribbled in HB pencil: "It's no use, I feel sorry for N. and the kids, but I just can't read it."]

The lessons Nurlihrt had intended to give her weren't enough. Nothing is for so short a life. Inés persisted in reading the worst translations, forgetting all the French she learned at the Lycée, her enthusiasm for Charles Trenet and Jacques Brel. In the typewriter was a page on which was written what one would have to consider a poem—hardly a last will and testament, since it had line breaks and didn't respect the margins. [It was difficult to remove: four carbon sheets were in the way]. Having torn it out, I compared the contents with those of the letter that was brought by the youth. The Hermes Baby typewriter had a font that imitated the childish curlicues of a schoolgirl's penmanship—but this was typical of Inés. Nurlihrt was the one who showed me her final drafts.

Of life, The Illness questions death

And someone says: Of nearly all there is of life . . .

Nothing suggests evil does his rounds like a beast

Without a spoor. The dog bites. If only Dos had noticed

As he left—that I die—

The illness won't deny.

But didn't the others notice?

Before dropping, the elevator door

Will have shut, my reach unnoticed.

A mess indeed: it was the Colasiopo brothers' Dalmatian that bit her.

For some reason—I can't recall what—it was necessary to head downstairs, so the three of us all went down together. Dos was fawning all over the psychiatrist again, particularly there in the elevator, but it was hard for me to feel comfortable around Schnabelzon, particularly there in the elevator. I remember timidly lowering my eyes and noticing his two-tone shoes. (I'm not sure what Doctor Marañón would say on the matter, but I've always thought that two-tone shoes were a form of orthopedic substitution, popularized to make up for the loss of spats; or else, with porteños anyway, to serve as twelve-inch *godemichés* to compensate for a similar lack.) He trimmed his moustache with obsessive care, like an actor from the forties. The elevator door opened on a young man. The fashions of the day didn't especially flatter any of us, but they seemed to have singled this fellow out for a particular savaging. Beneath his ample mane—which seemed to grow more outward and upward than downward—was a face adorned with metal-rimmed glasses, eczema, and a smile at once genial and glum. He wore a coat that was two or three sizes too large, a patterned neckerchief, low-rise corduroy bell-bottoms, and clogs. He approached us as if he knew us. Dos embraced him. As if he was an old friend. An intimate embrace, with every sort of clasp and clap, suggesting a practiced ritual, an oft-repeated rite. Afterward, Dos turned to me and said he felt sick. *How is it possible?* asked the kid. *How?* Only yesterday Inés had spoken to him, written to him . . . He had, folded up at the bottom of his coat pocket, her final piece of correspondence. We were standing just outside the elevator door, in the lobby, when Dos asked anxiously, "Has anyone told Nicasio?" immediately heading off to look for a payphone. Then, after pushing the doorbell first with thumb alone and then with the weight of his entire body [seek and ye shall find], in hopes of getting a look inside, a short gentleman entered (no doubt buzzed in by the doorman, Maglio, Wilson, the Uruguayan knew him) wearing a big raincoat and bearing a bouquet of flowers. On seeing us seeing him, he reacted with a "what gives?" sort of look, as Elena would have put it, before asking us "what happened?" Schnabelzon told him everything, and, turning to us, introduced the guy as "Doctor Perete." I had no idea who Doctor Perete was, but he offered us each a mint, as well as a consoling arm to the kid whom Dos had hugged, behind whose smile he detected, with professional keenness, a need for consolation. Then my sister arrived, also with a bouquet of flowers. What happened? Why had I called her at the office so early in the morning? Inés was dead. They supposed it was suicide. How was that possible? It was possible. It was enough to go up to her flat to see that much. Who else was up there? Did Oliverio know yet? What about Nicasio? Doctor Perete asked her if she was an acquaintance. My sister said NO, as if she was ashamed, as if she wanted to deny their relationship. Dos returned from his attempt to contact Nicasio with what looked like a pair of rent boys he'd picked up along the way. Not a bad day's work. The nearest payphone had been in a restaurant bar called 05 in Paraná in front of the plaza. It turns out the rent boys weren't Dos's latest conquests but actually two of Inés's neighbors, Richard and Charlie, who'd been having breakfast at 05 where they were informed of the tragedy. Dos hadn't been able to get through to Nicasio. Neither did he manage to get the whole message through to Astrid, because he got cut off and found he was out of change—likewise the two other guys. [One Christmas, they knocked on Inés' door to invite her over. Even their flat was bigger than hers. But she was on her own with no other company than the Winco turntable on which she was playing "Christmas" by the Who . . .]. They invited us up to their flat, the one opposite Eloise's, and so the retinue ascended ["we ascended"?] in three groups distributed between two elevators and a stairwell.

Their apartment, which was a little larger than Inés's, had a lounge, a single bedroom, and many framed photographs on the walls. In the early seventies, to own such expensive property could only have meant that one of them "came from money" . . . Charlie, the younger of the two, slept in the lounge. He was always pottering about picking up items of clothing, worrying about what would happen to Inés's dog, Carolo. I remember his older brother, Richard, objected to the notion that they "adopt" him on the grounds that . . . But Charlie said it was only right, that it was the human thing to take care of the

19

dog. They were both less than eloquent, as far as their diction, but of the two, Charlie was the better speaker. The intercom buzzed. Richard looked up and said dismissively, "It's nothing, it's only the knife-grinder." Dr. Schnabelzon recognized a former patient of his in one of the wall-photos. "My stepfather," said Richard. "He lives with my mother in Ibiza. He's an artist [reference: Banyalbufar, Majorca]." The door opened on Ivan, with Carolo in tow. He was barking. "I'm going to lock him in the bathroom." Peculiarly, the barking made the kid with the glasses start crying. Dr. Perete said, "He was a gift from me, you know." The kid turned off the waterworks. "Or, rather," the doctor went on, "I provided [gave her] the money to buy the dog [him]." The kid hiccupped, swallowing his tears. "I was told Nissus got her the dog," he said accusingly. Dr. Perete wasn't a man too much troubled by details. "I was getting to that, young man, I was getting to that," he said reassuringly. Carolo was howling. "I'll get the plastic bone Inés used to give him," said Charlie [[innocently or with malice aforethought (thoughtlessly or out of a sense of duty)]] and went back out. The contrast between the doctor and the kid, which Dos and I never tired of evoking, was notable: the kid—thin as a stick figure, sickly green in complexion, in temperament brittle as glass, unsteady in his clogs, nervous at the prospect of having to walk in them, insecure due to having already stumbled many times, and [above all] for having done so in front of so many people, in front of us mourners—had obviously been in love with Inés, and even seemed to have gotten some encouragement in that regard. It was something in Inés's helplessness that had brought them together, though what he would or could have admired most—as did we all—was the way she kept her vulnerability so discreet. Old Dr. Perete, on the other hand—short enough to rub shoulders with a midget, bald enough to share hairdressers with E. T., with a spine so misaligned he seemed perpetually to be staring at his shoes, and yet so full of nervous energy that anyone would have thought he was perhaps possessed of that prime-of-life, that "sexualidad perfecta" as described by the aforementioned Dr. Marañon—was also in love with her, but didn't show it, or didn't want to be seen showing it.

He told us that the breakfast ordered last night as compensation for adultery wasn't enough. And the administrator, Falduto (significantly in debt), my sister's future father-in-law. Extensive lobbying

The loose modality, the essential tolerance of the novel form invites pleonasm. NO—see the shift in narration from first person plural to third person omniscient in Flaubert's imitators (Bovary's pups), almost imperceptible if done skillfully.

Article in Lacanian journal: "The Scopic Drive and the Wandering Quest for the I."

Contest. A *Downbeat* "Blindfold Test." Charles vs. the narrator.

After all his many occupations and avocations, we finally arrive at the truth, the ultimate truth about Charles: jazz. His fanatical competitiveness—the pure form of that same quality which, more often than not, leads instead to enforced mediocrity among Argentine intellectuals—knows no limits.

Around the time María Elvira was captivating me.

—And do you recognize this one?

I had learned to adopt a poker face in this situation, whether the song in question was obvious or obscure, because my answering in the affirmative (or, I imagine, at all) seemed to send him into a profound depression.

Luckily, it was one of those Miles Davis records some of my other friends had bored me with before.

—*Kind of Blue*, I said.

I even managed to identify a piece by Chet Baker—thirty years since he'd last been "cool."

—Ah, but what about this one?

I listened attentively for a moment. John Coltrane, I told him.

—The dove is mistaken, cooed Charles triumphantly—and what

about this one . . . ?

It was a question of saving face. I didn't want to compound my error, but went all-in just the same. I tossed out all the names I knew, like a juggler with his pins, but I still managed to get several wrong in a row, mistaking Johnny Hodges for Ben Webster, Archie Shepp for Ornette Coleman, Cannonball Adderley for Albert Ayler, and Sun Ra for Lester Bowie, all to Charles's great amusement, as I went on trying both to win and to lose—hoping in this way to win either my friend's respect or, barring that, his gratitude.

—You're a phony. And Marina even told me you write a music column for *El Canditato Gauche*! The Madagascan Candidate, more like . . .

—I focus on rock.

—That's no excuse. Still, it must be hilarious. [a riot]

Then he made another thrust. Thankfully, I knew this one too. His selections were getting worse and worse. John McLaughlin, Mahavishnu Orchestra—a nightmare from which musical history is still trying to awake, and which continues to baffle and horrify neophytes. And then, my most reviled band of all: Weather Report. What they used to call "Fusion," a decade or more ago. All these played on a Revox turntable with tangential tonearm.

After the last piece (embarrassingly, I'd nodded off after getting another one wrong), I said:

—This one sounds like one of those interminable Beatles gag-songs, like "You Know my Name, Look up the Number . . ."

—No, you Neanderthal. It's Mingus.

—I may write for a jazz magazine, but I did say it was a rock column . . .

Sad skin of the universe / *Triste piel del universe.*

Then: Morecambe & Wise / Gilbert & George. Dream sequence.

Second story: "St. Mawr."

Vera Villalobos fax about what not to miss in London.

The D. H. Lawrence story Leavis was so enamored of (and, like-wise—though [Y.W., J.W., D.T.F., W.S.?] didn't mean to let this slip—Octavio Paz), and from which I derived no pleasure at all. Was I even capable? Have another look.

Get the cheap Penguin paperback. It has another story or novella included under the same cover. A no-frills sort of edition.

Kitaj's *The Londonist.*

Note: as I've already stated (I think), I read "St. Mawr" in the village of Tor, Spain, in an Argentinian edition with the title *La mujer y la bestia* (The Woman and the Beast).

Detective Stories

>   Venus Cascabel

>   Venus Rattlesnake

>   Regina Constrictor

Vernon Gish

>   Bruce—Bruno—Terrier

>   Inés

>   Completes first edit in Basavilbaso—

>   He worked as if piecing together court records (here or in La Plata?)

>   Nail-biter, like Ada

>   Ways of dining, both indoors and out

>   Maspero / Betelgeuse.

>   Basilio Ugarte

>   Someone confuses Basavilbaso with Virasoro.

Deafness: as used by Kermode.

O Viamonte. Ob-viously

Parallel confusions (i.e., the same ones): Barnett Newman / Wallace Stevens. Additionally: Jakobson on Nabokov. Samuel Butler / Pessoa: lies as imprecision.

Others: Lino and Lalo Scacchi. Remo Sabatani. *Eloi eloi lama sabachthani?*

Time to decide on our own, true name for Dos, a.k.a. Delfín Ambrosio Hurtado Iriondo. A transcription of the process. The minutes from some kind of rite or ceremony of initiation:

> *The Quintain*
> *The* . . . have a look in Chatwin and Pessoa
> *The Invunche*
> *The manipanso / maniputo / African fetish*
> *The Go-Between(er?)*
> Committee members present: Elena, Nicasio, Belisario.

And once you've come up with a good name: sell the rest, settle for the leftovers.

Parsnip & Pimpernel (Waugh): Auden & Isherwood.

Central committee, without Nicasio. "Sircular Cymmetry." Liturgical glossary. Lycergical glossary. The noise of many glossaries

The journey. List

Cheap Penguin edition: *The Virgin and the Gypsy.* The cover of *La Mujer y la bestia.*

Passive apnea: Monitor / Merrimac.

The passive voice, using "one" as a third-person pronoun.

What goes around comes around / Snowball.

The story of my friends visiting the dying Virgilio Piñera. Modest porteño scene of a man sitting at his desk writing, a scene very much like the one in that Kubrick film where a Marcos Zucker lookalike (Krapp?) is writing a book with the same title as the movie (or, anyway, the book on which the movie is based). With an Angolan nurse (male). Disease located right there. The comment: "What goes around comes around." The lumbar religion (Nurlihrt *dixit*).

Sluglike. Non-peristaltic virgin.

A pinnacle of elegance vs. the Mamarracho.

First catalogue of stories (written and partially written):
Early
The Imitation of an Ounce
The Scent of Thunbergias
America (The Fasting of Lourdes?)
Occupation (after Henry James)
Returns
The Old Bachelor
Semblance
Replicas
The Xochimilco Diary
Out of a Greek Gift
Did he Reach Thirteen?
Arriving Late

After Ibiza, we lived in Barcelona, where Elena had family. Hoards of cousins—both the docile and delinquent kinds. Mansions with outdoor swimming pools, omniscient beggars in the Gothic Quarter. Our short visit to Pere Ausic, a distant relative, who signed his name Zeuxis, posing not only as a sodomite but a sculptor (though his strong point was drawing), delighting in trivial cryptograms and impenetrable *repentismos*—songs with improvised lyrics. It was hard following him, but afterward, we were able to repeat a few of the things he'd come out with: something (a fib) about the Catalan painter Ramón Casas, and something else (a bon mot) about Sunyer. We didn't stay long, with our responsibilities moored like sailors at a riverbank, growing impatient; the sea beckoning them.

We went to Madrid alone, leaving our friendship with Eduardo Manjares behind. We visited an antique store and "ran into that specimen of graying Spaniard who knows a lot about diving suits," said Elena, "and who was asking us about books by some Argentine pornographer we'd never heard of." This anecdote always ended with us back at home, faced by Dos's wide, disbelieving eyes, and/or skeptically amused expression, after which he would proceed to explain the relationship between the pornographer in question and his avuncular herald [brother of the father of the protagonist-narrators in "Replicas"].

When we arrived in London, following Sebastian Birt's handwritten guide, it didn't take us long to realize we were lost.

Nicasio Urlihrt, *Diary*

"Dead Aunt's Diary" in "Out of a Greek Gift"?

A woman with her feet freighted in a new pair of shoes, growing impatient, the nails of a nautical excuse chewed away. Fingernails, that is.

To go unnoticed, as Aira once was; like Pizarnik; like Raúl Gustavo Aguirre.

Three intersecting diaries: the dead aunt's (Inés?), Nicasio's, and Xochimilco's (Prosan, Luini?)

The story by ??? In the "detective magazine" with the mask . . . ?
Black Mask. Haggard.

Elena / Teodelina

They were so alike that seeing them together compelled people to spout similes as well as point out the differences between them. Mere shades, nuances. Today's jasmines compared with those of days before.

Nurlihrt, a professional, had photographed them while they were asleep. They posed before the incubus, each with the same expression of docile acquiescence.

Do away with similes, as Flaubert wanted (this is in the letters, Louise Colet, look up)

Stendhal in *Muse and Thinker.*

Voices

Dress rehearsal

(baton, throat-clearing)

Agraphia / Alusiva, a journal founded by Nicasio Urlihrt (Emilio Mario Teischer) and his wife, Elena Siesta, with anonymous—or at the most, acronymous—contributors, to publish the best literature (statement of purpose rather than fact) according to the couple's own criteria. Their penchant for pseudonyms, which an essay in the first issue would account for with the phrase *ad usum Delphini*—in other words, for the education and diversion of the young, with an eye toward use in institutions of higher learning—was a [judicious] challenge issued to their era, as well as a source of wildfire gossip (with its usual roll call of the relevant phantoms, quotations, and parenthetical remarks). Urlihrt adduced a controversial synthesis of Giordano Bruno and Giambattista Vico to exculpate the culprits [and conspirators], and, at the same time, to demonstrate that creation and corruption are the same thing. From the middle of the last century to the beginning of this, *Agraphia / Alusiva* was, by and large, the leading exemplar, epitome, and promulgator of this bogus proclamation.

Agraphia / Alusiva, a journal founded by Nicasio Urlihrt (Emilio Teischer) and his wife, Amanda Corelli Estrugamou (Elena Siesta), intended to be entirely anonymous. It was to publish only the best literature, at least according to the couple's criteria. Their preference was for the use of pseudonyms—a legitimate reflection of their era's zeitgeist (and the cause of wildfire gossip once word got out), but a flimsy screen when subjected to serious critical scrutiny today. The contributors were known for—or ignored thanks to—the heresy they'd committed, and of which they took every opportunity to boast, even calling themselves "the writers without stories." They went around publishing books espousing the theory that it's better to simply write stories than to write about the writing of stories, and to illustrate this, they simply wrote stories. Few readers remember those stories today, but many recall the anecdotes associated with [adjacent to?] them. [Such that] Forgetting is not so serious an affront as long as we remember what it is we've forgotten. If it were [it was?] ever to become necessary to exonerate [the coterie, the conspirators], Nurlihrt would just publish a series of [unsigned] editorials to adduce a controversial synthesis of two seemingly incompatible theses, and at the same time, [to] proclaim that generation and corruption are one and the same. From the middle of the last century to the beginning of this, *Agraphia / Alusiva* was the evangelizing force behind this and other forms of casuistry.

Eiralis the Prologist, at arms:

Mar del Plata, 23 April, 1899 [sic]

Dear D. Julio,

Now that you've explained "the project," I'm less inclined than before to accept "the commission"—please excuse the scare quotes, but in this case I feel they are entirely necessary. I know that some of your best friends would, if having this conversation aloud, take the opportunity to pinch vulgarly at the air with their forefingers as they spoke, to make their disdain for such terms as evident as possible.

Of course I've heard of *Agraphia*; I've even had the dubious honor of being invited to work with the people "behind *Agraphia*," and the pleasure (although I didn't tell them it was so) of declining their invitation—a piece of information you should keep to yourself (like a whisper in your ear . . .).

I'm neither "proud" nor "flattered" that the Urlihrt estate is apparently so "flattered" and "proud" concerning the prospect of my "editing and introducing" the book in question, and look, I seem to have used more of those inevitable quotation marks, but then I would never have known how to word this long sentence if you hadn't yourself provided the—borrowed or invented—vocabulary. Don't forget, although I'm now a learner, I started out as a teacher, same as Nurlihrt and Quaglia. Well, thank the widow in any case for putting my name forward. (But do your best not to antagonize her—I know how bad your temper is, but she's got a chorus line of family lawyers on retainer.)

In any case, I'm getting by fine here, doing odd jobs, so am not nearly desperate enough. Still, if the book's already been signed on, I thought of two people who might do the trick. You know them, they're old colleagues: Inés Macellari and/or Corvalán's missus. (By the way, did you know that our old dictator Juan Manuel de Rosas's aide-de-camp was one General Manuel Corvalán? Go tell that to your "historical" editor, and if anything comes of it, be sure to send me my percentage.)

Anyway, I do appreciate the gesture and offer you my warmest regards,

V.

(The epistolary Eiralis . . .)

Belisario Tregua (or Basilio Ugarte) in a new draft of "Early":

"Say that again. Can't you see I'm hard of hearing? What was it? Glorify him? Vilify him? I met Robert Lowell here, you know. Now there was a man whose head practically glowed in the dark, a real bundle of nerves. Truly a magical thing, that brain of his—a brain that absorbed experience so rapidly the price was an early death, too early a death—with language blindly battening away at the pulp and marrow of his faculties, at all remaining potential, promise . . . I'm quoting someone or other. Look, I don't know if it was the same Salas. I told the CIA everything that went on. And I'm still pimping for my friends even today. See, right here in my briefcase I have the depositions of two friends who want to get a divorce. And look, these aren't newlyweds. But now they've come around. And believe me, they're doing the right thing. That's why I never got married—seeing my parents fight all the time. It'd be hell, no? My two friends say just the same. They live to ask me favors. And it's like people say, no good deed goes unpunished. Anyway, he asked me to translate a Russian story—from the French. And now he's asking me—because the publisher asked *him*—to retranslate it into a kind of Spanish flea-market slang. Christ, the shit they expect me to swallow . . ."

Bambi in *St. Mawr*

"It's all very well saying 'the sixties,' Mr. Rico, but the sixties weren't really the sixties for those who survived them. Looking back on them, now, from my place in the attic [of my life], I regard them with more astonishment than nostalgia.

"I made my debut in some provincial company, as an understudy. My stage name was 'Cyprian.' At fourteen, I was already capable of following Israel Regardie's regimen of anorexia and vomiting—so fashionable today.

"Soon I joined a traveling theater company, The Serendipitous Ashram, which staged plays, among other happenings. You know, Mr. Rico, as someone once said, all is change in this world—except avant-garde theater. So we started doing group improvisations, with disastrous results. In Amsterdam I almost got deported, though in Hamburg we had such a successful premiere that I stayed in Germany for three years. Then I started my solo act.

"They said the way I walked was like a dance, like the way Edie Sedgwick moved. And I used to mix LSD and cocaine, also like Edie [Sedgwick]. I would stay in Almería from time to time. By then the original company had disintegrated, each member going his own way. I worked in a bunch of movies, as an extra or in minor roles. I remember one movie scene in particular, a scene we rehearsed so many times—I don't even know how many times, perhaps a hundred—until it came out right. And it was so right, Mr. Rico, that I still feel proud whenever I see it today. In it, I'm standing in line with my brother, an attractive if unkempt boy, and we have to pass a message to one another during a funeral. To do this, we file past the coffin and cross ourselves in a particularly elaborate manner. If you ever get to see it, I'm the third in line—after my so-called brother and grandmother.

"I shouldn't have left Germany. After all, I was getting on quite well with the language, working myself into real verbal ecstasies. Rainer played the sax behind me, and I fell in love with him, then I fell in love with his best friend Brian. I wasn't ambitious, just couldn't sustain it, but Brian [Colin] was just the same—a Briton, he'd inherited a small fortune and some property in Islington, so by the early seventies, I found myself living in London again. And let me assure you, far from how it might appear to most adult mammals of our species, it isn't the best place to live. Perhaps the seventies wasn't the best time to be alive, Mr. Rico. I felt just like Ziggy Stardust did—or would."

Suddenly, the rather unfriendly James of St. Mawr, agitated and taciturn, sat down by us, but didn't participate in the ongoing conversation. He was supposed to come and collect us. But we hadn't imagined he'd arrive so early.

"I went back to Brian's home, Mr. Rico, but there was always something wrong. We would argue about this or that, and I'd think to myself, 'At least I've got a guy on the side.' I think real women must have other options. Nonetheless my lover was the unhappiest man I ever met. Lord Swindon—excuse my sighs—wrote an entire book just to show off—not just to me, but to a proper audience!— his clandestine love. Poor deluded man! He called it *The Naked Bed* and it was a complete failure. He went on writing other books, of course—*Loud City, A Beetle Called Greg*—as I'm sure you remember. And, soon enough, he'd found another lover.

"As for me, Mr. Rico, my high point and low met for the first

31

time like two stray dogs in the street, sniffing at one another then . . . humping, do you say?—a spectacle, to be sure, but by no means spectacular."

I have the worst ear in the world. The music was the same sort you'd expect to be broadcast on any FM station in the world. But Bambi gave me a special look whenever the first few bars of a Fleetwood Mac song began.

"Cocaine and adultery, those were for the eighties. I was ahead of my time."

I was ecstatic, couldn't take my eyes off her—her redskin profile, her Adam's apple.

"It's not me, Mr. Rico, but desire that's grown stale. Become old. I began to realize this in Rio about four years ago. I was on the beach one day and was suddenly overcome with boredom. The bodies I saw did nothing for me, they looked like barely distinguishable mannequins as they passed . . . and I remembered . . . The world is a grand, rickety monument erected by some mediocre architect, but the truth of the flesh was carved by none other than Phidias . . . That's what my Catalan friend used to say, Mr. Rico, a man far more interested in the subject than either of us, these days. But in that vaunting statuary, that beacon of human flesh, there was no substance, no delight, no heat. How I would have preferred to lick, bite, and suck at those delicacies until I choked to death, turned blue. Drowning, asphyxiation, cyanosis, are triumphs in comparison with the slow apnea of mere survival. The sublime course of the shark—I say, très chic. But there's nothing special about dying for love. Merely surviving as time goes by is the 'done' thing, these days. And, despite appearances, Mr. Rico, I followed suit. Swallowing my saliva, holding my breath, and heading to bed early."

We toasted again. She and I were drinking gin and vodka, respectively, and practically straight up—on a single rock each. We said all there was to be said in all those languages in which nothing need be said . . . But the clink of our glasses added little to these interjections. We might as well have been hoisting a couple of milk jugs in broad daylight.

"Our sins, Mr. Rico, are only of concern [and only start to matter to us] once we've stopped sinning. Then we reap our so-called reward. The preacher who married my mother made that quite clear. And so I'm always vigilant, always alert. I ended up going to Brazil with Mr. Quint, Basil Quint, Hugo's cousin—a businessman, among whose many deals during that time I'm afraid I would have to be counted [as] the least significant. Basil always went on his business trips weighted down by new theories regarding this and that: I used to call them his "carry-on baggage." For instance, he used to say the highest aspiration of any decent and honest citizen is to be a tourist, and also . . ."

Ignorance, license, laziness: who among them could so much as recognize it, who among them could take the hint? Not a single one of them: the gentleman of the jury! They knew all about what everyone was reading without ever bothering to read (let alone memorize) a single poem, a single line. The possibility that ordinary, quotidian language might ever be found in a poem didn't amuse them in the least—or even make much of an impression. The gulf separating us wasn't just a matter of passive consecration and active anonymity; it was in the view that the act of reading is an exercise in forgetting (the nuisance, the burden) all that doesn't pertain to oneself. And the things that pertain to *them* are prizes, tributes, reviews—more incentives not to read. And they wouldn't—they wouldn't read my book; they'd read *me*, or rather my *pseudonym*: Atrius Umber. And boy, he's sure racked up the points for me while I wait here in the dark; enough for them to hand me the prize. Moreover, I seem to remember having presciently, preemptively, commended the four of them—in reviews, in post-award speeches—with all the astuteness and patience of someone who foresees—is investing in—receiving a favor in return, someday. The conspiracy of gratitude would unfold in the Silvio Astier Amphitheater.

In this sense, *Accents*, Répide Stupía's book, was nothing more than the flimsiest pretext, but the best one possible, under the circumstances. Irreproachable on formal grounds, it had the virtue of going unnoticed initially due to the author's misanthropy. But, likewise, thanks to his misanthropy and his wilful anachronisms, his work ended up becoming wholly acceptable, plausible, to contemporary tastes. And if *he* could be plausible, then I, who am not, could begin at last to be a Somebody, thanks to [as a consequence of] the simple, relaxing occupation of plagiarizing him.

"Early"

"He's asking for a play."

"A play by whom?"

"He said (let me see, I wrote it down) by Ann Jellicoe."

"In that case, suggest *Mr. Logic & Miss Understanding.*"

(Lord Swindon)

"The gentleman has arrived a day early and would like to wait."

"Wait for what? I don't believe time is wont [able] to [oblige] suit [obey] him."

"The gentleman has decided to *stay*, I mean."

"Those are very different things. And 'I mean' reduces all meaning to ash. 'To stay,' on the other hand, implies location, a specific place, and only tomorrow will we know if such a place exists. For him or any other guest."

"In any case, the gentleman told me he's waiting for your decision."

"I can't make the decision until after the [his] arrival."

"But he's already here."

"A situation we sadly share."

"And he wants to stay."

"That [this] is where the similarity ends."

"What do you want me to do?"

"Depends on what you want to do."

"I mean, with *him*."

"That depends in large measure on what *he* wants to do with *you*."

"Sir, we owe him a response."

"How can I owe something to someone who shouldn't even be here?"

"He deserves it, poor guy."

"But, you see, to visit upon a victim his just desserts is an exercise of power I'd rather [I prefer to] avoid."

"If he leaves, something terrible might happen."

"I fear it's already happened. Simply on account of his being here."

"You have no respect."

"On the contrary: [It's] you [who] have too much respect."

"He has come with a proposition."

"And he can leave with it."

"He was invited."

"To arrive before being invited is a form of discourtesy that demands immediate reciprocation. One of the few for which such reciprocity is demanded, in fact. So get rid of him."

"We're not about to hand out the same information you could very well research yourself in any museum. And look, if you want them to understand what you're after, make sure to call her, '*Frah* Ann Jellicoe.'"

Biography of Lord Swindon

Ingenuity of lists

How do we appropriate?

Original Soundtrack

In "Early," listening to whatever (whatever, that is, Charles imposes on everyone). Contrast this with what the narrator listens to:

—The narrator, when alone: Incredible String Band, Joy Division, the Teardrop Explodes . . .

. . . XTC, Cockney Rebel, Duncan Browne—the Blue Aeroplanes?

Too late, in their roughest patches, they managed to sound like the Stranglers.

—Gilbert & George:

Noel Coward: "Poor Little Rich Girl," "A Room with a View."

Lenny Bruce, Tom Lehrer, Brute Force.

—The kid from the car: Django Reinhardt, Wes Montgomery, George Benson. He plays the guitar. "Caresses it," according to Gilbert (or George).

Cole Porter

When Marina's talking on the telephone, Penguin Café Orchestra:

"The Sound of Someone You Love Who's Going Away and it Doesn't Matter"

Rovira

Piazzolla: "Ode to a Hippie."

Luis Alberto del Paraná. Those who listened to him in London, those he listened to.

Keyboards: Alan Price (Animals), Brian Auger (J. Driscoll, The Trinity), Stevie Winwood (Spencer Davis Group, Traffic, Blind Faith), Garth Hudson (The Band), Mark Stein (Vanilla Fudge), Doug Ingle (Iron Butterfly)

The music we adopted to impress girls. The cube root of error.

It's pointless, him rehearsing
What to say in her memory,
when Koechlin's answer
Étude sur les notes de passage

still rests on the music stand.

Ironic too, anche
what the muse will say
in flight from everyone, en fin
(There was a crueller month than April).

In homage to what he heard, he listens.
Around the deserted isle, autumn fluxes,

he listens to what was (it's supposed to be music,
it is noise
But not for me).

In "The Scent of Thunbergias," Misia Taboda. *Lady Obstreperous.*
Bette Davis. Mankiewicz's *All About Eve.* W. S. Maugham's *The Letter.* Dotty Dabble. Mme Marasm. Mme Sarcasm.

There's no better place for hiding a secret than an unfinished novel (Calvino, Italo). Quoted by someone else, citation needed.

Voices: George Sanders, Tom Conway.

Finally decided on a title: *The X-Positions (Las equis distantes)*
    And, incidentally: no one else seems to like it.

(Appendices)

    1. *Concerning the enigma of* The X-positions

"Today I put an end to—which is to say, I found names for—two of the enigmas in my life, now banished forever," wrote Nicasio Urlihrt in his diary shortly before his death. "They were in a terrible poem," he added, "by a terrible friend: his worst, I'd say, although I admit its intended meaning was lost on me. Love's got to be good for something. Time's got to be good for something." Those who want to pursue this matter further (or destroy the evidence) can take a break from reading this apologia and seek out the material in question, as published in the journal *Agraphia*. If nothing else, you'll get a kick out of the punctuation.

X-Positions refers more to unresolved puzzles, the unknown, than to the old question of anonymity; this according to a somewhat biased interpretation of the second hemistich of the last line of the first stanza of the sonnet by Sabatani—"It wasn't yesterday the world we call old / Nor the secret lost on a mystery / Cult. Be grateful for the levity in the grave: / The bad poets, the x-positions"—that precedes the three Spanish versions of Mallarmé's "sonnet on X" in his chapbook.

The ability of the X to contain conflicting concepts is both a blessing and a curse, bestowed by accident and by amphibology, among other things. Xs are, according to Sabatani, "symmetries of opposition or denial similar to the phenomena of inverse relations studied by Lévi-Strauss." The genealogy of these Xs goes back to the "the Arcadian period" of *Agraphia* [Urlihrtian terminology]—to its very first issues, in other words, in one of those supposedly popular articles Lino Scacchi wrote for *Sherbet Aria* ("Todo Sobre la equis" [All About X] later published in *Idiomatics* as "Todo sobre equis, nada sobre Zeda" [All About X, Nothing About Z]), later translated into English by Hermione Hepburn and published in a journal called *Bible Black* (Tantrum Press, 1978) with the title restored to "All About X" (for a brief description of how all this came about, see "Early"). In his essay, Scacchi unleashed all the voodoo-erudition of a man who nonetheless ended up as the crossword-writer for a small-town paper. He ascertained, for example, that the *Dictionary of Defiance* by the mysterious L.F. [Louis Felipon], traces the sound of the letter X to that of the Greek word *chrestos*, or Christ. And according Scacchi, who cites "the best prose in the world," to adduce that the letter X "cheered and chastened the best man in the world, Thomas Browne, who said 'the letter *X* . . . is the Emphaticall decussation, or fundamentall figure.'"

After two pages of frenetically-written fustian, full of unconnected ideas and obscure references, Scacchi proceeds along the following line of thought: "It's curious to trace in the history of this feeble cruciate sign the adventitious influence that has led to its being given coronal rank in the hierarchy of letters. Nonetheless, in the majority of cases, writers, from Ben Jonson to Gertrude Stein, Confucius to Cummings, Argensola to Gerardo Diego, have rejected it with disdain. Ben Jonson wanted to remove poor X from the alphabet, saying it was 'rather an abbreviation, or way of short writing with us, than a letter,' and Gertrude Stein spoke of its triviality, its function as a simple strikethrough, swift deletion, blind shorthand. Some countries and languages—like Welsh and Gaelic, for example—have never felt its influence. Yet, its wholly gratuitous or fatuous acoustical expression is married to its striking graphical representation like no other letter in the abecedarian chronicle."

For more on the casuistry, the soteriology, and even the proctology of the letter X, see Edgar Lee Meaulnes.

NO

Felipe Luini, *Hunting Journal*

Ideas of Order, Wallace Stevens

Table of Contents

1. The Scent of Thunbergias

I. Early

II. The Imitation of an Ounce

III. Returns

IV. Occupation

V. The House on Calle Piedras

VI. The Cult of St. Mawr

VII. America

VIII. The Scent of Thunbergias

2. The Seychelles

I. Laetitia Pilkington

II. Hilarión Curtis

III. Doris Dowling

IV. Constantin Berev

V. Lord Swindon

VI. Irene Adler

VII. Venus Rattlesnake

3. SHERBET ARIA

I. Stealth//Centipede

II. Centaur

III. Arena

IV. Rhetoric

V. Karmapolis

VI. Ahnungslosigkeit

VII. Sestina

VIII. Pop Museum

IX. Portrait of a Tin Soldier

X. Chronoscopy

XI. Sircular Cymmetry

XII. Lycergical Glossary

XIII. Away with Them [Dead Aunt's Diary]

XIV. Epilogolipomena

4. POPULAR MECHANICS

I. Every Nerve and Sinew

II. Semblance

III. Replicas

IV. The Xochimilco Diary

Appendices

All About X

Fame, Polyonymy, and Denial in *Agraphia*

Photo Anthology

The Biographies

Epistolary

The Dry Martinis

Poem and Sestina

NO

Glenmorangie—Nicasio

      Better: Lagavulin

Or bourbon—Wild Turkey—prefers Jim Beam to Jack Daniels. Four Roses. Canadian Club.

Wyborowa. Stolichnaya.

Angostura. Negroni

dosage

Fernet or Negroni, Eiralis.

Red without question. And lots of it. Lalo.

The Dry Martinis

To sing sweetly then perish—"For Janis Joplin," A. Pizarnik

She seems quite despondent in that photo of her seated barelegged: an attitude of cloying introspection induced (more than likely) by the Southern Comfort

NO

Include "The Slow Ones"?

Because we were late in arriving, because we were late in departing, because we didn't care that we'd be late, and, above all, because those for whom we waited turned out to be ourselves, which is to say, the others, the ones we called "the slow ones."

There were whole days and nights during which we lost our way, during which we lost our purpose. We bummed around exchanging tales of days gone by, anecdotes, gossip.

Because we'll be late in arriving, because we are loath to depart, because we don't care that we'll be late. Above all, because those for whom we wait will turn out to be ourselves, which is to say, the others, the ones we call "the slow ones."

Neither drunkenly nor sleepily they'll call us—no, *are* calling us —"the slow ones."

And when the prize finally arrives, when it ripens, there will be music that will saturate us, sweep us from here to there,

reveal us to the women. When that very night suffocates us in its witching hour, the décolletées begin their long-awaited shift.

The night has plucked itself a jasmine, a gardenia, and we have vowed beneath our breaths to say now what tomorrow will catch (how this promise will bloom) in our throats.

It is now late (or expected) and obvious (or transparent)

the context to be demolished is night. Night, yes, but so close to the moment when she'll take her leave, as that old Egyptian relic begins nodding off, that it's practically day in the desolate dark.

They must conceal themselves. They are few, but they surround us. None can name them. They come, they float downstream, the décolletées.

"He dined on a mess of shadows," one of them said, "what a mouthful (placed out of the children's reach, yesterday—out of reach of their grasping nails). And now, once again, investors want to pluck out their own eyes, to be merely clients, but the kind that don't pay."

But we cannot be less useful than we are. We arrive late, but we don't care. We are content to dine on leftovers. We, the Slow Ones. We take in their necklines with inadequate glances. We used to be near-sighted—now we're farsighted; myopes become presbyopes (curious, is it not, the transit from a silent *E* to one with a stress?). That which we used to be, we are, in the high Sufic night, we, the violate relics. How we suffer to return.

[II] An eruption, a volcano. The scientific vocation is certainly wanting in mortals who commune closely with the gods.

Clucking tongue. The décolletées passing. Scapular. Swaying solemnly, that arbitrary souvenir, a volcano scapular from Storyville, the red-light district, which I still have. Why do I keep it, what will I do with it?

NO

Superimposition

of the bottom of my glass, a brief instant—a slick of melting ice, to the last drop—over the window of a Havana hotel. It's raining in the dry season.

Out of a Greek Gift

Ranelagh, 29 December, 1995/91?

"So Doctor Yturri Ipuche is also Doctor Purcenau?"

"Could be"

"And apparently he lied about everything"

"Don't know, maybe it was just *nearly* everything."

"Nor could one simply attribute this to the fact that they're all, well, fictional characters?"

"Hardly even that: they're floating voices, like in that Sarraute novel . . ."

"Some English writer did the same thing"

"*Les Fruits d' Or*"

"careful now, it's not like we don't have examples closer to home"

"since nobody understood a word they said"

"There's just no way it can be sustained for long. Four or five voices without social or political status to differentiate them, all chasing after the same chick, a muse with a capital *M*"

"Please stop"

"Ave María purísima . . ."

"Ave martini . . . dry"

"Maybe if they shared a real project, a political agenda, then you'd be able to include them. What did you say the book was about, exactly?"

"Well, it's centered mainly on her, as a peripheral figure—no, better to say a hidden figure . . . being a girl. But—in any case. Here they saw the potential for many roles, right?"

Hopefully it rained. It was raining.

"How learned you are, what did you say it was called, again?

"No, those guys were such navel-gazers. Completely incapable of telling a story . . . Look, if I'd actually studied . . ."

"It was psych, for me, lit for everyone else . . ."

"thing is, it was going to be a play, the title of which escapes me just now . . ."

"Urn something"

"and you called it . . . ?"

"oh, a . . . prolegomenon to an awful play. *The* awful"

"He was no stranger to them. And didn't those guys also do work with the Brits and the Galicians?"

"perfectly bilingual"

"well, there you are, Melchior, it's already getting hazy for you—he was Flemish, *un flamand*, he spoke six languages."

"with that stupid face of his? . . . Tribilin . . . [?lingual]"

"Come now, we don't want to let our reminiscing spoil your . . ."

"Spoil what?"

"The broth. This theory, hypothesis, or whatever it is"

"Wrong and wrong. Want another guess?"

"It's a monograph"

"The hell you say"

"Don't let the owner know, but that review of theirs keeps on coming out"

"and we two still contribute. Sporadically"

preaching to the deaf. My illegitimate father. Second chance, prayer of the river at the shores of.

how strange that I loved so . . .

"she's no less important to us. As a spokeswoman"

"But how old are they?"

"Who?"

"Look, they're coming down"

"How many miles has it been?"

"when did you finally tell the assistant?"

"So much the worse for us that we were picked to 'discover her' and 'tell the story,' in the movie by that friend of yours . . ."

"Every once in a while, or every so often, a novel, or a book with some political agenda is found . . ."

"the assistant"

"Lucky him"

"Politics in a novel, said Stendhal, is like firing a pistol during a concert. That's stayed with me"

"We won't ask for examples"

"But there are some"

"It's a can of worms, Inés"

"But isn't that all you do together?"

She wanted a glass to continue the argument. The other guy handed her one.

"that thing about the history of Prague—I read it too. And it was—what can I say? Bankrupt, inane . . ."

"Well, there are periods in history of which nothing survives. Or a little, just a little"

"Psychedelia, psycholalia . . . who the hell knows . . . experimental cinema"

"they leave their mark"

"*Vienna while in Prague*"

"who really cares . . . whether any of that stuff survives?"

"I disagree entirely"

"it all goes back to the father, see"

"what survives of that era? I noticed the other day . . . what's his name?"

"*Bergsonne*"

"So-so"

If I should awaken, I will try to go back to sleep.

Since the reader will find throughout this effort a lot of unnecessary, perhaps superfluous, punctuation, reflecting the anxiety and indecision of the writer, it wouldn't be entirely presumptuous to include a preface [note the inconsistency of this regime]. For what it's worth: I wasn't trying to write something experimental (much less spontaneous) when I commenced this journal. I was trying to find a structure in the mass of [modest, always modest!] narrative/cyclical intermittencies.

NO

Cryptodermia/deafness

There are none so deaf as those who will not hear

Strum away

Occupation

Auden, poem on Melville

As though his occupation were another island

When he saw them again, on that morning in August after returning from a visit to the city, he found them quite as submissive and
conceited as ever; and he, once again trapped in their especial variety of conversational antechamber (in which they oft belabored him
with successions of halting effusions), sought escape by firing off—or
more properly, stammering—a bêtise on the "perfumed scent" of his
butler's arrhythmic respiration, which was indeed perceptible to him
in more than one—and *to* more than one—sense. Not that George
Smith's exhalations were any more perfumed or arrhythmic than
usual, but his master, having grown accustomed to the salubrious air
of the city, and being somewhat distracted by his servants' tedious
divagations, judged his Butler's breath to be, on this occasion, especially noisome, which contrasted starkly with that natural air of
unbending courtesy that poor old George exuded in his manner, the
odor of which, in its many persuasive nuances, would, in fine, have
made any other man feel at home in his company.

Interruption: explanation/reasons/stylistic(s)

*A story in the style of Henry James—perhaps unnecessary. Tell-
ing a genuine anecdote from his life (it's in Leon Edel)—try to make
convincing and meaningful for the ever-vigilant eye of Agraphia, or
else discard. Don't just parody, like Beerbohm (hopefully, I can pull it
off). Try anyway.*

Could proceed as follows:

When George had finally left, it was only the two of them
at home, and he, nonetheless longed to evade that situation too,
and by the same exaggerated dissimulation that proved useful in
his escape from their suffocating antechamber. But Lydia Smith
wouldn't leave his side, debriefing him, as was customary, concerning his engagements for the coming hours, one of which, she supposed, would be a luncheon; and accumulating in the course of her

routine interrogation, was that mixture of "perfection and sherry" he'd once mentioned in a letter to his brother (a letter in which, with customary—or simply epistolary—reserve, he'd avoided giving too many details), which continued accumulating as they settled his provisional itinerary for the coming days.

Keep the action slow, focus on preferences:

He would have preferred—he muttered to himself, before repeating it aloud to Lydia—a simple dish, something *botanical*: vegetables, greens. . . and so he continued, spouting synonyms in triplicate until he made of simplicity a conundrum. Then, ignoring his interlocutor's indifference at this attempt to impose on their quotidian yet another one of his literary manias—and resisting the urge to answer the snub with a boast on his palatial refinement—he informed her that he would be dining alone this afternoon. His friends would only arrive the following day, while his gentleman acquaintance might arrive *as soon as* Thursday afternoon; on which day, in the event he should be alone—and safe, after all—(for there was always the possibility his friend might decline the invitation, or else arrive late, or else leave early), he would then *also* prefer a simple botanical collation (greens, vegetables), for he always ingested complicated fare when dining out. And, for him, dining out was not unusual.

He saluted Burgess with an expansive wave through the window, and when Max entered, he also saluted him, although he refrained from leaning over to do so. Nonetheless, after uttering some preliminary endearments that would have been unintelligible to Max even had he been human, his master stooped to pet him—a complicated act, from his altitude, especially given that his characteristically slight but by no means willowy frame had lately expanded to the dimensions of a prosperous entrepreneur—at which point, Lydia, with the finesse of an accomplished supporting actress, seized the opportunity to make a discreet if nonetheless theatrical exit. He straightened back up. Now steady, and with his eyes closed, he recalled again the scent of Lydia's breath—perfection and sherry—and judged it less offensive and noisome than that of George.

To be continued?

"Dos de Nosotros" gives an account of Nurlihrt's reflections on adultery:

He doesn't really care, he insists, but as with any issue where what's really going on and how it's reported vary depending on their respective subjects and objects—when we criticize others, it's called invective; when others criticize us, it's called abuse [Kingsmill]—adultery is a question best examined, dispassionately, with neither pleasure nor circumspection, as part of a larger phenomenon, in this case called—without bandying words, and *sans musique*—jealousy.

He doesn't really care, he insists, and insists I pay such close attention that I feel remiss in not taking notes as he tells me about Elena's imperturbability yesterday after he took her hands in his and remarked, "Cold hands, warm heart! Is there anyone in particular on your mind?"

He doesn't care. He looks at me, idly curious—putting on a mask of indifference to shield himself from the pain he knows he causes: "And what about Sabatani, Dos," I asked, "after the storm, when I got back the day before—remember? You know, I couldn't help but think of the enduring and astonishing validity of what Powell said about women, that their greatest show of fidelity was to start fights with their lovers."

The nearest some women get to being faithful to their husbands is being disagreeable to their lovers.

A.P.

Terror that *X-Positions* might end up looking like those hated novels *62: A Model Kit* or Revol's *Mutaciones bruscas* (Sudden Changes).

Both of which I read so fondly when I was at the cusp of adolescence. But it *does* resemble them, sad to say. We can't escape our early influences—there's my attempt at rationalization. And more: there's no denying the pressure exerted upon us at that most crucial moment—at the threshold between childhood and adolescence—by our reading. Just plain reading. The burden of those early devotions—like stamp collecting. And, even worse, the fact that your writing forever advertises every last baffling and muddy trace left behind by that confessional devotion: a sort of damper placed on your entire life, a humiliating expulsion of those errors you accumulated in the name of experience. To quote Lope de Vega's fundamental, eternal, infrangible enjambment: "That I have loved at other times / I cannot deny."

1971. Girri / *El Carapálida: Diary of a Book. In the letter, ambiguous forest*

We return to James

Lydia—perhaps because she had a genuine faith in his judgment, or because she was being indifferently compliant, or because something had alerted her to the exigencies of the day—had left before the end of his oration. It was startling, a miracle of indecisiveness. Even his questions were somewhat vacuous, empty, so that they sounded like irresolute twangs redoubling in an echo chamber. But it mattered not in those instances how obvious those empty spaces were, how provisional, how inane the suspense they induced in the hearer, for they reflected his own unwholesome diet, his discipline of misgiving, his false modesty.

In the study with Max, his first thought was that he need not wait for George's traps to fulfill their function, that Max could catch the rat on his own . . . And he recalled an anecdote of Doctor Johnson's—or only half-recalled, rather, according to his customary mode of recollecting—: It was strange, uncanny really, especially for it being a piece of prose, and more so because he managed to remember all the subtleties of accent and rhythm, the variable cadences of the piece, and yet none of its sense. No, it wasn't entirely strange: it was a confirmation of what he had believed his entire life, without realizing it, and certainly without regard for metrics or prosody; something that was difficult to explain without exhaustive preamble, for the belief required much correction and refinement over the years, during which time it grew like the spider's web that eventually ensnared him, disrupted his life. Life, with its senseless task. To grumble every day and night scratching one's head in an effort to apprehend what makes as much sense, superficially, as a black dog barking in the street. Because the substance of an event was never fully captured in the considered act of describing or defining as much as by a fleeting grammatical discharge, which reveals as much as can be revealed respecting an event's fugacity or fixity, *above all* that mobile quality, that acoustic quality, imitated again and again, although the meaning was lost, or was relegated to the limbo of one's memory.

Miracle of verbal effusiveness and emotive inhibition that so irritated Mailer (and, I suppose, Gorey too), "The Pupil" begins as follows: *"The poor young man hesitated and procrastinated . . ."*

Let's see if we can finish it today:

In the afternoon he dictated all he could to Miss Weld, everything he only half-recalled, with inadequate words, words like fading echoes and fragments of that immense inexpressible reality—intimations, as the ruffle of a curtain after closing on a scene—and worse even, of the ever diminishing recollection of what was said and of what transpired. Nevertheless, when Miss Weld had finally retired for the day, her hand stiff as usual, the late afternoon etched a sunset so false, so painterly, only a mawkish poet or adolescent (and perhaps the two are kindred) would, in attempting to exalt the scene, succeed in making it the more factitious. Although he was himself infected, he dared to admit to himself that the story he wanted to tell was in fact different to the one he dictated, and that his impulsive nature was an impediment to his telling it, that this was what led him to hide it beneath a bushel of vagueness, of imprecision, and that he searched in his pockets and found, to his dismay, only a dead mouse, a cork, and a fragment of eggshell. Was it his stifled imagination or someone else that told him this?

The story he'd originally wanted to tell was about a single house, and he certainly tried writing it in the past, but his attempts and successes had always been greatly divergent, and this was chiefly on account of that impulsive nature. The story he *now* wanted to tell should have excluded all impulsiveness, or not (it didn't really matter in the case of dictation, these documents acted only as spurs for his notebooks); he could keep it hidden in the background, in that empty mansion where spontaneous feeling takes refuge, and vapid, passionless words take their place on the page, battling it out like specters of slain soldiers. In this sense, the narrative mansion should be the opposite: there, the real forces would be *acting*, while successive proprietors and tenants, being subject to the passivity of the age—of any age, in fine—and poised on the threshold of an event, would have that freedom, that readiness that is so easily confused with aplomb, to respond to each daily challenge, each setback, in its proper manner, and with galling perfection. Critics and friends had already rebuked him for his honeyed volubility, and also that "nothing to say" which the terricolous Hardy suspected lay behind his ponderous, Tyrian diction. Critics and friends . . . , including one close friend, and one very distant critic, whose irreverence towards him snuffed out any possibility of friendship, for he accused him of the Pelagian heresy, after observing how little inclined he was to revision, lambasting his works for their serpentine, argentine oracy, and the author for his belief that they were "conceived without original sin." Another deviant tendency to be discouraged, he tells himself while inspecting, beneath the ponderous drapes, the motes of dust Lydia herself had so stridently taken exception to, but whose presence he takes as evidence of her distracted state of mind that afternoon.

He decided he must resolve the matter sooner rather than later. He sat down to write: Wednesday afternoon he'd summon a coach and tell George, or even better, Burgess, that he'd be visiting Wharton or Agassiz. He would prefer that Miss Theodora Bosanquet absented herself, for she cultivated an annoying habit of interjecting on every serious discussion with dreamy sentimentalities: the poor woman. Then he'd proceed directly to Addison & Ibbetson's office to consult the guide on contract waivers (taking for granted such a thing exists). After reading the various articles, he'd choose the most relevant, this being the one that suggests the most lenient way of terminating domestic service (supposing the archive had such a classification) in a house in the suburbs, roughly the same size as his. This last point should have been given the most attention, because the amount of redundancy is calculated according to how much work is done, on average, over the course of a period, and payment is then given both for the present period and the following one.

canNOt

Sounds NOthing like James. Reread those three short stories again, especially "The Next Time."

I feel more assured by the incoherent babbling of a panhandler than by the apodictic pronouncements of philosophers.

Good Day, Sunshine

He considered that, if such a law existed (and he presumed one did, for his is not an unprecedented case), and allowing for a considerable margin of error, the amount allocated should vary in proportion to the number of tasks completed and the number that would have been completed, during the remainder of this period and the whole of the next, adjusting for age, the relative advantage and disadvantage of being made redundant when young, when mature, or when not far from that permanent redundancy of death, and all in accordance with the terms of the contract. The figures, however, did not matter. These can always be altered, and the amount extrapolated adjusted according to the arbitrary standard by which justice is usually dealt out. Insofar as the redundancy calculated at the expense of one's dignity is proportionate to effort, he believed it to be just, and would pay that amount without scruple. The value of work not done, on the other hand, required of the employer an inordinate degree of generosity. Because the dismissal in this case was not unfair, it was a result of a conflict of interest. The scarcity of resources was the employer's first defense, and those he had at his disposal, could be called to visibly attest to his humble way of life, and furthermore, they would illustrate the stark contrast between reality and mere show, which was the *fashion* of his age, an age when the condescending image of the real, the superficial, had been overthrown by something altogether alien and antagonistic, although he, being an artist, would have certainly reduced the issue to a contest of wills, hoping that, in the struggle, in his writings, he could produce a better substitute, someone more attentive, more benign, and less distracted than himself.

An outside intervention, please

It had begun raining so he left off writing. How much better he felt dictating on this occasion! In reality, the lives of the George and Lydia Smith of this world mattered more to him now than before—although their situation was, in reality, less hopeful—and he came to realize that, in all the time since making their acquaintance, he had scarcely learned anything about them . . . He should allow himself to recover. He did so tentatively, at first, even fearfully, as those people frequently do who have spent or misappropriated their store of passion—and he remembered, could have listed many a case—with obstinate greed, and afterwards, wheezing satiety.

They first came to Lamb House recommended by Lucien Sordido, a Corsican gentleman of Napoleonic stature who in bustling London, where word so quickly turns to gossip, was unable to prevent news spreading of his broken reputation. But Sordido certainly held him in high esteem, although it was the kind of esteem a man with an irreparably broken reputation bestows on one who is careless with his. Lucien Sordido had sent the couple to his home with a letter of introduction; it must still be in the notebook in which he was working at the time. He vowed to go looking for it, but not at that moment, since there was nothing in the contents he didn't already know. During that first interview, he avoided interrogating them, for although he intended to improve, or at least not depreciate, the matrimonial economy, his sudden interest in them, after so many years of rebuffal, might have intimidated, or been interpreted by them as a prologue to a threat or a warning. But—taking into account the possible consequences, especially when fueled by a bottle of sherry—he wasn't going to bring them to task for former actions they could not undo. His careful scrutiny of them, however, might have yielded answers to queries discretion prevented him asking: how much had redundancy affected them, and did it correspond to one of those pathetic destinies he had imagined? For not being content with ignorance, he transformed a mere presentiment of debility and destitution, of desperation and crisis, into an augury. His only duty was to be alert, should their conduct betray any subtle confirmation of it, or should their claims induce in him any impressions of incredulity.

Since then, having succeeded in restoring them to that previous state in which their livelihoods depended on a meager spring (one that delivers only on a monthly basis), he eases a vellication of remorse with the thought that they would be amply remunerated with freedom of time and leisure, although he knows the leisure of redundancy cannot truly be enjoyed. He could dissimulate that his reason for dismissing them was to allow them the opportunity to find better employment, but he could not deny that the pension afforded them but little subsistence, and encouraged too much idleness. Worse still, a cocktail of sherry and idleness could precipitate their ruin. They could of course argue that an everyday existence vitiated by poverty, fatigue, and disenchantment need not be altogether intolerable. They could very well relieve the sting of privation by beginning a regimen of more healthful distractions. If they manage to sustain it, he could call on the Smiths now and then to check on their progress, update his case study, *in situ*. And yet, he would still call on them, even if their regimen came to nothing. The one certainty is there will always be a story. And no matter how long or short, it would always be interesting, for the events in their lives continually rapt the attention of the curious. And curiosity should be considered, in the case of these rigorously *factual* stories, the means by which their factuality, their consistency, is proven: for curiosity questions every revelation, accepts nothing on trust.

If—this very morning—Mr. and Mrs. Smith were to arrive again at his door, exhibiting all the symptoms of delirium tremens, despite their avowed sobriety, and if they came recommended by the same authority—the same Lucien Sordido who was unable to exchange a broken reputation for a new one—*he* would certainly receive them with the same apprehension, the same mistrust, and the same pretense of goodwill as during that first interview, suspecting that, due to Sordido's notoriety as an author of operatic librettos (a craft not dissimilar to his own: the only variant being the notoriety), they were introduced to one another at a party, and considering them too dull and tasteless to be among his own cast of caricatures, or believing, almost superstitiously, that they were practicing the art of evasion, of dissimulation, and that this was the means by which truly singular personalities concealed their exceptionality, he recommended them to him—perhaps naïvely—as living models. Living models, indeed, but for a novelist. And as always, *he*—disinterestedly—availed of them.

If his memory were as reliable an instrument as his imagination, he would have recalled that Lucien Sordido had in fact sent the couple at *his* request, and that he had afterwards muttered to Sordido in a restaurant—during one of those myriad occasions they dined out that year—a slight of *their aristocratic pose*, which required an almost anonymous fealty to borrowed habits, a wavering confidence in the performance of those habits, and a similar irregularity in the upholding of one's convictions and scruples.

For now, he could dream of Mr. George Smith, with his threadbare coat and perfumed breath, as a citizen borne of his own inventive memory: as a guide or cicerone to a gallery of facetiae chosen with more haste than judgment, and afterwards replaced with variants whose verisimilitude relied more on his degree of inebriation than on the appraisal of critics, or, above all, of future biographers. The biographer, in particular—being tethered to the past—is a class of professional whose imagination retards his recognition of the present moment, though this is the first door on which every casual observer knocks. As George himself—although not a biographer—had done . . .

By contrast, he was never wanting in charm and elegance; indeed, it could be said he had more than his share, something he made pains practically to exhibit during postprandial conversation, while enjoying his demitasse, when a distant onlooker might imagine he was descended from rural nobility; and this was justified, almost as much as the paradox of Burgess's mundane beauty, or his own treatment of realistic tragedy according to the conventions of fantasy, imagining there was neither conflict nor contradiction. True, conflict—which was real in the case of the Smiths—brought with it a kind of superfluous scaffolding, so that the course of events, whether suspended or delayed by that cumbrous stage machinery, forced him to anticipate every flaw, every error in that machinery. How instructive and misleading are errors! How the terricolous Hardy erred in believing he had to bury his hands in the loam of misfortune to prove that he had suffered! Dirt under the nails was the ultimate proof. But Jurisprudence was for him a secondary calling, one whose emblems solicitously evoked a fealty to justice and the public weal, and whose symbolic acts were so amply displayed during the ceremonial openings of law firms, whose founders took care to choose a splendid Latin motto to suit the heraldic monogram surmounting the doors of their establishment, an establishment whose end was not justice but commerce.

In any event, planning the married couple's future allowed him to distance himself from a problem only Addison or Ibbetson could resolve, each one of whom dealt with the kinds of technicalities he believed were at the core of the issue, but which he could never fully apprehend, since, from the time of his earliest instruction until his removal from the Polytechnic school in Zurich, such things were always lost on him due to his natural inaptitude for systemized learning. No, for him, any attempt at indagation or inquiry into such matters would condemn him to circumambulation, frustration, and endless raving. And, after some time following his own steps, he would find himself once again going down the path already beaten by Musset, who discovered *il s'absente trop de l'Académie parce qu'il s'absinthe trop.* Although, he could adduce in his defense a monastic temperance so commendable, the casual drinker's tipsiness—or if he be Irish, the not so casual, for an Irishman would pursue the matter along an entirely different course without ever encountering a Musset—would seem Bacchic by comparison. In this sense, his sorrow, grandiosity, and style were all consistent. And someone who wasn't even intelligent, but were only a link in a system devised by others, a man who maintained his place only by fear and trembling, would have no difficulty in recognizing him. Even in anticipating him. This is style, and cannot be taught at the academy. If he could hold a conversation with his brother without the usual pretenses or recriminations, they could surely come to some agreement. And especially now he had begun reading *The Varieties of Religious Experience.*

There was always gossip concerning the two of them, whispers sprayed like shrapnel, for without at least one of their deaths, there cannot be an autopsy, or afterwards, a museum of commemoration. It was said that it was impossible to mistake one for the other, since "one was a novelist who wrote treatises on psychology," and the other, "a professor of psychology who wrote novels." The derisive chiasmus of fools.

Tomorrow, enough

The other benefit was to incur an immeasurable indebtedness to life for visiting on him so many woes. Curious he would think it a life's work, and not a novelist's, to repay that debt, as if his writing could remedy or at least assuage the wounds he accumulated with experience. What is certain is that all his possessions together could not discharge that debt, of which the most valuable, the most powerful, was also the least ponderous—his splendid art, his sad profession.

The days passed, the ceremonies were repeated, the guests arrived and then departed, but it was only after they were gone that blood once again engorged the arid channels of his heart. So with impatience arising from bewilderment of desire, he awaited the arrival of the gentlemen guest who would prevail on his hospitality. Or, in the event he didn't come, he would celebrate the prospect of a full day dedicated to solitude—a Saturday—during which, after initial speculations as to why his guest had failed to come, his imagination would be free to follow its own course. Once, a fellow conversationalist—a Spaniard, he recalls—made the pronouncement in English that Saturdays were days of the imagination, speaking with such orotundity, his words seemed to dress the invisible air in the flounces of that paralogism. Curious: time requires more space than space itself for those who were once close to become estranged. But for *him* to be estranged from those spaces of time when he was made the victim of posturing and casuistry, requires nothing at all. But it doesn't matter. *Trop.* His account of the most decisive days was now complete, although it was lacking in vigor, although it seemed puerile, and vacuous, and although his fingers reached into the pit but did not feel the loam.

And though a guest were to arrive, expectedly or unexpectedly—or not, since an absence, expected or unexpected, was always welcome—solace remained his constant companion ("his mutual consul," they said, mockingly, of Dickens), a friend that eased the dyspepsia of too much living, enabling him, without guilt of pride, to etch—for any guest, any companion—a portrait of himself that were as crude as a silhouette or complete as an incarnation. Without guilt of pride, yes, but pursuant to what he believed was his legitimate hatred of the real and its eternal trappings. Thence, on that particular August afternoon, at the hour when the demiurge oft goes handing out empty promises—so many trappings—he resolved, with aristocratic disdain, to ensure his reciprocal and utter destruction.

Back Cover sent by Eiralis to D. Julio

Christmas Eve on which the wolf howls

Fernando Tapiols

Circumstantial Island in Claveplana is an enchanting paradise in the middle of the Mar Izquierdo [which is hidden behind Basílico Bay]. [Those] responsible for maintaining its high standard of luxury are Iris Oratoria and her [twin] half-sister, Mateluna, [who's] the bellwether of a flock of [hard-working, enigmatic] girl-scouts. Everything is going splendidly until Saverio Onofre Trápaga arrives on the island, [a] taciturn writer with dirty fingernails who drafts [imprisons] the girls into literary workshops with the apparent intention of re-educating them [morally] for the job [his ulterior motive being to corrupt them]. This is the story that Isabel Semiramis Errázuriz writes in the Hohenzollern mansion [castle], near Darmstadt, while her half-sister, Hildegarda, tends to a flock of Jewish girls in Zagreb, although using a whip instead of a staff, and with the help of Abravanel, a black German Shepherd of uncertain origin, who studies the Pentateuch. (Important details: the custodian of the land on which the Jewish girls pasture is an unscrupulous Brazilian magnate from Manaus, Ouroboros [Kniebolo]; a worm that grew into an anaconda during the rubber boom.)

This is the tale written by Matilde Moura, nom de plume of Matildo Amancio Miura, an old pederast who shares a room with Medellín, a young Latin American boy (the suspicion he may only be Peruvian limits his prostitutional prospects), who maintains a long-term relationship with Don Federico Loane, a vaguely Argentinian man of mainly French-Basque origin who is writing a novel on the side. This novel plagiarizes Fernando Tapiols (a Chilean writer living in exile in Barcelona, "disgruntled by failure"), to keep the most vocal detractors of the junta, Pedestrian Square Root, *happy. Tapiols is the author of a vast oeuvre, the highlight of which is an epic poem, "Christmas Eve on which the Wolf Howls," a merciless chronicle set during the Christmas of 1974, written in* nona-*metric lines [distichs] of variable feet, a metrical pattern devised by Tapiols in homage to Nicanor Parra and to commemorate the passing of Pablo Neruda.*

Annick Bérrichon was one of the most prestigious literary critics; (which is the only reason why) Nicasio had been greatly interested in her. Besides this, she was also a professor of Balkan literature, although no one knew how she obtained the title or with what institution she was affiliated. But this last mystery is what piqued Belisario's interest. Annick's friendship with Elena soon led to her being introduced to the most prominent committee members of *Agraphia*, including Nicasio. One afternoon in June, almost seven months after Eloísa's death, they met with a medium in the house on calle de las Posadas (*not* the one on calle de las Piedras).

Miss Bérczely's face was a grotesquery of warts and other excrescences, an especially nasty case of what Elena termed "lunarism." She spoke with what sounded like an imitation German accent with a hint of French in the guttural. Everyone pretended to understand what she was saying.

Those present were Dos, Oliverio Lester, and someone else who came with them; Elena had dragged along her best friend, Sofía Sarracén, who was even more superstitious than she—a pianist with certain mediumistic talents, who brought along her fiancé [Eloy Armesto: Lupanal . . .]—a student of Bérrichon's—to introduce him to the rest of the group.

At last, Nicasio arrived. His system of responses resembled those adopted by Elena to translate Blevgad: quibbling, nibbling, double negatives—disagreeable in any language—delivered in the passive voice . . .

As it was a commemorative date—June 23, launch of *Oxyrhynchus*—the committee was hoping Hilarión Curtis would attend (who not only owed the journal answers, but also his fellow Argentine citizens).

According to the more or less reliable testimony of those present—particularly Sofía's fiancé—the first to induce a fit of histrionics and table tapping was a confused little girl who was communicating with the medium on the subject of writing. Suddenly, the medium began coughing and choking, perhaps because there was a change of . . . "visitant," or because someone had taken off their shoes . . . [???] A high pitched voice then spoke in impeccable Castilian: "I am Zelda Bove, grandmother of Benkes, and the legitimate proprietor of his falsehoods . . ."

Annick Bérrichon's spiritual ancestry has been discussed in an essay by Eloy Armesto. Suffice it to say the literary critic's grandfather—whose *nom de plume*, Belén Mathiessen, is better known to the uninitiated—had been complicit in the activities of Dunglas Home, who had duped many nineteenth century positivists. Today, we can conclude that Annick Bérrichon and all her pseudonyms—so suited to *Agraphia*—was born, as Blevgad prophesied, to unpack this piece of history, although her [personal] activities would succeed only in blurring the chronology. Her grandfather died in a pitiful way, although not as Luini described—nobody will ever know if her account precedes his—in both "Lemurids, Cheiroptera, et Cie" and *Sherbet Aria*.

Two weeks later (after this encounter), Elena is elected (with respect to this story) as the keeper of secrets. It's funny how little time it takes to become accustomed to risks; perhaps because they're not truly risks, or perhaps there are no such things as customs. Nothing can be a custom that has a habit of perishing. Antúnez Irrusmendi's lover (of six weeks), who's the patron of Irene Picabea—Nicasio's lover—confirms and displaces a crass fantasy of the servile novelist. See the disadvantage in the following light: Elena and Nicasio were, on this occasion, made the victims of this bungling demiurge who used them as theatrical doubles. The obvious correspondence condemned them not so much to the gossip of associates but to the twisted commentary of biographers and other forgers of their destiny.

NO

61

Bourgeois squabbling disguised as intellectual pride: they're capable [CF, above all] of explaining away anything, even a gift . . .

Exercise in baffling symmetry

Moving up or down in an office building (after an initial humiliation). Hesitantly, he carries the photocopied documents to a nurse who is leaning from the balcony holding a less burdensome charge (a joint). It soothes and comforts. But then the horrible process of forgetting. For it's necessary to: summon the elevator without success, climb and descend the stairs, check the baffling symmetry that prevents them knowing what floor they're on, what level of negotiation their colleagues had reached, casually enter the disabled bathroom, offload the burdensome artifact, send it the way of dead goldfish . . .

F.'s anecdote about McLaren-Ross and Dylan Thomas in an elevator. Bad memory.

Eiralis to Don Julio:

[I went to the bank to try cashing the check, the one just around the corner from the house in which I'm now writing this. Two fat heifers told me the bank didn't cash checks, and that I'd have to go to the head office or a parent company. I went to the head office or parent company, or whatever it was, where, after waiting in a long queue, an employee even more clueless than I told me I couldn't cash the check, that I had to deposit it into my account. But as you very well know, I don't have my own account.

NO

Cryptodermia / Kleptolalia. Insist.

The precursor's mission, the successor's mission

The letter ending on a semicolon

Rejected.

Weariness. Self-indulgence

Luckily, nobody noticed the allegorical didacticism in *El Carapálida*. Charlie had instructed me (nobody suspected the narrator's name, Leboud, was an anagram of Double; no critic noted the ingenious cipher). And although political readings abounded in my favor, and superficial ones even more so, I have to be the one (*after* Eliot, Deniz and Empson, *after* Feiling) to throw light on the *backstage* so they comprehend the *miscast* and staging.

I understand the resistance—the animosity—of readers and critics to texts that are conceived and arranged by tendentious principles. But just as the reference to Ph. Holland in "The Aleph" is a clue to be pursued, there is nothing in Argentine fiction to indicate where to go next, it is at an impasse: of mere storytelling, straightforward narrating, having lost sight of that profundity of vision that inclines one to the implicit, to allusion, elusion, paraphrase, and veiled quotation.

If literature is strengthened by its referential commitment (if we love Latin literature because it is derived from Greek literature, if Spanish and English literature occasionally surprises us with profound evocations, invocations of other literatures that informed them), *El Carapálida* presented, according to the author's plan, a practical dilemma (practical because it offered two modes of inquiry) between the carelessly written potboiler and the Thomas Mann approach (profundity, difficulty, their consequences . . .)

The two masters were leading the pack: Ricardo Neira and César Quaglia.

In contrast to the weight of those initial sesquipedalian surnames—Beaumarchais, Bauvebrouillard—the pungent brevity of the biforked: Piglia, Aira.

NO

There was something evasive, annoying about Inés Maspero. Firstly, her protrusive eyes—that askant gaze—secondly, her mismatched teeth (the left incisor broken on the right side), thirdly, her taking care to always maintain a standard of inelegance, fourthly, the coarseness of her knees, and lastly [definitively], her bad manners. When Inés Maspero opened a packet of cigarettes, it was like watching a ravenous lioness quarter an antelope [Ogden Nash, in "Dead Aunt's Diary"].

Spanish translation

Foreground anything to do with taste (other poem of Ogden Nash), if there is anything.

NOt found. The account:

The poem says a *gourmet* challenged him—O.N.'s "lyrical him"— to eat, god help us, a piece of rattlesnake meat, assuring him that it would taste like chicken.

And O.N. (or the "lyrical O.N.") ate it. Now he ("the lyrical he") says he can no longer eat chicken since it reminds him too much of rattlesnake meat.

Lead with the poem which has a part called "question of taste."

Inés Maspero was the kind of person no one imagined [being in love] falling in love, the kind of person with whom no one had wanted to fall in love, the kind of person with whom everyone fell in love. One morning, or perhaps it wasn't the morning, at least one person discovered they were not in love with her.

Or was it she who believed this and so everyone around her was led to believe it too?

If there were reasons, some were perhaps of her own making—with the rabid elegance of an Egon Schiele, who for a time completely forgot about the love angle, the rectilinear lines of the Viennese baroque, its *serpentine* effect. It couldn't have been because of Nicasio's influence, because no one knew he was the second person that didn't love her. The truth is, it was a long process that clearly entailed some psychological manipulation, but which also needed a little magic—the elusive and unhappy process described in "Returns"—at the end of which the insignificant skivvy of the reception desk had become—by the intervention of her Pygmalion and Svengali—Eloísa Betelgeuz[s]e, the inspirational muse of *The Place of Apparitions* and inspired poet of *Chrysalid Simulation.*

Inés Maspero (*ci-devant* Eloísa Betelgeuse), who died in a variety of ways, all of them tragic, all anthologized in at least four stories in this book, died by accident (as one of the survivors liked to stress to the protagonist's father), after ingesting alcohol, a lot of alcohol and medication (since she never referred to them by name), more than likely—according to a reliable witness [Dos]—an un-prescribed and dangerously high dose of Tryptizol (the suicide hypothesis should be discarded for the sake of a reasonable alternative . . .)

It was a dimly-lit apartment Nicasio Urlihrt hadn't helped her choose and which, according to a letter by a frequent visitor (Dos, a member of *Agraphia*'s second committee), was like "a cave made for a pygmy who obsesses over Jackson Pollock monochromes." The stuff that was shedding from the walls is called *skip trowel.* And indeed, whoever visited would have shared the letter writer's sentiments. Even those who spent an evening with the intensely private couple, playing those domestic games Nicasio—despite appearances—particularly enjoyed, would soon begin to miss their own hearth in the grim atmosphere. *After the first death, there is no other.*

Eduardo Manjares described Nicasio Urlihrt's curiosity in women using the adjective "proboscidal" [in . . . ?]. The zoological term is apt for a man with a large nose, corpulent frame, premature wrinkles, and a clumsy gait. This should be of concern to us because Manjares, who was passing through Buenos Aires, was guilty of an attempt at courteous dissuasion, citing Proust: "Let us leave the beautiful women to men of no imagination." Nurlihrt, who was good with a riposte, and imaginative (or perhaps just in love), twice emended the citation with the intention of improving it, first saying: "Let us leave the imagination to men undistracted by pretty women"; and then: "Let us leave pathetic theories to men of tragic nature." Oliverio,

Felipe, and someone else were also present.

A few ideas in stories already written (I'm not surprised by the notion that stories aren't just motivated by ideas: Mallarmé to . . . Degas?). In "Early," the first thought in the morning doesn't correspond with the last one at night (Urlihrt's program against random ideas). In "The Imitation," we understand time by the substantive construction of history, not by looking at the clock (whatever that means). Nothing is understood plainly, needs elaboration, explanation. When the crystalline fails us, use the humectant and adhesive capacities of reasoning.

"The division of one day from the next must be one of the most profound peculiarities of life on this planet. It is, on the whole, a merciful arrangement. We are not condemned to sustained flights of being, but are constantly refreshed by little holidays from ourselves. We are intermittent creatures, always falling to little ends and rising to little new beginnings. Our soon-tired consciousness is meted out in chapters, and that the world will look quite different tomorrow is, for both our comfort and our discomfort, usually true. How marvelously too night matches sleep, sweet image of it, so neatly apportioned to our need. Angels must wonder at these creatures that fall so regularly out of awareness into fantasm—invested dark. How our frail identities survive these chasms no philosopher has ever been able to explain."

Iris Murdoch

Scherzo

Elena told me before entering the bathroom about her weakness for bespectacled men, men who don't wear watches, men who wear neckties. I caught a glimpse of her removing her clothes [balancing herself, climbing into the bath.]

Near the bath was a pile of Nicasio's magazines. He could hear her body's dialogue with the water, her sigh of gratitude for its embrace. Twice I left and twice returned to the same place. Elena said children inherit the way their parents sleep, and their way of getting into water. [I furtively got in, got out almost immediately.] I don't have children. Elena does. It was raining.

Staccato

Books [abandoned] on the floor: Elena had not been a disciplined disciple. Betrayal in Trilce, inconspicuous satellite.

Approaching the windowsill, a German cockroach's deafening saraband, the silence of the world I didn't want to hear, didn't want to hear, didn't want to hear. Elena already left the bathroom. Her legs to the iliac crest, her eyes closed.

NO

Parallelism: "The Old Bachelor."

NO

Elena claimed husbands should either be poisoned or deceived (if possible, both) between the first pregnancy and the (second) tale of Scheherezade.

Mustn't go back to where one was abandoned. One should know better. Because the right opportunities are scarce (the wrong too plentiful, if one sticks around).

Buried keys

Examples seen in Nabokov, hidden in James. The genius of that other Jeffrey Aspern—the maestro—Ray Limbert, is to be always suggestive, elusive; the opposite in V.N.: visibility of the other's genius: Sebastian Knight, *The Gift*, John Shade and also the protagonist of *Bend Sinister*.

He was acquainted with the jury. There was an ineffective trio of persons who ignored the fact there was a natural bias in favor of bestowing the prize freely.

O Lord, don't punish me for that.

Lord, you've already done it.

Russian Story. Semblance.

Onomastics, renown, polynymy, and denial in Agraphia

Eloy Armesto

[Extracting the *Thursday* from *The Man who Was.* Biannual Newsletter of the Universidad Autónomo de Los Sunchales]

Going against Occam's razor, the nominative entities of *Agraphia* are born to reproduce themselves, to proliferate, and after a short time, be discarded. Their life-cycle can be compared with that of the common cold. "Each syllable of their names, a germ, a potential pandemic." Categorical proliferation, diametrical. The names function as algebraic permutations that make no difference to the final result. They accumulate, are collected, arrayed, and then *spent* (in the double sense). The metastasis occurs where fame is unevenly distributed. A whole argot of sectarian terms to designate where: first, the "paludinal glitterati" in *Septic Midrash*, then the "phalansterian demographic" constructed to "contradict the anecdote." In the journal, "there is no theory," except what makes you rich. Theory, they proclaimed, plagiarizing Proust, is the price tag on a gift. Nicasio Urlihrt was quoted in the newspapers as having said that admission into *Agraphia* relies not so much on intellectual common ground but on the postulant's mandatory baptism at the font.

So, at the "Sestina Session" they began laying down the (criminal) tracks towards what they believed was an amoral approach to anonymity—the pseudonym—a meeting that ended in compromise instead of unanimity. *The uninterrupted progress of those tracks,* according to "The Change." For his final choice, Eiralis removes some, alters others. "Notes for a Plagiarist," by Belisario Tregua, summons those *eroici furori,* four of the nine forms of love, both blind and blinded. With retrospective rage, one or another dissenter will sometimes change even the precursor's name, exchange it for another. Who is Hilarión Curtis? The anecdote goes that he was a predecessor of Nicasio Urlihrt, although he is not. And in different places the *apic ancestor* appears to make the story seem apocryphal, to submit another dossier to the lore. So that Belisario Tregua, the original Glaucus of Urlihrt, can quickly make the exchange with Sabatani, the *Glaucus et Diomedes permutatio.*

Insofar as *Agraphia* is an extended discourse on the insignificance of names, real or invented—as a Traherne, Arthur Paul Clerkwell, Jacques Derrida, Lord Swindon, Guyotat, Gayelord Hauser—the name or title is an indication of this, and the activity most often adopted by these personages is trying to remember the names of things or, failing this, coming up with new ones . . . As in "The Dreadmist": "What name could we have chosen for what was going on. I suggested to them: Gobi, after the desert. Or after the tanguero, Alfredo Gobbi, with two Bs. One of them said aberrations don't make good names. Optical aberrations, as I recall . . ." On most of those ruled pages Tregua had specifically chosen for recording the *Agraphia* committee minutes, it's apparent everyone is involved in the act of coming up with names for people, stories, and various other things.

The other "perdurable aspect," besides the Arcadian myths, as the members saw them, is the ceremonial, or liturgical, for which they gathered together countless emblems, constructed a host of personas, prepared myriad refutations to any argument that might be leveled against them. There are three tribunals: the first, consisting of three judges, is the casuistical; the second, consisting of twelve judges, is the episcopal; the third, consisting of the nine malic molds, is the diametrically surreal . . .

When Nicasio and Elena Urlihrt were trying to come up with a name for the journal, they had firmly in their heads the name of Georges Bataille's review, *Acéphale.* [*Still needed*, Belisario's letter to Dos, anaphora. Seven times.]

Agraphia was then forty years old. "Longevity and solipsism have gradually transformed it"—declared Oliverio Lester—"into the strangest and most idiotic literary journal in South America." Many agree. Its longevity seems to be a result of its strict discretionary code, and a policy of nonintervention so severe, most members have developed hormonal disorders. As only a few other journals have done, *Agraphia* dispensed with all matters concerning the outside world—or according to Lester in an interview, "barely sensed it." Its members spent their days engrossed, their faces bent towards the page, their thoughts reflecting back from it, as if *Agraphia* was scripture, and everything else Apocrypha. Such interiority results in those *indoor games* which Rómulo Stupía and Répide Sabatani never tire of reproaching, citing examples of the behavior of characters in the stories, and the suffocating absence of chronology. Their output—in "Early," "Imitation . . . ," "Xoch. Diary," "Out of a Greek . . ."—has been thanks to a pseudonymity that guarantees the absolute identity of the precursor, the template, distinguishing him from the list of alternative names, which are dropped, as it were, throughout a narrative that makes biography, or the story of a single person, read like a "family romance." As for the length of that story, it is determined by an almost trance-like focus: a focus on the self that admits no external influence and on events that takes no account of any chain connecting them. Luini, who was consulted for a poll by an even more obscure journal, *Jolt*, affirmed that *Agraphia* is "apolitical, glabrous, almost oligo- . . ." A nice bit of opportunism considering the glabrous and near-oligos were expelled from the platonic republic during those years [Lesiva Víctima: pseudonym of Teodolina Teischer, in *Political Readings*]. It's curious that so many who scornfully renounce their past services to *Agraphia*, do so in a way that's characteristic of the journal—with scorn. Rare excursions are sovereign kingdoms [choosing one's own books, people, situations], small exiles, exclusions . . .

His first ("anonymous, collective") task is still only *half-accomplished*. At the height of preparations for the seventh issue, all the compromises, the petty alliances, the underhandedness that so often stymies progress on "the task," were once again brought to bear for an obligation Nicasio and the apostles didn't want to be burdened with: writing an editorial. [They would say later, "We didn't want an editor or a publisher, but we were forced to be both . . . So we committed parallel crimes pseudonymously, and came out looking like spotless lambs."] This explains their cross-purpose rationale of both affirming and denying responsibility for what they do. Nevertheless, having not failed to tell the truth, nor tell a lie, they inadvertently found the median, a word in between deception and honesty (perhaps it was in the first anthology). Of the best stories published, three were written anonymously—"Too Late," "The Fasting of Lourdes," "Vienna while in Prague"—three were collaborated on—"The Candles," "Dominion," "The Scent of Thunbergias"—and five were anonymous collaborations—"A Double Celebration," "Houdini and Cravan," "Supporting Acts," "The Cold," "Quodlibet" (although the *non plus ultra* of such a collaboration, "Out of a Greek Gift," appears in the latest issue). Their insecurity, impatience, paranoia—said Luini in the aforementioned interview—made them feel obliged to put on "a show of invincibility." Buenos Aires: a world already dimming by the late sixties due to the influence of psychoanalysis, according to Urlihrt. But, in the profession, there was a stammer, a nervous tick, a hint of uncertainty. Of Urlihrt becoming more assured in the following decades: "After so many years beating about the bush trying to get noticed, we finally began writing with an eye towards posterity, instead of fame or notoriety . . . and that happened once we exorcised our insecurities, our fears." The practice of condescension is tied to prophecy: "As we said without really understanding: *we do everything by halves.* Yes, as we said: it was mainly the programmatic nature of the formulation [or affirmation] that made us take a step backwards, recoil." In implementing these misdeeds—these "adulterated truths"—there was some fruition; as when Urlihrt used that example from his youth to vindicate "the journal's ethical principles" . . . The idea "It's not what God wants but what God is" that we see in "The Scent of Thunbergias," and which is distorted and amplified in "Returns," and seems in both stories to be "an infirmity that walks hand-in-hand with death," is part of the orthodoxy, the religion of *Agraphia* . . .

The dogma, mysticism

Only *Agraphia's* rite of initiation, the transporting of those orphic vessels of ceremony, demands academic candor; the rest is eschatology: the situations conceived, the roles played, the rigorous sentimentality, are repeated indefinitely. On the threshold, motionless, stands the invunche. The introduction of the *go-between*; the divinization of the *feticheur*; the tribunal duties of the nine malic molds; the transformation of the *Septic Midrash* into a gospel ministry [paschal]. Urlihrt's shamanistic character is revealed in his managerial approach: he responded to every polite request with an act of tyranny. When asked to be merciful on Belisario, he published "Early"; denounced all the conspirators in the lycergical glossary; in advance

The anamorphosis: "the distant far away." Sister Juana. Baphomet.

From the beginning, Urlihrt wanted to do away with "loose ideas." His aim: winnow the "spellbinding grains" from the chaotic mass of apathetic, indifferent, dogmatic, "tyrannically unwarranted" chaff . . .

Irene: Lemprière's Dictionary . . .

"I'd like to transform this journal, which is a pandemonium of columns and pillars with no personality or style, into a paradise where calumny is warranted, and pillory is praised" (A purpose met by other contributors, collaborators, deuteragonists).

Reproductive entities

Meaulnes's grammatical question; to those he knew as "the inventors of modes." He's no master of style: all he does is imitate, practicing the modes of kleptographia and kleptolalia

The gratuitous and the fortuitous

Those tireless reproductive entities continue to "breed" catastrophes. And catastrophism, that lovesickness, reproduces itself in the gratuitous sense of a *flatus vocis*, a mere accidental. So every effect is the product of at least two causes. Thus, the propensity for imitation and plagiarism proceeds first from the masterful work of Francisco Aldecoa Inauda—a contemporary of Rodrigo Caro—Francisco de Herrera, and the Argensola brothers; and second, from the maladroit bungling of Hilarión Curtis [no notable contemporaries]. The ancestors of the first are Urlihrt, Luini, and Lester; of the second, Tregua and Prosan. One name is missing, and that's the person Lester had insisted be excluded lest he "overshadow the genealogy." Outside the system is, for example, Sabatani, thought a heretic—a heresiarch in fact, for he was around before all the corruption began.

At the same time, "textual exposure" is what really concerns us. And *Agraphia*'s "texts" give the impression of thematic *foreclusion*: "The Dreadmist," "Sircular Cymmetry," "Out of a Greek Gift" . . . For every decade of tolerance, there are always three or four exceptions we overlook.

These interferences are outside excursions for *Agraphia*, holidays from their seclusion. Times when nothing is concealed.

Beginning with libel—"Sircular Cymmetry," which can only be found in two places: the issue of *Agraphia* in which it appeared and in Uribe's anthology ("Holy Fridays")—there is a categorical imperative of considering *La Colunnia* (Botticelli's painting in the Uffizi) as a parable. There is a terrible scene showing Apelles being dragged by the hair before a tribunal, consisting of a single judge, for he knows not what crime (the title gives it away), escorted by the Graces—the always beautiful, always gracile Simonetta in her various guises—and a Venus (the Anadyomene, one of the few works the maestro managed to complete). It's difficult for laypeople today to determine the nature of Apelles's slander. Lemprière, in his dictionary, offers the following anecdote: "They say he was accused in Egypt of conspiring to assassinate Ptolemy and that he would have been executed had the true conspirator not been found." Only a few people involved with the journal are aware of the anecdote. Otherwise, more than one would have admired and followed in the steps of Remo.

All the styles are one, and *one* is the unquantifiable "whatness" of *Agraphia*: its penchant for idealism and anonymity. The reserves, which together make up this singular subjectivity—defended at all costs by Elena—comprise the list, the partial compendium of cast members of *Agraphia*, and descriptions of them [using pairs of adjectives] are adapted from descriptions of favorite pianists. Nicasio—or rather his style—is "tentative, proboscidal"; Luini, "dark, erratic"; Tregua, "complex, trivial"; Lester, "exuberant, introspective" . . . Elena herself, "tender, neurasthenic" . . .

73

In the zigzagging genealogy, Nicasio does his best to justify the sententious approach that's characteristic of the journal ("Ysir is not visibly Ysir, not what God wants but what God is"), for it is the fulfillment of a promise, of a prophecy, a malediction: Nicasio Urlihrt is, in the twentieth century, the cryptographical, the cryptogrammatical incarnation of Hilarión Curtis: the consonants throttling the single vowel.

The number of heretics

And also, finally, the hypochondria, the ills, the diseases of *Agraphia*—cryptodermia, kleptolalia, cryptophasia, Elena's migraines and tachycardia, Inés's asthma, Belisario Tregua's gout, dyspnea, and partial deafness, Luini's stammer, Urlihrt's crustaceous deafness, Zi's prescription telescopes [28]

Family doctors. *An addition?*

After many years, and countless investigations, the mystery remains. What was it that was so modern about *Agraphia / Alusiva?* Despite its longstanding resistance to signing and dating works ("practices to which it has become inured as one would a chronic hernia," to quote the first manifesto), the year can often be deduced by examining the many scathing, self-indulgent references ("Early" is the best example): "if what I told you comes to pass, if the Manchurian candidate wins, I'll either go into exile or kill myself"; "It was better back in the day," the *dernier cri* of belated followers of Guyotat and Derrida; the trophies of a previous decade recovered on the beach of a future one like jetsam after a wreck: late eighties, early nineties, difficult times for the journal (*facts, deeds*) . . . The "actualization" of "The Imitation of an Ounce" had little to do with the story that was published under another title—"Specular Soup"—in issue number (?) [Eiralis: "I don't remember the story having such a title"]. I think Nora Fo's original submission was in the late sixties. But there were many changes, including the addition of a tribute to the co-author [dates: the days leading up to Inés' death is reflected in the children's timetable in "The Imitation of an Ounce"], so the final submission had to be in the mid-seventies.

Birthday mission

Elena Siesta:

"Sweet Fatherland, fountainhead of chía,

I have carried you away with me for Lent . . ."

RLV

What do we learn about the author from reading his novel *Las Patrias*?

1) That he was born December 15, 1858.

2) That his death was neither by murder nor accident.

3) That he's of Irish, Spanish, Portuguese, and Jewish descent.

4) That he fell in love with a married woman (whose name isn't mentioned), and fearing for his life, [was forced] felt he had to go back—exile himself—to Montevideo in 1878.

5) That he never had [didn't have] to work for a living.

6) That he began writing *Las Patrias* in 1914 [1904?]

7) That his father was a friend of Juan Crisóstomo Lafinur.

8) That, on various occasions and in many different cities, he met Paul Groussac, Emilio Becher, W. H. Hudson, Hilario Ascasubi, Euclides Da Cunha, Ireneo Funes, Alma-Tadema, The Prince of Faucigny Lucinge, Doctor Parkinson [Sinclair?], Foucauld.

9) That he also wrote a play in Alexandrines, *La Calumnia*, and shorter play in three acts that he wrote in French (*Une Petite Gare Desafectée*) [but not in that order, says Eiralis].

As one sees, they [these biographical notes] don't even reach ten, which are distributed among twelve chapters. Perfect economy. Rightly or wrongly, one can complain (in other words, give thanks) "that the sparse information deprived me even of those two guides that remain after I empty myself of everything else to begin the writing process: ignorance and unpreparedness" (Chap. I). And then: "that the questionable dates and chronology in general will relieve me [exempt me] of those two circumstances that are fatal to writing: Continuing to live [Being alive], being awake" (Chap. VI).

The Excluded

The Reference The Referent

He lived at quite a distance from her body (1), which suited him because his body had become (or he transformed it into) a kind of [surd] transmitter of resonances, the majority [of them] going unanswered. For a while it was believed these resonances or vibrations were meant for someone in particular, until the belief became a solid conviction (2). That someone, the recipient of these transmissions, might have been the daughter of a certain accountant [Elvioapeles Momigliano] (3), a girl he admired unreservedly (4, see after "La mia figlia"), who worked as an administrator in one of the schools, whom he pursued determinedly, or instead of a girl, it could have been a diffident youth, one with a furtive gaze (5, Proust), a student of a subject he cannot recall (6). The first case is intriguing: we can only guess that she must have extracted from these messages some small or mysterious residue of what was communicated in the originals; of the latter case, through his prudence and *obstinacy* [*tenacity*], some flattering suggestion was perhaps received, something propitiatory though inhibitory (7, Lampedusa). But let's forget about them for the time being. There will always be another *occasion*.

Of the various principles and scruples of conscience that governed the life of Enzo Nicosi (1913–1979/80), or at least the scruples he mentioned when he was alive, there is one in particular that casts light on his [predominant] tendency of speaking about one thing with reference to something else (in order to affirm that this other thing [always] evokes the former, whether because of the aptness or remoteness of the comparison), which is illustrated by quoting the following: "Latin literature is the most important solely because it was preceded by the Greek" and "I cannot speak or write without disorientation" (8).

That the first (9, Galileo, *Dialogue* . . .) (10, Hume . . .)

In 1958, when most of us first got to know him (11, Funes, second hand, Flaubert, Bovary—description of school briefcase), he was [already] "the man who would help guide us in life," which was expressed with a kind of negative clairvoyance [like the capability] (12, Keats, Shelley, Coleridge) by our parents in those circumstances in which most of us, being part-time pupils at the Balmoral of Adrogué, were demanding explanations for our extraordinary regimen of study. Even then he was incredibly antiquated, pompous, withered, and lacked any peculiarities to set him apart from others. His moustache was trimmed according to the fashion of the times; it resembled that of many others of a certain age (including Miss Aserson) who kept those kinds of moustaches, which our parents admired for being like those of Errol Flynn, Clark Gable, Laurence Olivier, Ángel Magaña (deleted in final version, 13) . . . Many years later, once we saw through his mask, that symbol of his claudication, we summoned the image of Von Aschenbach, as interpreted by Dirk Bogarde in the Visconti film (14, reference to Gathorne-Hardy, anecdote in the book about English public schools).

We first learned that Balmoral should be stressed in the second syllable, correcting the local habit of stressing the first syllable of every foreign word that looked Anglo-saxon in origin (or the last syllable of every word that looked French). Then, being a wise instructor in the ideals of Benjamin Constant's, he left us alone with a bunch of riddles to solve.

The origin of this strange calling, this way of instructing pupils, this way of addressing people in general—never directly—of dropping clues without ever hitting the nail on the head [the mark], seems to be in the way he himself was educated—or technically, in something he learned before receiving any formal instruction, something that happened not too far away in Lobos.

Orphaned at a young age, he was adopted by aunts who got their money's worth when they sold, for a good price, the umbilical cord that nearly strangled him (15), for he spent his early years listening only to them. "Girl, open the shutters so Phoebus's rays can unsettle the Lord's diadem," he remembered the eldest asking her younger sister when she wanted some light in her room. Pilar Rosario and Adelaida Barriolo . . . referred to eggs as "homemade abortions"; to rides downtown in a sulky or tilbury as "baleful journeys to the ninth circle." Adelaida's only suitor, an Englishman in the merchant navy, was received by Pilar with the question, "A vicissitudinous journey, was it?" The two women were known as the "Belfry Owls."

After his aunts—who always repeated the same not very bookish stories—dates and people seem to have evaporated from his life. Perhaps it was because the people he met made his aunts seem bookish by comparison. But, some fifteen years after his first class at the Balmoral, and fifteen years before Enzo Nicosi's death, certain anecdotes, like suspended whispers, began repeating themselves in places suited to abuses such as repetition (Kingsmill). A mascot, an English Setter—named Bramwell—was given to him as a thank you gift from Mr. Netbro's [T. Lebron's] daughters, and not only did it become his pet, but it was perhaps the only living creature about which he ever spoke with true affection. The fact is, he was going through a phase, whether he knew it or not, of wanting to be part of an English tradition (Ackerley, T. H. White). That symmetry, marked not so much in geometrical terms or by the equable disposition of objects in space, but temperamentally, as in the feeling of surprise one gets in discovering hidden objects [treasures] after years of searching, and seeing they are located at equal distances away from two equally terrible catastrophes; somewhere herein lies the indemonstrable [indescribable] artistic temperament others persist in attributing to him.

A game of tennis is perhaps the only way to see it in the open, one without a commentator. He'd learned to play in Lobos with his aunts, and his playing was—according to those who witnessed it—a perfect testament of that apprenticeship. A witness told the story many times [Bioy *père*, *El matrero*] of when he played a game of doubles and tried handicapping his opponent—one of the accountant's daughters—by aiming for her ring finger, specifically the sovereign in the ring her godmother Barriole gave her for her confirmation. He and his partner—a young man who had also been taking lessons— were winning emphatically (*score*: ?), and it was one of those happy occasions he'd later recall with avid boasting. But the accountant's daughter wanted to quit before the second set, convinced her side would be routed; whereby he, her instructor, had to suffer, earlier than he expected to, the absence of his favorite pupil; and so, for the length of an entire weekend, he was divorced from her, separated from the ring that betokened her, the only seal that approved his existence, the only emblem that secured his identity. According to entries found in his only known diary, the separation resulted in,

by turns, nights wracked by insomnia and sleep wracked by nightmares. The following entry records his bewilderment: "*The ring, not
the book.* But I wake up groping, knowing they're the same. That
I've kissed her, not him. *The atrocious derelict.* What made me kiss
her. The hope of a result is the strength that gives us a weakness for
rejoicing. Mutual."

He kept vigil in one of the college classrooms

The latter was the first instance where reference was made to a person without naming him, at least openly, a man who would remain
anonymous, despite his cultivation, his supposedly great intelligence
and learning, refusing to be honored at every opportunity, or to be
the subject of some discourse or panegyric: it is the result, some say,
of his timidity; it is a stratagem, others say, of his inordinate pride,
a form of display in the refusal to display, a show of the romance
of seclusion. It was to him Miss Aserson alluded, indicated, and
pointed when she spoke of the many times they colluded together
in a Brighton bar—he with a dry martini, she a gimlet—and despite
having learned by then to remove her moustache with minimum
violence, she retained the aspect of a doll, trembling, irreal, one who
only came alive in the hours she was with him (Kleist) . . . At the end
of her talk, she had the bad idea of recalling the secret conversations
they used to have in English—confessing [honestly] that her English,
which she learned from a Welsh aunt, was abysmal—and then citing
from memory a wicked remark of Nicosi's about Eliot that was in a
style that parodied his verse [true].

The murmurs that followed him weren't intimations of dispraise,
nor were they intimations of immortality. They were, as one might
expect, murmurs of relief, of good riddance. All were a little weary of
the legend by then, which held but little fascination, little relevance,
considering it propped up what was now a faded old gentleman,
who, even in his youth, was never very handsome, and now—to
top it all off—he was dead, which was a reprieve, for he would have
continued to fade further and further into obscurity, thanks in large
measure to Nicosi's devastating slur: "If it is not exercised, permitted
to fall,

To recover "The Old Bachelor"

to soften or die—with a dying fall—is going to be [will be] his unbending ally in all his defeats. I'll have you all know I'll not give in to silent defeats. Come little ones, you know what I mean. It's not a matter of guessing. It is on the tip of your tongue[s]. Say it."

Je renonce à Satan, à ses pompes et à ses oeufes!

Paul Verlaine

Lugones, "El Solterón"

Swinburne,

Betjeman,

George Herbert

Ater Umbrius, De Quincey

Faulkner, The Bible, Aeschylus (Alter)—book of David, Christopher Smart

Pedro Leandro Ipuche; invented source, Clemente Colling

Superstitions

If a man succeed at completing another man's Librarie, he shall surely perish

Worries mount as volumes of Books, so that it bee common-place in the lives of Men that loss of cares occasion newer ones. For Men are such vain and deceptible Creatures that many will fain embosom Misery who are loath to suffer injury of Pride, as certain Schollers, whose Pride of intellect causeth them to hurry after wind, seeking augury in the disposition of figures in Holy Books, or mathematique patterns in absurd Chronologies. Such Men are but slow discerners of the Truth, since that even Children quicklie learn that Books and Calenders are but

the fruits of our unperfect Wit, which hath never procured unto us a
perfect means of reckoning Futurities, but only useless Prescriptions and
Formulae that touch not our salubritie, nor inform us on which day we
breathe our last, but indicate only the passage of Years, the assurance of
Infirmity, and of our absumption unto Death. Nor should we reckon
the years to come by historical deductions, since that even Janus seeth
not the same Symmetrie twixt the Future and the Past. Thence the great
Mutabilities of Time must needs be recorded as they transpire, for Vani-
ties adulterate Remembrance, and Errors multiply with each Recollec-
tion. So Man should remember only his Negligibilitie, and heed not
the sophisticall advisos of Prejudice and Superstition, since that Time's
vengeance is to render these as mutable as Bone and Flesh. For upon
His long Journey between Diuturnities, Enlightenments accend but
rarely, as the fabulous adjections of succeeding Ages, the heroical deeds
of singular Men, or the life of the mortallest reputation, since that all
are but the flickerings of cressets.

After the style of Sir Thomas Browne

Instill

There were some snatches of English poetry translated by commis-
sion of Benigno Uzal for the Ur anthology, Nurlihrt's first publisher.
Poems by Dylan Thomas and George Baker, Philip Larkin and
Anselm Hollo. And a poet with the pseudonym: Gabriél Donovan.
Donovan was his mother's maiden name.

His name was Gabriel Sebastián Lubriano [Cecchi] [?]. Donovan
was his mother's name. Sebastian Birt [via *Concluding*] . . .

[But some began suggesting it was jinxed: *Trib*]

On a trip, Bambi falls for him [???]

I remember they divided the translations between Belisario Tregua
and me ["him"]. "I got to know Belisario the same day I got to know
Nicasio . . ."

The narrator has a book belonging to the old bachelor. Read the
highlighted parts, the annotations.

Inventing the book

He'd thought about leaving with his books. Or rather, he'd never have thought to leave without them. The forgotten, the unread, everything was a pretense of death as the two of them read in the same room together without acknowledging each other. And they did so with neither a show of reverence or nonchalance, as they would have done in the presence of their enemies [solicitous, smug, thought themselves ahead of everyone]. Sometimes a general overview is all it takes. After which, one discovers—he discovered—how many victims could be disinterred.

At some point, after all the trials, the stumbling blocks, [and mostly] all the anger and frustration, he finally attempted to make a record of his experiences as a bibliophile. But there is little left of his notebook; in fact, all that remains is a single inscription, brief but desperate, which perhaps cannot be properly conveyed in the indirect style we've adopted here (and which he'd also adopted). On one occasion, the loss of a very precious collection—the five volume study by P. Uslar on the libraries of Jesuit missionaries: source, P. Pastell, who succeeded in reducing the number of volumes to four—obliged [forced] him to commit a "surreptitious crime." For him, it was a point of honor that he never stole a book without first consulting the price tag, and fortunately, when he got to the bookstore, everyone was too distracted by the man who came to sign Uslar's collection to notice the indiscretion. Everyone, that is, except Birt, who was standing three paces behind him, with a look of irritation that quickly developed [distorted] into an expression of outright disgust, as he watched the incident unfold. The judge of appearances residing in him [Birt] disapproved of the ostensible buyer [shady fellow], who was neither a collector nor a noted bookseller but one of those fatuous men [and adventitious] who was, perhaps [at best], only a very distant descendent—the genealogical branching, formalist in design, blessed Uncle Toby—of P. Uslar or Pastell.

Where was he wounded?

Shandy, not pointing to the anatomical ubicity of the wound [the groin], instead disclosed the geographical ubicity (or name) of the battle . . .

It wasn't so much the loss of his precious books that distressed him, but being deprived of his closest companions; he felt as if he lost an entire kingdom. The irrevocable absence in his library spread like a contagion in his person. He spent days in mourning. He neither bought books nor consulted his own. He was content to read only those he carried in his briefcase (never fewer than four). But neither penitence nor abstinence could repair the gaping wound [left by the loss of those precious books] of his ravished library.

Anecdote in "Early" and "Replicas"

Many years later, he was horrified when one of the boys who wrote for the school paper—being alerted by an older boy—referred to him as one who had been "investigating with gloves on." And he answered: "I've never done [carried out] any investigating whatsoever. And that's not to say I don't fear infection, [*au contraire*, I know all about the terrible diseases one can contract . . .] and for that reason, I never felt the urge to investigate. I fear the gloves are only used by arrivistes. The seeker doesn't need to rummage or even touch anything: he need only look in order to see. The spines of books are like tombstones. Even the least discernible ones, those with faded inscriptions, will not escape his notice. And as regards the ones stacked on desks or piled on floors, they are detected, as tiny pebbles in a dense forest, through the gaps between leaves. Even what is imagined, what has never been seen, is anticipated by those spaces that are yet to be filled . . ."

It was the longest answer he gave, and the most emphatic, for the written questionnaire. He'd even tried to find the first fake editions he'd done [for Frederick Prokosch (*NYRB*)] to make the answer more exhaustive.

He came across some publications of Edith Wharton—the ones with those illustrations by Maxfield Parrish she'd rejected . . .

He looked with familiar disdain on the books from his last trip, still wrapped in a Galigani bag.

He had on his wall a photo of Arthur Waley playing the flute, or something that could be translated "flute" as a penultimate punishment [*reed*]

[And although he was a big fan of Hollywood movies, and especially Westerns, he was cautious about making sweeping generalizations. It's true he liked Hitchcock, but he felt that when his movies were bad, they were horrid. But the director whose films he really couldn't stand was Brian de Palma. He far preferred a conventional movie with a strong cast, directed by someone like Adrian Lyne, to some florid art-house adaptation of the *Hitch-hiker's Guide to Europe*. He advocated films like Karel Reisz's *Sweet Dreams*, because, for one, he loved K. Reisz generally (the first time I saw that particular flick, at an open-air cinema in the provinces, he spent the whole time raving about *A Suitable Case for Treatment*), and, for another, because there's no film that succeeds so well at divesting myths of their splendor, he said: not by censoring them, but through a stripping away of the rich patina of common belief to reveal the underlying pith]

NO

He was raised by two spinster aunts in a large [and cavernous] house in Lobos. The Donados [the Vieytes] [Chola Quaglia: Barriola, Fanfarlo, Arribalo], his FATHER's sisters, were known for their euphemisms, which although frequently incongruous, seemed to leap from their mouths with such éclat . . . "part the shutters so Phoebus's rays can unsettle the Lord's diadem," said Soccoro to her younger sister, Milagros, when she wanted her room to feel less like a monastic cell . . . // "Milagros, narrow the shutter, so Phoebus's rays can wound . . ." [Chloe Quaglia, las Barriola] As for the eggs in their henhouse— and eggs in general, for that matter—they were called "homemade abortions." And Gabriel was content to recall their turns of phrase, the majority of which were taken [extracted] from Don Quixote or the Vulgate . . . "Either Sancho is dreaming, or Sancho is lying," is an example, and also "Tomorrow, God will bring back the sun and we will prosper," and "see you remove the mud from your feathers after swooping on serpents, and if you can, be sure to trim your talons]."

And: "No manna, no manna . . ."

And, on one occasion, he heard: "Look, here they come . . . the belfry owls . . ."

[But] he had a good childhood, thanks to his orphancy, and he has many fond memories of playing outdoors with other children, or alone in the garden with bugs—earthworms, beetles, and smoking toads. And if the world was made up entirely of earthworms, Doctor Natchez once said to him, it would suit him to the ground [find in *Book of Merlyn*]. When he hung out with other boys, they were either at school or bathing in the lagoon. One time, the bonetudos stole their clothes from the branches of the trees that circled the lagoon. It was on a sunny afternoon in November, before classes had finished. A surprise attack, for no one expected the bonetudos to be on duty until later.

There were [public] outrages committed behind the carnival mask. And indeed, it was a grotesquery of disguises—tall hats, stilts, shiny pants, and feathered masks—that ensured the malefactor's anonymity. For the carnival time is when small offences are forgiven, crimes encouraged, and outrages lavishly rewarded. [At sixteen, he was very precocious,] *The foregoing was about Firpo. The brisk night air was riven by howling. But he vowed to stay silent, and he did.*

Before going to study in La Plata, Gabriel got to know the first and last names of some of the bonetudos. It was one of the most astounding discoveries he'd made in his life up to that time; but after two months in the city, it seemed the most banal. How strange it is to live at the mercy of time: before he died, and just before he found the Forbes Mallacombe edition of the Progresse of Sicknesse in Rubio (bookstore), GD recalled the name of the boy who found the clothes (it didn't matter that they weren't his clothes) close to Fiñuqui's property, nearly two miles away from the lagoon. Finnucan [*surname*].

When he got back to the house, the Donados . . .

Three days later (so begins the anecdote), on Holy Thursday [?], Gabriel went with Socorro to the market to lend a hand. The market . . . "maritime or fluvial?" enquired his tutor. And Gabriel recognized the voice of his benefactor [masked, lacunar] hoarse after shouting from the kiosk: "twenty for a pair." She was his first love.

At his fiancée's insistence, he went to see a psychologist. *"Your motivation is your salary."* Adelaida's suitor had given her a gift of stamps (*Antigua, penny, puce*). In *El Carapálida*'s lycergical glossary (I forgot the codes), Patrick Hamilton and the postage stamps they gave him

Suite of names

Wanda Landowska. Conlon Nancarrow.

Vivant Denom. Bonomy Dobrée.

Include the scene in A. de Mayo's bookstore.

He couldn't think about them without remembering a certain epistle of Lope's, and he couldn't think about this without being reminded of Lugones's poem, "The Old Bachelor." He'd pocketed these anecdotes in order to share them with others he confided in, the people he most wanted to impress. He'd repeat them frequently to those who'd already heard them, but in changing certain details here and there, his interlocutors got the impression they were hearing them for the very first time

In the town, Pondal [Pividal] used to call them "belfry owls"

Until he was sixteen, he never went a day without seeing them. After he left, he only returned home after hearing of Alina's death, which happened the same spring he went to study in La Plata. They died in the order they were born, although Lourde's sickliness seemed an omen of her passing not long after. They bequeathed to him many memories and stories, but also a strange uneasiness he always felt while he was living in the house, which others felt as well while under that roof: a feeling each of them provoked, and which was only enhanced when the two were together.

(. . .) In the period before he left, when he was at the cusp of adolescence, Lourdes used to request it whenever she was in the shower.
He'd gotten used to seeing his guardian through the frosted glass
partition, but he'd yet to grow weary of seeing her youthful body.
When she knocked on the glass screen, he understood it as a request
to regulate the water heater. Once, she drew the screen too soon and
he was able to catch a full-on glimpse of her for the very first time.
Her body looked more youthful in the vaporous brisk air than it did
through the opaque barrier. She seemed flawless, her skin, a marmo-
real pallor rarely violated by the sun. And although the image lasted
but a second's glance, a glance he tactfully removed before she felt it,
it left an impress on his mind he never lost.

Alina, he recalled at the wake, was more than just a stockpile of
euphemisms and abstruse paraphrases: she'd been the one to instigate
his habit of collecting, beginning with words and sayings in various
languages. And she, the weaver of his destiny from the following day
onwards, was responsible for uttering what he deemed an unrepeat-
able insult: "Mr. Mies has his quincunx aspect badly disposed."

Later, when he was moving in more lofty circles, pushing his luck
amidst the movers and shakers of the Buenos Aires elite, Gabriel
Donovan would often repeat the story, but censored himself from
uttering those secret foreshadowings his overactive infantile brain
once associated with that word, as if the uncertain and the certain
had, in the intervening years, become equally demonstrable, equally
representable, as a blank page and a written page; or an arrangement
of dots and an exhaustive interpretation of those dots. So he presented the story as a comedy of errors, and his vaguely astrological
quincunx took on the significance of a Jewish prepuce, his sexuality
cold-blooded, reptilian, for there was a weakness in the susceptibil-
ity to derive pleasure from a woman's body, immorality in that for
which he was once grateful, now the quincunx became a *shibboleth*
he couldn't pronounce, a goddamned reminder of his former self . . .
[a reminder of the one that held the sword above his head] Reread

Cavafy

Mr. Mies was a Dutchman who stayed in the barn at the back of the Donados' house (which, GD found out years later, was also where the bonetudos kitted themselves out [where they stored their face-masks, their wagons]). The first time he saw him he was chewing on the bit of his bubble pipe

He was amused that his close friends were so amused by his "bad quincunx aspect," although they were guilty of their own blind superstitions, which was reflected in the books they read, books by authors as important to them as any on the university curriculum (Arendt, Sontag). He himself enjoyed a semester under the saturnine influence of various authors . . . There was an astrological clique emerging in his circle of university friends, and he felt he had no choice but to go along with it. "Saturnine" is a reference to the editor, Saturnino Calleja. But it wasn't really a case of peer pressure. He always reserved a hint of admiration for those who can spell and who respect the basic rules of grammar.

They interrogated him about the bonetudos and he gave them away. Now that he'd moved up in the world, he didn't care. He also wanted to know the names of those involved in the conspiracy against D.

Before going to bed, and before making what he called a "moral choice," he recited "Prayer Before Birth," by Louis MacNeice

Anagrams, pangrams, double acrostics . . .

[Arribalo, Barriola, Donado, Ventimiglia] the Andovers' residence with his girlfriend, a young woman (daughter of Ventimiglia Donceles, the singer—remember?) who was very much in love with him, and an avid reader of everything he wrote. And he wondered, but refrained from asking aloud . . . How could she be in love, the only condition for which reciprocation isn't a law . . . ?

Combine hearing / / Conversation

—She's in love with him because he writes.

—Does he write so well?

—For sure. She reads everything he writes.

And then he asked himself . . .

Conversation with the *editor*.

—It's Balmóral, everyone pronounces it wrongly. I'm surprised at you.

The aunt. Everyone was living in a state of shock. Shock that overrode the fear.

After returning from his last trip, he saw his door had been forced open. He was [NOt]

surprised at what was taken [by those freaks]. He knew what they were looking for. *Honor among thieves.*

He stepped over the threshold and tripped over the books from his last trip, still wrapped in a Galignani bag. Jet-lagged, he moved through the house with a weary contempt of the all-too-familiar. He was humming a song.

In the bathroom, he found the dog-eared though still unread journal he bought on the train from that youth who reminded him of *George*.

End of P, bad marriage to an awful girl. Chesterton's biography of Chaucer: William Morris's edition of Chaucer's works. The smell of cat piss hit like a brick wall. At least other urine smells only erect a semi-permeable barrier. And having some way through is always better than having none. He had to get rid of his slithering, reptilian comparisons: repudiate them. And he was here. *There.*

A not-unexpected death begins the story (disease, obviously)

The three factors. The conversation in which we learn: X is the accountant's daughter's boyfriend. The house broken into during a trip to Europe. The angelic girl in the Pallemberg bookstore. Passing by a poster of Belgrano in Peru ("The House on calle Piedras," "Replicas")

A lengthy tribunal negotiation (on the same day Luini saw him) concerning the movement of the inheritance southwards, which couldn't happen until after July 9 . . .

[Eiralis sets the date . . . in the preface or the letters?]

Luckily he liked walking . . .

So that he went down, as he liked to say, as he liked to believe, for Esmeralda, then he got to Piedras—with the cars and buses before him, daring him—and he got as far as Carlos Calvo, at which point he doubled back.

Include the booksellers in "Early"

Accents has the original strip of paper [a valuable addition to my bibliophile's treasury], which contains a false enthymeme or [involuntary] syllogism:

"A completely original work that will endure in the memory: all its readers will be friends of the author and one another and so complicit in ensuring its endurance."

I'd already managed to acquire some gems in that unassuming bookstore with its unprepossessing old proprietor. Most were on the tables with the other cheap books, but, occasionally, there were one or two great volumes to be found on the shelves. Of course, they'd remain there unsold for several months before being demoted to the plebeian tables. Some of my best friends were witness to the regularity of this process. The most observant of them called the period of caducity "the fall," and he'd usually announce its arrival out loud. But it was still the middle of spring. Behind me, the two sisters and heirs of the establishment were conversing—a pair of redheads who looked like they came out Dante Gabriel Rossetti via Zwi Migdal or the Warsaw Ghetto. They were speaking in intricate detail about some family matters. But there was an anger or furor in their voices (perhaps they were just being loud) about information one wouldn't expect two siblings to disagree about. The indirect way they related that information didn't help, but any auditor would find it hard to believe that two sisters who spent nearly every waking hour together for the better part of fifteen years, would be ignorant of their father's eye color, the ages and genders of their cousins, or the fact their mother was bald. But I swear that this was the nature of their exchange.

That day, each of them discussed how much they disliked the noise and heat of their respective houses, in the process of which they gave away not only their addresses, but how long they'd been living there, how many rooms they had, the location of the television, etc.

I thought that if this absurd display was practiced, merely an exercise of redundant communication intended for the casual listener, then I should demand a refund for those four issues of *Accents* I bought (the most recent hidden under the ponderous weight of a copy of Papini's *Final Judgment*), the contents of which were lame by comparison; but if they weren't practiced, intentional, then I regret having admired their pleonasms and redundancies for as long as I had, which seemed to go on for as long as I'd been in possession of a mortal coil.

Temporal convergence of "Early" narrator / "Replicas" narrator ["The House on calle Piedras"?]. *Stop. Stet.* We're still in the "The Old Bachelor."

He knew the bookstore he established there—Columbo, Pallemberg, Palermo—would, on many occasions, provide him with surprises [*Ethics of the Dust, Galleries of Whispers, Black Lamb and Gray Falcon, And the Name of the Star is Wormwood, The Goshawk . . .*]

The Finnish biography of Maturin: *Charles Robert Maturin, His Life and Works*, Niilo Idman (Helsinki, 1923).

On the near empty shelves of the bookstore on Montevideo street, there were copies of books that he purchased at a surprisingly low cost: the first volume of Rabelais' *Gargantua*, translated by Thomas

Urquhart [*7 Types of Ambiguity*, first edition with dedication], a first edition of Eddison's *The Worm Ouroboros*, two books by Meredith (*The Shaving of Shagpat, The Ordeal of Richard Feverel*), and almost every volume of I. A. Richard's *Modern English*. The Milton is in the dead aunt's house

Meredith's monograph on Siegfried Sassoon.

He was about to leave with a bizarre and [little known] treasure, a book of Armenian grammar that was signed by one T. Anlunle in Mexico City in 1965, when from a distance, he noticed [the soft glint of stealth in motion? Try thinking of a concrete comparison] the slow descent of a spider on a book inside a tray he'd already explored. He was well known for his fear of spiders—even amongst those who barely knew him. The creature swayed back and forth pendulously, dexterously, before finally alighting. The book on which it stood seemed to glow under the overhead lighting.

Then he saw the spider stretch out its forelimbs, as if it were the girl, the Donceles's daughter, inviting an embrace . . .

He approached the tray into which the miserable creature dropped, and warily examined the book it seemed to select for him: William Morris's edition of the works of Geoffrey Chaucer. With the spider nowhere to be seen, he quickly stowed the book in his sleeve. He was looking forward to thumbing through it, as he did when he was young.

The next row of books was so disappointing—for example, three volumes of the works of that impossible poet they tried persuading GD to translate into English, the *novelettes* of Herman Wouk, Vicki Baum, Hans Fallada—he felt he had to check if the "treasure" he had under his sleeve was really the book he thought it was. He looked at the timeworn, almost non-existent binding, the near-extinguished glow [like the liminal glow around a flame: his reason for taking it]. It was old, but at least it was the right book. Then Gabriel Donovan suddenly thought he was too hasty in judging the row of books disappointing, for while flashing his eyes along the upper shelves, past some old gazettes and anthologies of English poetry compiled by Patrick Gannon, he happened upon the very paperback copy of Henry Williamson he needed to complete his collection. Then he found a copy of *And the Name of the Star* by Oliver Stonor, and that hard-to-find French bibelot—which French booksellers gloated was actually impossible-to-find, a claim he not only disputed but which he vowed to confute—*La muse demi mondaine et les antibiotiques*, the first and last work of Luc Crespin—a kind of Radiguet figure to Lucien Rebatet's Cocteau; that's to say, a last intimate acquaintance [but we must specify what we mean by "intimate" lest it be understood with the same unscrupulous literality the French scandal-mongers derived from perusing their Littré].

And in another tray he found [the works of Swindon listed before and . . .] Then he suddenly got the impression he was in his own library and was afraid he was no longer in the place he thought he was . . .

Because whoever arranged or mixed up the books would never have thought to do so in the following order: [unrealistic books, Sebastian Knight, Herbert Quain . . .]

An ordering that inexplicably corresponded with his own—with Donovan's—personal, interior, library

Time, air, and substance, aspects of the real we take for granted, but which seemed unreal in that single volume initialed [prepared by] HQ [Herbert Quain] containing both *April March* and *The God of the Labyrinth*. When his fingers found the well-worn edge of a copy of *The Prismatic Bezel*, he lost his breath, and his heart skipped a beat . . . with a sense of foreboding aptness, there was a copy of *The Tragedy of S. K.*, by John Goodman, lacking a jacket and balanced precariously on a shelf's edge.

And then, slowly, with a characteristic swaying back and forth, which his best friends had detected when they accompanied him on his bookish excursions, [on their way to Esmé's] Gabriel Donovan was fading away from, crumbling out of the dream he'd been dreaming. When he found himself again . . . , he realized he'd arrived, as if by magic, in his own house . . .

He hadn't regained his calm after the return journey, which he made believing himself laden with treasure, a journey that felt like a swift descent; nor had he lost sight of those images of private devotion from which he was so rudely awakened . . .

#??? He was found dead: a happy suppression of consciousness and all conjecture, passively accepted in every tribal dialect [the following day]. [Circumstantial data] No one believed, etc.

No one wanted to believe.

While others—puffed with bombast—appear
To lash the sea's shoulders, skirt the poles
Though blustering of all things tropical;
They lantern the moon, lend Apollo a taper
Worse than the lady of my mind, my Earth,
Who, once baptized, foreswore her place of birth.

These you will see depicting battle scenes
Full of gorgons, griffins, and centipedes
Invoking Scylla, their runaway harlot.

Lope, "Epistle to Barrionuevo"

With a grammar book signed by T. Anlunle in which were copied the following lines [from the second sestina]:

Because it was the touch of a distant stream
That made his visible [palpable], broke its surface
As a body falling in the concave glass of night,
As dreams mirror the last day's wayward steps
Leading to a false awakening [dawning],
To the icy sting of awakening without him

A kind of parody or burlesque of Elizabethan writing

Inquiry about the Progresse of Sickness[e] and the Behavior of Death. Elizabeth, [Jean-Marie] Maurice Schérer, Gallimard, 1946.

Lord Swindon: *Early Fiction* (André Deutsch, 1964).

Lady Centipede, Religious Matters, The Game and the Solitude, Before & After Firbank, Auday & Ainchil,

Dreams that money can buy

"Disney contra the metaphysicians . . ." Perri

The Referent

By Nicasio Urlihrt

Followed by notes and commentary

By Oliverio Lester and Ema Teodelina Wuhl

Epilogue by Luis Chitarroni

Ema Wuhl

Magritte

Apple: western communism

After visiting the pathologist

Inscribe Miss Gee's verses in a Gideon Bible. See original draft of "The Old Bachelor"

In February 1971, the French journal, *Alusif / Imposture*, launched a short-story competition. Instead of using a panel of judges to arbitrate on their suspiciously nepotistic, allegedly venal, and indisputably subjective standards of taste, winners were chosen for their ability to fulfill two very special criteria. The first was quantitative: whoever managed to adulterate their story with the most references and allusions would win. A key to these allusions should be sent as well, in a separate envelope and signed with a pseudonym (or, if the story was submitted under a pseudonym, a *different* pseudonym), specifying for each allusion or reference the title of the work in question, its author, and, where possible, the appropriate page number, chapter, publisher, and year of publication.

Considering the literary atmosphere of the time—the days of *Tel Quel*, Barth's "Literature of Exhaustion," and the *Ouvroir de Littérature Potentielle* . . . the era stretching from *The Waste Land* to *Ada* (which latter would have been published right around the same time the contest took place?); not to mention that of *Finnegans Wake*—the second criterion was a patriotic one: French literature might have felt a little depleted, not quite the [roll call] starry firmament it had presented in previous centuries. Why weren't these great precursors more appropriated [drawn upon]?

The funny thing is an Argentine won. Nicasio Urlihrt, a temporary resident of Paris, wrote the winning story in twenty one days (eight less than Stendhal) with no other library at his disposal than the one in his memory. He was lucky enough to befriend an excellent Antillean translator, Iphigenie Andromaque [Girri, *Je pense a vous*] Prévost, who could translate as fast as the story was written.

The author's notational convention is given at the beginning

Even stranger, the first writer mentioned is also Argentinian: Osvaldo "Lalo" Sabatani, author of "Sircular Cymmetry," a type of dialogue borrowing from the Ulyssean theme. Sabatani had had more difficulties. Firstly, his translator happened to be Urlihrt's wife [Raquel Elena Salafia?], Elena Siesta. She was a fine translator but a slow and painstaking redactor. To achieve his unusual feat, Urlihrt used a detailed notebook. As Oliverio Lester discovered later, he used such a notebook in order to include, with a minimum number of variations, as many allusions as he could to the books he'd read in the previous three years. It was surely the variety of these references, and the way they were incorporated, that won favor with the judges. But what especially impressed them, was the way he adapted these references to his own language in such a way that made them appear fresh, original—it was as if they were being read for the first time—and the way his cryptic style made the writing seem almost inscrutable, the references almost undetectable, but with occasional lapses of more direct and coherent prose which, although less lively, functioned as a series of interludes.

The conception of Urlihrt's story had little to do with Walsh's story, "Footnote"

Careless verses

[*Pushkiniana I, ode to Istómina's foot*]

A foot lightly touches the floor
The other, delicately crooks—
As the pause before exhale of air
From Aeolian lungs—; they prepare
To ripple-trail across a brook.

Istómina danced [,] to purge her body
Of desire, her soul of apathy.

Too showy
NO

Poetry
#1 Careless verses
#2 Mid Sixties
#3 Poshlost
#4 Social life

St. Mawr (by Javier Manjares)

It wasn't long after we finished our meal that Henrietta [Bonham-Carter / / Ormsby-Gore, Gome-Hornsby] once again showed her disapproval in that familiarly ambiguous fashion: free of disdain but not repudiation; of fastidiousness but not disinterest; one of those English ways of objecting that offend more in the performance than the remembrance, but which nevertheless leave an impression. For the objection is always timely but never pointed, well-expressed but barely relevant, and if it is offensive, it offends no one in particular. Henrietta only rarely showed her disapproval, but when she did, it was with practiced accomplishment (the key to which lay in her economy of expression). I had mentioned something about the portrait of F. R. Leavis when her back was turned, and my expression must have reflected a somewhat faded admiration for the author of *The Great Tradition*, which I had read passionately in my youth, a time when I was becoming acquainted with D. H. Lawrence and when his poems (the "local" version, I mean, translated and published in a volume titled *Phoenix*) were required reading. But Henrietta disapproved of my admiration, or perhaps I should say, she implied her disapproval of what was left of my admiration.

In that not too distant past, Henrietta [it's Bonham-Carter] held the position of [consul] "sympathetic interpreter" (although she couldn't speak Spanish) for the British Council's department of cultural exchange. And I had converted one of her nieces into an avid cineaste, for we often went to the cinema together, although I rarely looked at the screen, the object of my gaze being not a projection of light but a girl of flesh and blood, a girl with whom I fell in love not far from where that cinema was located—in Cambridge—while on a picnic beside a stream. But despite the romantic setting, there were no declarations of love, only intimations. Neither were there declarations of independence (I say this because, the previous evening, we had discussed the famous picnic that, according to Auden, inaugurated literature's independence: the July 4 picnic of 1862 which the Reverend Dodgson and three little girls had in a narrow boat.)

But the evening that concerns us—that of Henrietta's disapproval—we

(Henrietta, Melchior, Nigel, and I) had conversed for quite a long time, and not on academic topics, but about French *chanteurs* [and American *songwriters*], particularly those Henrietta liked best—Brassens and Brel—but also Trenet, Reggiani, and Gainsbourg. [[and Leonard Cohen, [Loudon Wainwright, Harry Chapin, and Gordon Lightfoot]. We stuck with the French ones]] And Tony Gaos, my Argentine friend, also mentioned Polnareff and Dutronc, boasting of his meager knowledge, for which he was forgiven because he was a greenhorn, while I was dueling surreptitiously with the overcooked lamb, trying to forget the taste of the undercooked potatoes, which the wine had barely masked. It was a French cabernet, awful. I expected a lecho de piedra.

I am Spanish. I work, without much passion or conviction, in the publishing industry. I'd like to say our publications are all commercial failures, the kind of literature that must be wary of success, for I certainly have an intuition for such writing—a feel, a nose, if you will—and I'm not bad at the business side of things, and if it weren't for that pretentious clan of pseudonymous scribblers, here (or I should say "there," for I'm writing pretty far from where it all happened) we call them "hacks," and if it weren't for those tightwad publishers, whose trust [in a noble lineage] helps me to recognize my colleagues under the veil, I can honestly say, and without boasting, that things would be going great.

F. R. Leavis looked like the kind of man he was, or must have been: like a guardian of integrity, a professional who knew how to do his job well, and a man who had a special dedication to his art. Moreover, the old photos I saw of him were a record, despite their weathering, of a man who ensured even his posture should attest to the probity of his criticism, a man whose corrugated features were an index of his candor, of his contempt of ostentation (although there are various anecdotes that give lie to some of these descriptors). Work by Peter Greenham, the varied palette, the tense, nervous brushstrokes: a less rustic-looking Augustus John. The Metropolitan, Urbana. [*Farouche and Uncouth* cancel each other out—the names of those two jokers who made our stay in Stratford-upon-Thames so uncomfortable]. It's [truly] convenient to be born late and be able to calumniate our precursors and ancestors who rest silent in the grave.

It's terribly convenient, easy even, or it was back then.

And I recalled an observation of Hugh Kingsmill's, a man who was always ready to calumniate. He even compiled an anthology of abuses and invectives in which he assured the reader that "invective" is when we do it to them, while "abuse" is when they do it to us. Despite having child-like fingers and a face like a porcelain doll, Ada Antonia (Nonham, according to an Argentine friend) tore apart her bun with as much grace as ferocity, before doling out the same treatment to one of the compositions—seasoned, thanks to her reading, with useless inkhorn terms, vague nonliterary importations, portmanteaus, archaicisms, provincialisms—which I condemned as violating the criterion of those of us who resolved—who were chosen—to dwell on the isle of *understatement*. We *happy few*, of whom there were still a few who were suspicious of immediate happiness. The world is still just an expensive toy we share among us. A large toy, but free, and amusingly adjectival.

I voiced my opinion guardedly, for I knew it was quite possible I was mistaken. But despite trying to appear modest, I was lambasted for the fault; and in being quick with a reply, I was then lambasted for being vain. Commentary between the lines, *footnote for DrScholars*. And not for my sake, but in order to dissuade the others of my opinion, Ada Antonia showed her disapproval in the same idiosyncratic way her sister did. And I was beginning to feel that anything else I said would invite the condemnation of a hypothetical third sister. Of course, I later learned there was indeed a third sister.

But I too had my chance to disapprove. I had objected to Tony's long tractate on Spenser's *Mutabilitie Cantos*. It wasn't just his writing on English poets that irritated me, but his way of speaking the English language—and it wasn't just me, but quite a few of our friends. But, luckily, none of these were present that night. Take, for example, his odd anachronisms. When he answered the phone, he wouldn't say *"Hello,"* like normal people, instead he'd say in an affected tone, *"Well, are you there?"* His cinematic counterparts were definitely David Niven's Phileas Fogg and Peter O' Toole's Mr. Chips. And if a waiter happened to serve his whiskey neat, he'd ask for a "single rock."

The story was one of Gerhardie's tales from *Pretty Creatures*: "The

Big Drum."

Tolstoyan, was how Melchior described it; Chekhovian, insisted Henrietta; at which, my Argentine friend rolled his eyes and sank into his chair with weary exasperation. Seeing that he wasn't paying attention, I brought the subject of Leavis up again. Malcolm said he doesn't merit consideration let alone denunciation (Henrietta had already denounced him without the need of words), and that he had the same opinion of Lawrence, at least the Lawrence who wrote *St Mawr*. I recalled my first reading of Lawrence's *nouvelle* in an edition (I believe it was Argentinian) entitled *La mujer y la bestia*, which I found on my uncle Rafael's transatlantic bookcase, where it rested alongside works by Joaquín Belda, El caballero Audaz [*The Bolshevik Venus*], Barón Biza, Pitigrilli, and the elusive pornographer, Dionisio Aranciba. I wanted to consult my Argentine friend, but he was in a world of his own. And although an expert on cheap editions of books, I'm not sure if he'd have agreed that in certain cases—translation, for example—Argentine writers are any better or worse than Spanish ones, but I believe in the case of D. H. Lawrence, who for some reason he called "the English Arlt," his contempt for the writer would've only prejudiced his assessment.

Finally we (the survivors of that night—Henrietta, Malcolm, Melchior, and I) discussed *St. Mawr*, although, by that stage, our patience and our level of intoxication had reached saturation point (I suppose I mentioned this already), so that none of us were then innocent of the sins of exaggeration, repetition, superfluity, and digression, and none guilty of the virtues of ingenuity, perspicacity, or insight.

The place in which these events took place, by the way, was Downing College. I mention this because once we finally gave up our ramblings and left, the noise of some students rehearsing a play could still be heard coming from somewhere. But at that hour of night, even Shakespeare would be disagreeable. So, walking down the corridor, all I could hear, all I could think about, were (the bard's) words, words, words. *Treasons, stratagems, and spoils.*

But maybe the play was offensive for being crude, as all drama coming out of Oklahoma: a challenge to the audience to forget where we were, where we came from, and even where we're going, as if a representation—or the cosmetic or zodiacal parody of a representation—could instruct us as to the extent of the will, or better yet, its limits.

We left Downing College, passing through the inconspicuous gateway it shared with a psychiatric clinic. We always enjoyed passing through that gateway at night, moving through the shadows, pretending we were in a spy film.

We (Tony and I) were ambling along casually as the drizzle began to descend, neither of us rushing to get back to our rooms (one of those casual walks we privately relished, during which we avoided all conversation), when we suddenly heard—or, at least, *I* heard—a noise [coming from behind us]: soft plashes, as if our shadows had fallen behind and were playing catch up. I quickly spun around . . . nothing. Some minutes later, while continuing our walk, I was startled by the recollection of what I believed I saw. It was a face. But the glimpse was so brief, I dismissed it almost immediately. Eventually, I broke the customary silence and said casually to Tony, "I think I saw a face just there . . . when I turned round . . . but the features seemed to blend with the backdrop, as if camouflaged . . . it was like it wasn't even there." At which he said, "Really? I just saw the same thing. But it was in front of us." And it was true. A face with angular features was watching us from the heath; waiting for us; the same face [or countenance] that had followed us at such close distance.

—Allow me to introduce myself: I'm Bertram Fortescue Wynthrope-Smyth, chimney sweep . . . a quite fortunate fellow really . . . and in possession of a great fortune too, thanks to all those English chimneys, and the sooty little whelps in one's employ. And because one is such a busybody, running about the city here and there, one was lucky enough indeed to have caught a part of your conversation. Yes, and one couldn't ignore the fact you were speaking of something that pertained to the Society of St. Mawr . . .

Tony looked at me, stupefied: in trying to figure out what exactly was going on, he'd missed part of what this apparition had said. It all seemed like a bad dream, but I knew very well that it wasn't. And Bertram Fortescue Wynthrope-Smyth seemed to appreciate this.

—As times and fashions have changed—he continued—so have all the [obvious] signs; but the most important ones, the less obvious [hidden] ones, have existed since time immemorial, since before there was any fashion. Nonetheless, when the ephemerals entered one's consciousness, one tried to behave as if nothing had changed. But one has to admit things are certainly better now that we have words. One is aware you have many questions, but one would rather not answer them. You already know the answers. You may have noticed one speaks English. This is one's greatest limitation. Indeed, it is the greatest limitation one can possess, but never mind. The reason one came was to extend to you an invitation to a meeting next Friday of the society you so modestly spoke of.

He spoke with that aristocratic accent I despised. "One" this, and "one" that, avoiding at all costs the all too plebeian "I."

—You must understand it *cum grano salis*—he continued—; if you manage to decipher the words they use, you will be forced to join. But know this: chimneys and books are not so dissimilar; the same skepticism follows from the realization of the bland inconsequence of both ashes and words. There will be no talk of literature, but we should be honored if you choose to accept our invitation.

He gave us a card on which was printed the name of the society and the address where the meeting was to take place. Then he disappeared, leaving us perplexed and almost completely sober.

Until

[Perplexity guaranteed we wouldn't sleep that night, but not that we wouldn't be drunk. Tony had a bottle of Tamnavulin in his room. It was standing on his copy of *Old Mortality*. Bertram Fortescue Wynthrope-Smyth had addressed himself as if he were dictating a letter to an esteemed editor (it's true, we were both editors, but esteemed?) . . . And Tony was suspicious of this icy character, the chill of his formal diction, his low stature. "Don't forget, my good friend," said Tony once the bottle was empty and I was getting ready to leave, "the college and asylum share a gateway." With no more whiskey to offer, I suppose his generosity prompted a parting platitude.]

[I spent most of the following day in my room. Tony had given me his old TV set. First, I watched an English film that I remembered having seen before on Spanish television. I was surprised on recalling what it was about, and had to conclude it was a sign, a portent: it's a film about a boy who rides his rocking horse until he almost goes mad, and was inspired by a D. H. Lawrence short story.]

Henrietta knew nothing about the society of St. Mawr; Malcolm knew even less; and neither ever heard a word about Bertram Fortescue Wynthrope-Smyth. After dismissing the possibility he was a patient at the clinic, they thought it must have been a [practical, elaborate] joke. The intrusion sounded puerile to them, and the idea of a chimney sweep being part of a secret society was scarcely credible. Although Melchior (who was about to begin his journey back to Amsterdam, from which he came the previous day), knew many a ghastly tale about the horrors and abuses suffered by boys employed as chimney sweeps. "Back in the Victorian Age," said Henrietta, interrupting with a self-conscious harrumph. Afterwards, we began discussing the many idolatrous sects that are active in England today. Some are innocent enough, like Man o' War (although there was a fanatic among its members who happened to own the Books of Last Reason, which of course we'd all read), while others were quite dubious, like Henry the Horse, which was only a cover used by a group of heroin addicts for whom the syringe was both emblem and institution . . . and which claimed, as a badge of merit, to have some Argentine doctor at their disposal. Tony was the one who paid most attention.

Melchior, an expert on Slavic languages, interrupted with an observation taken from the novel, *Petersburg*, by Bely, in which it is claimed that the single most important person in the bureaucratic hierarchy of St. Petersburg was the chimney sweep. After reciting the passage [to us] in Russian, he continued with the *pushkina karta* [read in the Tarkovsky film], and [then] concluded with something from *Eugene Onegin*.

Luckily, that afternoon I received the first file on *Agraphia*, and the first report on *The Megalithic European*, Tadeus Oliphant, born in Yden . . . , about which I once heard him speak . . .

Friday, Tony and I decided to go to the meeting and attend to all the formalities. We had on the necktie and jaspé sash the committee requested we wear. In the Badger & Boar—or was it the Ferret & Bear?—we met up with our guide, a Terry-Thomas lookalike, who led us through an alley into a dimly-lit premises. The alley was so dark the single candle that illuminated the place dazzled us to temporary blindness.

A few flights down, Bertram Fortescue Wynthrope-Smyth presided over the meeting, as if he were the mad hatter (whom he resembled somewhat). He spoke with a high voice, and that impeccable accent, which—perhaps because of his explicative tone—now sounded like that of a BBC newsreader . . . Truth be told, we understood very little (we should've also given a necktie and sash to Malcolm so he could come along and interpret), but from the small amount we [from the little Tony and I] managed to decrypt, we concluded that:

a) The fictional St. Mawr from Lawrence's story had actually existed, but had been dead for some years.

b) Then he was reborn in the United Kingdom—in Wales (*of all places*), to be exact—since his father, who was of uncertain origin (a stallion, apparently rejected by the Spanish equestrian school in Vienna), was grazing in a sleepy meadow a few miles outside London.

c) Given the society was non-profit, and since it was so expensive looking after a horse, after six months, it required the radical intervention of a couple of prosperous American entrepreneurs (and philanthropists) to ensure the mating was successful.

d) Once the cult of St. Mawr was born, it committed itself to what was called "the small instauration" and to "the little idiom." No one ever mentioned St. Mawr's mother.

From the back, an elfin-looking creature came out dressed like an altar boy, his surplice trailing along the floor, carrying an object covered by a type of serviette on which everyone presently swore an oath. When our turn came, Tony nervously tried to repeat the words he heard muttered by the others. The object turned out to be nothing more than a well-thumbed [Penguin] edition of Lawrence's book. It wasn't even a first edition, but one with an introduction or epilogue or additional commentary (I forget which) by the great Leavis.

Bertram Fortescue's closing words were:

—Like Numa Pompilius, one presides over this society with the assistance of a muse. Latinisms aside, she will never attend these meetings unless some great calamity befalls one, in which case, she will take one's place . . .

Afterwards, Bertram Fortescue Wynthrope-Smyth gave us a leaflet from which I learned how to spell his name [correctly].

Three days later, a letter arrived. It was addressed only to me. Offended by the apparent snub, Tony resolved never again to mention anything to do with D. H. Lawrence or even the ridiculous name of that emperor of chimney sweeps.

I took a train to St. Pancras, and from there, grabbed a taxi to Durward Street. I was beginning to get the impression I was in a film: the changing scenery, the developing plot, the cinematic sequences—particularly on my journey through the city—it all seemed so contrived, I felt I was in a movie theater watching myself, waiting to see what would happen next. In the taxi, I passed by some posters of Kate Bush peeling off the buildings, advertising yet another comeback. How sensitive we are to every second of our aging. The London I saw will already be old by the time this is read. The taxi dropped me off in front of an enormous warehouse. I rang the bell and the door was answered by Mrs. Prothero.

The house was done up to appear as homey as possible, although it wasn't very clean, and the wallpaper told only of the proprietor's dubious taste (apologies, Chesterton), a typically English, middle class residence, with a steep staircase and hallway decorated with watercolors depicting uncertain scenes from an English countryside that exists only in folklore.

I was told to wait for my contact in a room with two facing chairs of very different design, a small table, and a china cabinet adorned with trophies, badges, a diploma, and some statuettes of canines. Out of the jumbled mess on the table, there protruded a book about children's art by an author whose face—which appeared on the cover—looked as if it was once used as an ashtray. The small bookshelf in the corner contained nothing of interest—tourist guides, cookbooks, the Gayelord Hauser diet—except for two Penguin publications [from the Tschichold or Schmoller period] of Anthony Powell books that were written before his *A Dance to the Music of Time* cycle— the one with an illustration by Osbert Lancaster—both delights for any collector, especially one as obsessive as myself, who was tempted to steal them [+*who stole them, afterwards*]. In the other corner (the one to my left, from where I was seated), there were stacks of old records. I walked over to have a closer look [at the covers]: Vera Lynn, Matt Monro, Engelbert Humperdinck, Helen Shapiro, Patsy Cline . . . Then I suddenly heard a noise and [swiftly] returned to the seat Mrs. Prothero had assigned me—a rustic armchair that was facing the second staircase.

From there, I saw a pair of shoes descending, the tips of which were parted to look like hoofs (I believe I saw them advertised in a shop window on the King's Road), then a pair of magnificent legs [atavistic, oriental], then a body sheathed in a leotard, which was either brown with yellow ocellations or yellow with brown ocellations— either way, alluring, either way, entrapping, consuming—a pattern to excite the male libido, the ashes of which are trampled underfoot (or hoof). She really kept me waiting. I was already five minutes late on arriving.

I scanned her from head to foot (or hoof) and judged her well-endowed, despite her very angular features and aloof expression being under a thick layer of what looked to me like makeup removal cream. Two tightly braided blond pigtails fell across her naked, pallid shoulders. She had a distant though penetrating look, as if she were pointing a sword at a louring horizon. And her eyes seemed to communicate [directly] to my gut which forwarded the message to my brain.

—You seem a lot younger than the person Hugo described, and much less handsome. There, there, don't be discouraged. I'm Bambi—she said, leaning over to kiss my cheek.

Then she slid into the large, medieval chair opposite mine and crossed her legs tightly, which made a loud, near-comic, and abrasive sound—which called to my mind Rita Renoir and Benny Hill. Then she took up a scone and began gnawing at it like a mouse with those perfectly formed, lipstick stained incisors. (Was there an urticant substance in that red lipstick? My left cheek was burning.)

—Our mission is simple—said Bambi—as you will soon discover. You mustn't tell Hugo I told you. But everyone's supposed to think *you* are the one who bought the horse and that I am your wife; that *you* are a Spanish gentleman—Mr. Rico—established in London, and that the horse is for your—*our*—daughter.

I said I knew nothing, not even who this Hugo was.

—Fortunately, he's not aware of this, she said. For a Spaniard, your English isn't bad, Mr. Rico . . .

I said I intended to improve it. But from the start, Bambi acted as judge of my every word and gesture. And although my opinion of her was to change completely [my presumptions about her were to change] in the course of our evening's adventures, only now do I know (having not been fully aware of it then) that everything I said and did from the beginning onwards was said and done only to please her.

—We have to wait for Hope, who'll be here soon. She's going to take us where we need to go. But don't worry, there's still plenty of time to spare. You don't mind waiting while I finish getting ready?

She took three or four steps towards the china cabinet, chose a small bottle, unscrewed the top, and extracted a small brush. Then she took three or four steps backwards, like a funambulist, watching her balance in her hoof-like shoes.

—You will be amazing, Mr. . . .

I said my surname.

—Don't worry about that. Just keep calling yourself "Mr. Rico" so we don't get confused before the adversary.

I said that, for convenience, she should call me by my first name (which I repeated). And that there's no need for the "Mr."

—You must be patient with me. I'm not good with names. Now regarding St. Mawr, it may seem like an incredibly strange society to you. And since you're ignorant of so many things, I presume you don't know that it's a totally non-profit, extremely permissive, heterodox society, and that although they meet in secret, the reasons they meet aren't exactly simple: you see they love keeping secrets, Mr. Rico, and I'm not exactly the most tight-lipped of people. Quite the contrary, in fact: I'm the kind of person who likes to share them, to spread them far and wide . . . As a result, Mr. Rico, I attract a lot of attention, you know? So remember, the Society of St. Mawr is a permissive, heterodox, non-profit organization. I couldn't be a member if this wasn't the case.

There was a picture on the wall that was directly in [purposely put within] my line of sight: it depicted a little man standing with a crumpled figure resembling a dragon at his feet, looking out towards a kingdom on flames. Fleeing in the opposite direction, as if to avoid his gaze, as if to disdain his courageous triumph, was the aery silhouette of a fairy or princess. Behind her, a winged chariot—like in Marvell's poem—seemed to be sweeping away her footprints as she fled, while a young child, a cherub, looked on in amazement.

I asked her about the risks.

—No risks, Mr. Rico. I promise. Hugo would warn us if there was any danger. We've been devilishly secretive, and moreover, deliciously perverse.

I asked her if she meant to say "perceptive."

—I said perverse, Mr. Rico, and that's what I meant. But at least you're listening to what I'm saying.

She carefully passed the brush over the nail of her left ring finger. Then I feared she'd suggest we go to her room—for whatever reason, not necessarily sexual—where I'd have my suspicion confirmed that it was still kept as it was when she was a teenager, as if she—a grown woman—were reluctant to let go of her adolescent angst, her maudlin existential search for a self: something depicted all too often in contemporary cinema and literature, and symptomatic of a soulless age.

To break the silence and allay my fears, I sought sanctuary in a casual question: did she know any other Spanish people?

—Of course I do, many; and Latin Americans too. They are, as Hugo says, "my specialty." I know quite a few words in Spanish, or *en castellano*—she mispronounced (which the italics should indicate without the need of a footnote)—but I couldn't give an entire speech in the language, your language. You'd have to help me with that. I know "medianoche" and "destino" and "corazón" and "certeza." And, let me see, I also know "la hostia," "carajo," "matador," "después" . . . and the phrase "apaga y vamanos." O yes, and "color quebrado, color quieto" . . . and let's see, what else . . . did I say "después"? . . . And, by the way, I also know Triste's parents' names.

—It's a pity my friend isn't here. He's an Argentine linguist, and he hates Spanish almost as much as you do . . .

—Ah, Argentines. After the Falklands War—the Maldives War, I mean—someone suggested I should "make friends with an Argentine." And so I did. I even moved in with him. And we often visited the Tate Gallery and the British Museum. He knew everything about Turner and Constable, you know: in fact, he was one of those people who seem to know everything. Which reminds me of a compatriot of yours, Mr. Rico, from Barcelona: he was my best friend when I was living in Banyalbufar. He's an architect and wanted . . .

I interrupted her to say I was from Valencia not Barcelona.

Then Mrs. Prothero entered to announce that Hope had arrived.

—Don't worry about it, Hester: Hope's always a little early. If she were ever on time, she wouldn't be Hope.

And once Mrs. Prothero withdrew, Bambi continued addressing me as if she—Hester Prothero—was now overhearing our conversation:

—If she didn't trust me, Mr. Rico, if she didn't take words at face value, you and I wouldn't be enjoying this intimate exchange in such a nice house. Well, it was nice until *you* arrived. Come, sit on my lap.

I already said that my desire was to please Bambi. I didn't need any prompting. But when she slapped her thigh so hard it emitted a sound that made me start, I was ready to obey her every whim. Suddenly, I saw a mass of fur move towards her, and leap onto her lap. An eerie creature, it looked like something from another planet.

—Falina's been my companion for years, Mr. Rico. I've never been able to manage without a companion, or a mascot, if you will. Falina's an award-winning Cornish Rex, you know, and she's very well-trained. Before her, I owned a little pug—since I like both cats and dogs—and before that, a Frost Point Siamese called Procol Harum.

So the trophies, medals, and rosettes all belonged to her pets. Animals: creatures of that other kingdom. I was so caught up with everything she said, it was like I was *of sense and feeling dispossessed.*

—Mr. Rico, where in your country . . . let me say it right, where in your *país*—she mispronounced—are you from again?

Once again I said Valencia.

Then Bambi spent some moments talking to Falina as if she were addressing me. She seemed to ask questions about bullfighting or something, but I got the [distinct] impression she was interrogating me. So we spent these last awkward moments together—she talking to the cat, blowing her fingernails, me sitting nervously, gnawing mine—until (thank goodness) after putting on her raincoat, we finally left the house and climbed into Hope's car.

During our journey in Hope's Daimler, the two women engaged in one of those dull conversations that invariably (and perhaps purposely) bores the passive interlocutor to tears: so I sat through the

111

journey, quietly, reflecting on the events of the day so far, wondering what else would transpire on "that adventure."

—If you get bored in London, Hope can show you around, take you places further afield than the museums. She knows the city like the back of her hand. She could take you to Mornington Crescent, for example, where Sickert and Auerbach lived.

—It's actually my sister, Honor, who's the art aficionado—said Hope—. *Honor among thieves.* But she hasn't the least scruple about admiring foreign artists. I mean, look at Sickert and Auerbach: they're both German, for goodness sake.

Soon, we were in the outskirts of the city, or as far as the suburbs, where we finally saw some green—the color of insularity, of self-sufficiency, but not truly green or truly insular as that autonomous isle of Erin. What was it my Argentine friend used to say? *The truth is never too green for a corruption.* Hope drove at medium velocity over a hill and then accelerated. I guessed we were approaching our destination. Moments later, Bambi proved me correct by pointing to a cottage in the distance and saying that that's where we were headed. I asked her if she'd been there before, and she responded by grabbing both shoulders and shuddering. Whether it was to her advantage or no, the woman was pure instinct.

The cottage, which was painted all white, was partially obscured by a tall fence, a hedgerow, and some trees. Hope parked her car. Bambi and I got out, passed under the arched gateway, crossed the pathway flanked by roses, and rang the bell of the front door. Two men and two dogs answered.

One of the men was short and fat, a ringer for Bob Hoskins; the other—well, he was the opposite. Both dogs seemed to have been following the first man's diet. We approached and Bambi said, unhesitating:

—You must be Careclough, and you James.

—The reverse actually—said the Bob Hoskins lookalike, whom she mistook for Careclough. On entering, I saw it was a large country house with—I discovered after a quick peek—a sumptuous kitchen.

We spent quite a while with the horse. James refused to stop brushing him until his coat was lustrous. The future father of St. Mawr was a large but tired-looking stallion. It was very dark, almost black but not quite: the Spanish have a name for the color but it escapes me. Burnt or charred. I should probably ask my friend, Odriozola. There was nothing to predict how powerful the son would be, except there was a distinct advantage of his being born in Wales, apparently—in Cardiff specifically—even though his father was sired on a farm in Maesteg.

—To be honest—said James—it's my first time looking after a horse of this caliber without the proper facilities. In fact, I used to breed horses in Clydesdale and Suffolk. —Then, as if he couldn't perceive an arc connecting his proven past with an untested future, he added—: So Careclough will take on most of the responsibility.

Careclough had been born in the Orkney Islands—a small archipelago in north Scotland—not far from Balfour Castle.

—Just like Eric Linklater and Angus Swain—he suddenly vaunted.

—Tomorrow, Hope and James will come and collect him—said Bambi.

—His name's Triste—said James.

—What a silly name, like that ugly city in northern Italy.

—No, "triste." It's Spanish for *sad*.

—Whatever—said Bambi—neither makes much sense.

—Triste. *Sad. Blue*. In Spanish it sounds nice: Don Quixote, *el caballero de la* triste *figura*. I don't know how Smollett translated it.

—exaggerating, as always: *The Chevalier of the sorrowful countenance*—said Hope.

But no one was paying attention.

The place to which we then headed was (I later learned) formerly a pub called The Eagle & the Lad, which had been renamed Bird & Child (in fact, the neon sign over the entrance read Hinterland). When we arrived, the event had already begun. So, with her shoes in hand, Bambi scurried to her dressing room.

Cornelius Sacrapant was speaking, affecting (or seeming to affect) a foreign accent: a bald man, jovial—a mix of Elmer Gruñon and Pepe Grillo in appearance. He seemed to be telling jokes, switching between two voices, one of them addressing a person called Wallace. It was only when I saw the redheaded puppet propped on his knee, that I deduced he was a ventriloquist. Wallace seemed to twist everything his master said into a joke. His voice was certainly the strangest I've heard from a creature of his kind—at once surd and resonant, clipped and lyrical, with euphonious vowels broken by brusquely stressed consonants that reminded me a little of Careclough's Scottish brogue. As for the ventriloquist, it turned out he was also a magician. Whenever he did a trick, he'd utter a catchphrase—"I can't do it any slower"—before once again drawing a bird or rabbit from his hat, or running himself through with a rapier and turning in profile to show us the pointed end—covered in red paint—emerging from between his shoulder blades.

—One of the many superstitions of my land is to make sure and salute the priest twice each morning (so he doesn't come blessing us in the afternoon); another is to only practice on our carpets in the small airfield that's located just outside the city. For the route laid out for the flying of carpets out of Baghdad [Hagrabah. *Spell*], as recorded in Burton's translation of *Alf Laila Wa-Laila*, is dangerous and restricted. Now I admit Wallace and I have never needed magic carpets to fly. Especially Wallace.

Then he flung the puppet in the air. But he did it so crudely, the erstwhile invisible wires that allowed the puppet to walk alongside him on the stage, could clearly be seen by the audience (which, in the dark, looked a sparse congregation of pearl buttons and dentures), and resenting the spell being broken so abruptly, they all began to boo. Cornelius Sacrapant reacted as if he'd intended the effect—standing center stage, proud and erect, grinning smugly, waving his hat, and bowing to receive the occasional projectile on his bald pate. Once the puppet was back in his hands, he made it say goodbye with a sober wave. Then, not knowing what to do next, the magician's proud veneer began to dissolve, as he remained rooted in the middle of the stage, raising a nervous hand to fix what remained of his hair, and stepping from side to side. As the booing continued, he set the puppet on the ground and manipulated its strings so it ped-aled its feet, performing the action of climbing a falling ladder. No one was amused. Nevertheless, thirty seconds later—I counted the seconds because I was bored—Cornelius Sacrapant had gotten rid of his nerves and remained on the stage, suspended five feet above the heads of the audience, and although they continued jeering, he dis-missed their jeers with one of those ambiguous gestures characteristic of Henrietta Bonham-Carter, and cheerily finished his routine.

Five minutes later, on the same stage, Bambi began performing a routine of disarming delicacy. There were various allusions to the past and present in her dress, which everyone thought marvelously quaint. The little space she had on the stage didn't matter. Her lithe slender frame moving around the stage seemed to cause time to throw open its arms. My eyes pursued the outline of her cygnean nape, the taut muscles of her back through raven mesh, but when she turned I saw she had a sad face, with false lashes and lips smeared with wax, like an abandoned doll, or an actress in a silent film playing the role of a garreted spinster. Then she began her performance. She opened with a recitation—interspersed with oscitations and eructations—of a monologue by the teenage actress in *The Seagull*. Then she turned to the audience and mewed some passages by Brecht: the effect being of a cat that fell down a sewer, surprising a plague of rats. Then she performed a Bovary that was worthy of a dose of Arsenic, a Karenina deserving of being flung under a train, and the audience responded with a muted applause, hoping she would end it there. But she con-tinued with her own version of Cathy Berberian's *Stripsody* vocal. Then she performed imitations of Marlene Dietrich, Patsy Cline, and a tango vocalist named Libertad Lamarque, before concluding with an a capella from Wagner's *Ring Cycle* that was so lugubrious we all demanded she transport us back to the present immediately. The performance ended with a last vocal flourish and a gesture of painful defiance. All that remained was for the DJ to yodel his own farewell. During the set, I suppose the Diva was explaining her life to me, a tragic life, which had been preserved only by the most delicate means.

Then James, [apparently] invigorated after his third pint, finally told us everything. But his account was confused, clumsy, inarticulate, erroneous, and—in many respects—untrue. It was an account in which he described people of dubious intellectual accomplishments, but in which he made use of every superlative to exaggerate those accomplishments. An account moreover obscured not only by alcohol but by his insisting on playing a cute rhetorical game (which I tried to ignore to get to the heart of his narrative) in which he reversed greater and lesser degrees of comparison. So, for example, "extremely" was less extreme than "very," "tremendous" less tremendous than merely "good" or "nice," "invaded and usurped" more lenient than "landed and solicited." Most of the time, success in these sorts of exercises depends on the personality of the performer. Homer, for example, paid no heed to the sequencing of events when it came to their telling and retelling. And Jesus, whose biggest *hit* was the Sermon on the Mount, suggested a disproportioning perspective on the qualities of the blessed. And so it was with James, sitting there with his flat face and want of a neck—far from Byronic—hardly a profile to be printed on freshly minted coins. He was more a Jeffrey Aspern lookalike. In brief, from his terrible account, we managed to decipher that we had to hit the ground running if we wanted to save the father of St. Mawr.

An hour later, the rescue party had been organized. Thanks to Honor's intervention, we managed to secure the services of Hulot, a magnanimous canine, a *chien de St.-Hubert*, or what the English call a *bloodhound*, whose owner had been absent from the meeting. Arthur Conan Doyle's famous story is often translated in Spanish as "The Bloodhound of the Baskervilles." But when the reader conjures up the image of a bloodhound's face—those drooping ears, those melancholy jowls, those large compassionate eyes—he forgets all about the monster of the story. He thinks instead of a loyal companion, a friend, dedicated to searching for what's lost, to sniffing out any false trails. He thinks of that little mongrel mascot who's first introduced in *The Sign of Four*: one of the most memorable scenes in all of Holmes.

—Christine Knowles—said Bambi—now calls herself Charmian to seem more distinguished. I knew that sooner or later she'd show her harpy's claws. I got to know her on the West End—the worst actress I ever saw. Onstage, she looked like a useless piece of furniture, one of those garish ornamental pieces collecting dust in the mansions of impotent inbred aristocrats. Poor woman, she eventually married an American professor [of English Literature] and dedicated her life to her kids . . .

—What's wrong with Americans besides the fact they're all born with a natural incapacity to properly speak *The* language?—said Hope.

—They speak with an accent—said James—that's their only fault. And, as long as they don't become fans of some baseball team or other, it will remain their only fault.

As if she wasn't listening, Bambi continued:

—Now she forced her kids to do horrendous doodles, assuring them they're enriching contemporary art . . .

—Not that there's anything original in that—said Hope—. The task was begun years ago by Sir Herbert Read.

We entered the deserted house, a shed or hangar with a gigantic sofa in the middle. The tip of Bambi's cigarette was our only source of light, and that was swallowed by the darkness after every drag . . . until the bearer of the torch managed to find the switch. Dazzled, we glanced in every direction. Hulot began barking. As Bambi anticipated before entering, there were no ashtrays; and, as she foresaw in her earlier comment, the walls were covered in childish doodles resembling those of Dubuffet [genre, realist]. One wall, however, the one we happened to be facing, was the only one depicting something symbolic, a fairy tale. It was a cartoon of the cottage in which Hansel and Gretel lived after they poisoned the original owner with a blowgun they borrowed from Beddoes, and afterwards, burnt her with the help of Giordano Bruno. Then, from the doorway of this Trompe-l'œil, emerged a very tall though fleshy woman in dowdy dress, a fashion victim in every sense, holding an aerosol can in her hand.

—Who are you people and what are you doing in my house?

—You're ruining our fun, Sophonisba—said Bambi casually, looking straight at her—. Perhaps you don't recognize me?

—If you don't get out of here right now, I'm going to scream . . .

—You're already screaming—observed Hope.

—Get out, you tourists, you gawkers! This is the house of St. Mawr!

—Mary and Joseph didn't own the manger, heretic.

—Ever since we got married, Woodrow and I wanted to give all English children the opportunity to get to know their favorite literary characters . . . That's why St. Mawr had to be born here, because the children deserve to be surrounded by their favorite literary characters.

—If all that's true, why didn't you kidnap Bambi?—asked James sensibly, surreptitiously.

—Shut your mouth, I'll have you know the president of the institution supports us.

—You take a risk at covering up what can be easily uncovered by us.

James rushed the sofa, which no longer faced us but seemed to have us corralled in the corner of the room, provoking a mock chase and a change of position worthy of comic scene in a silent movie. Now Christine Knowles Kinsey stood where we were standing thirty seconds before. Hulot spent the whole time reclining comfortably on the sofa. The second period of the shouting match began when Bambi said brashly:

—Triste, the father of St. Mawr, belongs to us. Malanoche, the daughter of Noctámbula and Padrenuestro, and Nabucodonosor, the son of Casualidad and Monaguillo, together begat Comino; and Comino lay with Aldebarán and begat Úkase, and Úkase lay with Solombra or Sansueña—sister (night)mares—and begat Triste. The sky was indifferent. The clouds were like ash. Or maybe chalk . . .

—Just because you know his ancestry doesn't make you his owner, you jumped-up whore!

—Are you going to make a moral issue of it, Mary Poppins? I'm not the one who dedicates every day of her life to corrupting kids.

—Look at yourself. You're a mess! Haven't you heard of clothing?

—Haven't you heard of a mirror? Or do you think looking at yourself means bowing your head whenever you see a reflective surface?

—Fucking Olympian slut among whores!

—Fucking bitch! Dowdy old cheesecloth-wearing Calvinist . . .

—Whore of Babylon! Fucker of multitudes!

—Miserable nun! So easily found out by a pathetic copyist, and now he's going to ruin you . . .

To prevent the duel [between the two] going on [indefinitely], James once more intervened. But when he did, it seemed Christine was no longer our only opponent. Accompanying her was a short man with his fringe combed forward. Like Moe from the Three Stooges.

—Onanist altar boy . . .

—Let's resolve this issue once and for all—said James.

—Doing so would require us to be reasonable. Lower the weapon, my dear—said the man with the fringe. Then he turned to address us—: Forgive poor Chrissie's want of eloquence; she's rarely well-spoken when she's nervous . . . but within a society of which we're all members . . .

—I'm sure *he's* not a member—interrupted Christine, pointing at me—. I've never seen him before, Woodrow . . .

—He must be an invited guest, then—retorted Woodrow, before continuing his explanation. But he was interrupted again [by something unexpected]. Bambi leapt behind the sofa, and

NO. St. Mawr was by no means where she thought. Dragged on longer than expected.

Early

The Referent

Xochimilco Diary

[Her strict sonnet]

Sodomy / allegations
#???
Contre-rejet
A sonnet Nicasio challenged me to write,
Not about me—a thing completely alien
A concept too remote to penetrate—
But about the things I see, the laws that govern

Outer spaces. The first law discourages
Me to love a man who only gives me bitter
Looks. But being full to rupture with desire
I let a trickle fall upon these pages.

For the small space between the gut and heart
Is like a city state whose frowning prince
Forbids desire's polluting influence.

Yet, a silent blush [frown] is all he need impart
To silently renounce [confirm] the looks he gave,
And I'll write a different sonnet to my love.

Elena Siesta, *Errands*

Then include a proto-prologue / procto-prologue

XOCHIMILCO DIARY

Sunday, March 23, 1100 hours. Solstice, Xochimilco.

We should've arrived early for the celebrations, but Luini and Zi Benno didn't want to. So we'll have to wait until after one p.m. to witness the (second) Grand entrance of the Great Chihuahua of Xochimilco.

Aída and Hernán were waiting for us at the exit of the metro station. Then we took Hernán's car (driven by Aída) to our destination. Some cajolery, talk of the festivities. And then: "This is something our rivals would never think of doing (Hernán knew we'd spent the previous evening at Sherman's, Septimio Mir's executor) because they'd say it's . . . what's the word they use over there?" We concluded the word they use is "vulgarian" (but we [three] neglect to add that we'd already suggested the same word to "his rivals" the previous night).

11.15. At the pier. Last minute doubts dispelled by Aída or Hernán. Exploring the boat, Luini was delighted to find a large table flanked by long benches. Then he thought he hit the jackpot when he saw that Hernán brought eighteen bottles of beer, five bottles of tequila, two of rum—apt, since we now comprised a naval crew—and [thrown in for good measure] a bottle of sangria.

[11.18. *Rum, sodomy, and the lash*, we cheered. We threatened.]

11. (20, see below). Beautiful, detailed notation by Aída on pulque and the agave plant. We all cracked open a beer, except Luini, who moved tentatively for the sangria. Once finished, he seized the bottle of tequila, and poured himself a reckless measure.

11. (23, prime numbers). Toast finished. Zi Benno (after yielding to his obsessive compulsion of applying lip balm to prevent his lips from cracking) steered the conversation towards topics of interest to him . . . "In what language did Traven write?" he asked. "German," answered the room. Zi took a seat. "How weird," said Luini, who held that B. Traven and Arthur Cravan were one and the same,

and that he decided to remain a célibataire when he was in Mexico (the reason he never traveled to Buenos Aires to meet up with his betrothed, Mina Loy). No doubt Cravan became Traven in Mexico, and that it was Traven's shadow we see cast over Marcel Duchamp's journals.

Aída was put at ease by her husband's comment (a comment she herself should have made): "But then, at some point, the bachelor must've emerged from the shadows. He has a legitimate daughter who looks after his estate in Mexico City."

"Estate?" asked the room. He meant the author's royalties and copyright.

11.28. After some idle talk by Luini, the day's first nautical incident. Our boat was almost swept under the hull of a very large, very luxurious yacht ("when describing a boat, should I refer to the draft?" I'll ask Captain Bonzo once I'm back in Buenos Aires). Its occupants (crew would be an exaggeration) hardly noticed the incident. In fact, they seemed to be getting on with having a good time. We signaled them to pass us by.

"What a bunch of shitheads!" said Luini [with his usual impertinence] after they were gone. "It wasn't that big, no bigger than the billiards table inside. Speaking of which, let's have a game." "It's a *snooker* table," said Zi emphatically, the only time I'd heard him speak so emphatically, which caused my admiration for him to grow. "If it wasn't that big," interjected Hernán, "you wouldn't have noticed that it nearly capsized us."

11.33. Got back on track. Before long, finished first bottle of tequila (thanks mostly to Luini's animal thirst). Hernán tried to recall last the time he played snooker. "It was in the Hirsute in San Diego, no . . . the Champlines, no, no . . . in the Venusón in Guadalajara!" We asked what that was. "Was? *Is*" said Aída, who then proceeded to explain: "the largest and most densely populated brothel from Acapulco to Laredo, I'll have you know. Tell them Hernán." So Hernán continued the hyperbole. We seemed to be in Brazil, where I'm from, where everyone's prone to exaggeration. "Not very often," Hernán hastened to add [confess]. "But I used to go once in a while."

11.40. Then Zi remembered that he was supposed to go see it the last time he was in Mexico. Not for pleasure, [he assured us] (none of us suspected otherwise), but because he was invited to the Guadalajara Book Fair and the Venusón wasn't far from where he was staying. But while in Guadalajara, he also intended to pay a visit to a convent that apparently houses the best preserved mummies in the world, because the previous time he went, way back in 1985, when he was accompanied by a friend, Quatrocchi, a sinologist—whom he introduced to me one morning during their visit in the Colegio de México—he was in a rush and didn't get a chance to go either to the Venusón or the convent . . . , so they planned to go last year . . . , because he thought that would be his last ever time in Mexico . . . , and once again forgot . . . , about both! Only when he was on the plane back to Buenos Aires, did he remember . . .

Prolonged silence. Then tactfully, furtively, with dignified misgiving, Zi added: "Of course being with friends at all those literary conferences, whether in Mexico or River Plate, helps make the time pass by more quickly . . ." But Aída and Hernán were still suspicious so he finally confessed that everything he said was actually [in reality] just the précis of a story he was writing called "The Motive," that he intended to publish and distribute in the form of fliers around Buenos Aires. For free, of course. We all demanded copies.

11.48. Initial assertion on the artificiality of memory followed by [simpatico] effusions on said topic. Photos taken, then more toasting.

11.51. The Venusón of Guadalajara, they say, was built at the start of the twentieth century, and is distinguished for having been modeled *a la manière* of the most exquisite houses of ill-repute in New Orleans. For this, they gathered together three architects, two painters of the academic style, and a gringo [Greek] pimp: Milos (afterwards, Eros)

Catsaunis, who brought along the first employees—Hungarians, made available by the generous Zwi Migdal Foundation. In 1901, there were already one hundred pupils. As a principle of order, the first madam (ex-principal of a rural public school) decided to give them all new names, using a triadic or tripartite alphabetical criterion (Amanda Albéniz Amadis, Fátima Fajardo Fez, Zenobia Zilphia Zardos), and to group them accordingly within stables, each group's designation being the first names of each of the five ladies in that group, the designation being pronounced rhythmically after an iambic or amphibrachic pattern, with all groups together, of course, forming part of a single group, that Fourier-inspired phalanstary called the Venusón. In the early days—the *Belle Époque*, specifically, but above all in Mexico—the Venusón was run by a committee, each of whose members was supplied with a catalogue (basically, a large photo album). Aída still has the one she inherited from her grandfather, an eminent hygienist who'd made a memorable contribution (I can't remember the year, but Aída wrote it down somewhere) in enforcing the use of Venusiline (or Veniciline, as it's called in old manuals and dated encyclopedias).

Famélica Fátima íntima, crooned Luini.

12.02. We hear a distinctively whiny voice coming from outside. Turn to see a boy on the pier, leaning over the gunnel, holding a basket. He was watching us attentively. Such serious eyes, he smiled a toothless smile. Luini passed a [frivolous] remark about the poor being more varied and interesting than the rich [the poverty of enrichment]: the rich look the same wherever you go, but a city is made distinctive by its poor. Indeed, it is the poor we erect as models to be imitated, it is they that easily pass through the eyes of needles. He gave some examples, to boot (the castle, the museum, the oasis) . . .

The boy offered us corn, marijuana, axolotls, magic mushrooms, more tequila, Angostura bitters, a mercury or cinnabar casserole (which came with a clarification: *specular soup for the reptilian brain*). Zi wanted to try it, in spite (or as a result) of Hernán telling him it had hallucinogenic effects (similar to those brought on by severe fasting, according to a mendicant monk he knows who spends his summers on Mount Athos).

Asked to describe it, Hernán said it was a colloidal substance, with a taste like rolled oats mixed with a drop of sacramental wine (Nebbiolo or Semillon), which he remembers from his boyhood. He said he got used to the taste of the soup during a long trip around Patagonia with his stepmother. As regards its consistency, he tried to be precise (recalling his studies in chemistry) and therefore once again began by insisting it was a colloidal substance . . . something he had as a boy . . . like rolled oats and sacramental wine . . . In the end, we bought a parrot Aída fell in love with. It flitted from shoulder to shoulder and then became like the Paraclete of scripture or Felicité's little mascot in that sentimental though charming provincial parable of Flaubert's.

12.05. A look at the watch, then the sky. Clouds like nurses escort the sun unhurriedly in this climate. We were all sweltering in the heat, panting; moving was too much effort, speaking . . . cyanosis. Then, mercifully, a warm breeze's caress, delightful and refreshing as a cold spray, and Aída was enlivened enough to point out the jacaranda and bougainvillea flowers joggling in response outside. Then a butterfly floundered in, hairy and (begging forgiveness of lepidopterists) repulsive, lighting on Aída's tanned elbow. Once settled there, Aída took aim and burst it like an apricot or an overripe persimmon . . . some kind of fruit in any case.

Then Aída—who had a talent for persuading others to abandon a trite subject—performed a quiet gesture to suggest we forget the incident. But, luckily, Hernán brought his camera.

Haiku, improvised (drunkenly) by Luini: *The butterfly / angel in my sleep / demon at my wake*. Not a proper Haiku. According to the rules, seventeen syllables.

Having been abandoned by *Psyche my soul*, I was reminded of the book (*because I do not hope*) that led us to go to Mexico that first time: Zi Benno and I; not Luini. Luini was, *is*, in every sense of the word, a *parvenu*.

12.08. A gathering of geniuses in Tlalpan—Einstein, Niels Bohr, Heisenberg, Max Planck, Pauli—and later (as if answering a casting call)—Crick, Oppenheimer, Fermi, Watson, Pauling, de Broglie, etc. This absurd convention defied all rationale: it was the crazy whim of the most important writer in Mexico at the time (whom our friends from the previous night prohibited us mentioning in their presence... luckily we were now in different company!).

Zi and I completed our monographs on time (which were published in *The Notebooks of Tlalpan* in summer, 1992, and for which, more importantly, we were remunerated). Without the need of Psyche or headphones, I could suddenly hear mingled unsettling cadences from the recent past, the sounds of Amon Düül and Ash Tempel. Howling hordes traversing the steppe [between things forgotten and remembered] avoiding the others, but charging straight for "me."

Yma Sumac, anyone? Aída to the rescue. A DJ persecuted us before in a similar boat. Then Luini seemed to vanish as my soul rose up and up.

12.12. From a great height, I could see the tiny dot of our boat, and I prayed to return to myself. We all prayed to get close to one another. But the supplication was to no avail, for the prayer was quenched in the utterance. For afterwards, when I opened my eyes, I could see the jungle stretching in the distance, the water of the river lap the shoreline. And then, still presbyopic, I squinted on a little bark where four were tirelessly rehearsing sham civilities—imperceptible *in vitro*, but, otherwise, obvious—and a fifth, forcing himself to cooperate in the farce, which would seem less ridiculous with repeated exercises in loyalty.

Then I peered at the telltale oval of my watch (sixteen after twelve) and made an effort to rejoin the conversation.

Postscriptum, airport: look again at my wristwatch. Not much elbow room inside that little case. How the hell does Time cover so much ground?

12.17. We spoke again about the Venusón of Guadalajara. At the end of the fifties there was a change of ownership. The girls could now call themselves whatever they wished: Glenda Brian, Pussy Brain,

Bermaine [Vermin] Greer, Xenia Brainiac. At the end of the seventies, the establishment itself got a new name (although it seems the large neon sign at the front wasn't taken down). It was a time when many changes were made, and many shady deals. There was also a newsletter released revealing the names of many notables who'd once attended. Aída jogged her memory again: W. C. Fields, Haile Selassie, John Garfield, Greta Garbo, Elvis Presley, JFK, Ian Fleming, Lee Falk, Lee Hazlewood, Serge Gainsbourg, *TL* (Tom Lehrer? Timothy Leary?), and an Argentine (to whom I'll also refer with initials because of my strong bond of friendship with his direct descendant): H.C.

12.22. I recapitulate. The reforms were initiated in 1969, *année erotique*, when it was rumored the place was bought by one of Hugh Hefner's henchmen, who renamed it the Venus Club. "The business didn't change, but the decorations did: the naturalist engravings were all replaced by paintings with an abstract motif, and all the bidets had to have printed on them the signature 'F. Mutt.' The interior decorator was an American conceptual artist," said Hernán (none other than Bob Guteron, he eventually said after making us guess). "It's still possible to see the originals today," he added, but then immediately regretted the disclosure. Aída shrugged it off though. She wanted to finish her account: "The business is now owned by a group of Germans," she said. "And like an old family heirloom taken out of the attic and restored to pride of place, they decided to reinstate the old alphabetical custom of naming the prostitutes. Except now, the names are all gringo: Ada Adcock, Fiona Farlow, Zaida Zorn . . . a consequence of globalization, no doubt." "But it was just the same before," yelled Luini . . .

In 1980, a certain fugitive called Lady Lumumba had jeopardized the integrity of the entire city-state. She transformed Villa Venus into a kind of mini-Cuba—not the free Cuba, but the communist one—with herself as Fidel Castrobarbarella. Luckily, someone intervened and restored things to normality. Hernán knew her. He didn't provide any details.

12.29. "Are those names real or did you just invent them?" asked Luini, almost beside himself. And Aída answered him with calm disdain, adjusting her sunglasses with casual precision, "No, I didn't just invent them. In fact, let me think . . . O yes, one of them happens to be my best friend." "O really, which one?"

Samuel Johnson called those people most susceptible to enjoying the privileges and tolerating the hardships of a vulnerable institution "*clubbables.*"

12.38. After reading the Excelsior, we learned that Federico Prosan (who, at last, had learned how to ride) was heading from Chiapas to Mexico City. That our compatriot had managed to overcome this difficulty was, to Zi Benno and me, a cause of immense joy and patriotic pride. (And we remembered Belgrano, who, before embarking on the Northern Campaign, could only visit the city by dog-cart.) That Prosan—after his marriage to the Mexican—became a righteous leader seemed incredible to the people of Buenos Aires, where, while he was still living there (some time before we'd arrived), everyone believed (as one of his best friends told me) "he had the social conscience of an electrical appliance." But Mexico is different. Mexico changes everyone.

12.42. An author of works I've rarely encountered, Federico Prosan had great success in Mexico and the rest of Latin America with a series of novels whose titles were inspired by the argot of a local sport: *They're Copacetic, From Chaco to Pollack, Me to Ye.* Then he used another system of naming using ordinary words in unexpected ways: *Later, Mirror, Scout . . .*

His last novel, *Ingle*, inspired by the life of Doug Ingle, the organist of a seventies psychedelic band called Iron Butterfly, was a complete flop. Their most famous song, "In-A-Gadda-Da-Vida," a mondegreen recently deciphered as "In the Garden of Eden," thanks primarily to the investigations of Holden Caulfield, who maintains the original was a phonetic rendering of an intoxicated Ingle's slurred pronunciation to the first literate person (rare in California) who happened to have a pen.

12.46. I spent some time thinking about yesterday (which, through the alcoholic haze, seemed no different than today—a horrible day, whose unfolding I seemed to control at every opportunity by consulting the oval on my fragile left wrist, to verify that within that small space behind the glass face, only you and I exist).

I completely forgot. The evening spent at the home of Septimio Mir's widow had been exceptional. The refined Uruguayan poet asked with oriental courtesy what had happened to the hototogisu in Zi's novel . . . "The what?" yelled the poet's husband, posing like a River Plate sodomite. Zi explained that the nightingale is in fact the cuckoo. The poet's husband thought the words didn't sound alike: the cuckoo, a scoundrel according to his moral lexicon; but not the hototogisu. How is it possible that within a belletrist culture like that one, there was so much admiration for the works of Zi—with their soppy sentimentalism and bumpkin sophistication, their bad grammar and archaic anacoluthia, and all those gigantic leaps away from the slightly credible to the wholly fabulous? Why him, a mere essayist, a literary seamster, a sower of gaudy patchworks, of varicolored doormats . . . ?

As always, Luini showed his true colors. For example:

12.55. In fact, there were many at the widow's house: first, he attempted to steal a work by Gironelli (I doubt he'd have appreciated it, but it was the only book he could fit in his pocket); then he spent the whole night flattering guests and then backbiting them when they were out of earshot; finally, after slobbering his food and swilling his drink like a cuirassier, he soon had his face in the toilet, one of the two complementary seats of capitalism, the other being the bank. He shouldn't have banked on us defending his actions though.

14.35. The widow's house on Edgar Allan Poe Street, in Colonia Polanco, was like a museum. Paintings of the highest order.

14.36. (Wolfgang Paalen, Robert Motherwell, Adja Yunkers), portraits of the widow before she was widowed (posing with her husband

as proof), and then, next to the latter, the former, the antecedent—
the last—another of her posing with some friends—more like acci-
dents of geography (who were clearly, unmistakably, indissimulably
Cuevas, Fuentes, Ríos). There were also some other paintings there:
autographed eyesores, according to Zi.

13.00. Enrique Gelzhaller, the husband of the Uruguayan poet, took
advantage of the widow's momentary absence (she went to speak
with Sherman, her executor, on the phone) to tell some hilarious
anecdotes about other literary widows.

In Montevideo and Buenos Aires (the Berlin of South America), there
was one who boasted that her husband was with her everywhere she
went, that she couldn't blink without seeing him; and, indeed, it was
true she was never seen in public without her distinctive eyelashes.
Since none of us understood what he meant, Enrique, a verecund
polyglot, hinted: "Poil pubique." Laughter. More laughter. "Watch
out," said the poet, at the cusp of an epigram: "if the widow over-
hears, she'll widow me."

"You watch out," he retorted. "I'm not the famous one here." Someone suggested the title of a River Plate bolero.

13.04. Enrique took his wife's advice: after all, he was [looked] much
younger than she. The topics were [being] covered in quick succession: Communism and Amorim's good fortune, the conjugal relations between Felisberto Hernández and the KGB (via África de las
Heras). Juanele, Juan Emar, Juan Almela. The widow returned and
the conversation switched back to her favorite topic of discussion,
her widowhood. "Did any of us know Federico Prosan?" We all said
yes. Later, we all went out onto the balcony to see the empty Edgar
Allan Poe street in the dim moonlight. ("If you're standing alone,
don't lean against the balustrade. It's dangerous.")

[stretch-marked] Hagarene supplemental: celibate alabaster scimitar.
Secret mission accomplished. Melancholy—the *Ultra*ist's melody
[Borges].

Someone indicated that my watch had stopped, died. Ah, I return abruptly to the present. "Now let's see if we can pause long enough to see it. That's to say, pause long enough to see if we can see it," said Hernán oratorically, seeming to look at us panoptically.

Later, when the Uruguayan finally said the last word on the last of her serious topics, Zi and I began discussing our own: Francisco Coloane, Pablo Palacio, Pilar de Lusarreta, Pedro Leandro Ipuche. No one was paying attention. Our conversation ran its course.

13.10. In the middle of the Xochimilco event (nobody could tell if it was really the middle, considering where we were and our level of drunkenness), but we were actually in the middle of a perfectly blue, perfectly oval lake, a perfectly reflective lake as would be found in the northern land of Zembla. Zi, on returning from somewhere far away, or, according to Luini, a distant and unchartered X that encroached on the letter Z—for Zembla—was in good spirits, and he broke into a recitation, chanting the measures, counting the beats for the synod's delectation. At the expense of the parrot / and forgoing any Latin / this sonorous feat / by Aurelio Asiain:

Salvador Novo was suppressing his laughter
as he proudly unveiled his smiling Mona Lisa:
A photograph of José Gorostiza—
Fair-haired pharos of fishermen's trawlers—
flanked on both sides by many a señora.

And as time went by, it was as if Zi's words were filling an old scrabble board sustained on Xochimilco's noonday shoulders.

13.14. Then suddenly the drunken boat lurched towards a topic already discussed the evening we were at the widow's house, Federico Prosan. But one of Luini's imprudent interruptions saved the day. Who are the ones responsible for the literary supplements over *there*? A bunch of kids, we said. Explanation of what we meant. Gave examples. Then we came to a unanimous conclusion. *Just like here,* we said.

13.27. The huge head was the very first thing we saw. The legend goes that when he leaves his [ancestral] bed *for the second time*, he does so feet first. But no. The great mythological monster slowly emerged according to the normal conventions of birth, top to bottom, looking like a huge stuffed animal that was custom made for an acromegalic child . . . Without hair! "Residual alopecia," said Zi, taken aback. Then there was a rumbling noise like the sound of distant thunder, or a seismic event attenuated like a wave by the very air, the breeze transmitting it.

True, the circumstances demanded more than cheap suspense. There was supposed to be introspection. I was distracted by the sight of Zi looking at the giant head. There wasn't an iota of energy wasted on those commonplace reactions of amazement and wonder. That's right [he was introspecting]! He seemed to absorb the image like the pages of my Mexican journal absorbed the ink from my pen. Ah, my Mexican journal. With such beguiling voracity it absorbed [drank, swallowed] the ink from my pen! I bought it the day after I arrived on Donceles Street, in one of those stores that always confuse tourists because they sell different things and things under different names to the right, correct, and just way they're used to back home.

13.41. The Great Chihuahua of Xochimilco wasn't a Chihuahua per se (that, in itself, would've been horrific), but something worse, something more appalling: one of those ugly hairless dogs they (in the United Provinces of Río de la Plata; in the northern part, that is, where they use them to heat the bed) call *perros pila*. In someone's chronicle of the Indies—or an apocryphal chronicle, certainly not one by Bernal Díaz del Castillo—it is stated that, when Hernán Cortés saw it for the first time, he christened it Egito. Perhaps it's in Prescott. The fact it didn't have any hair, made it look eerie, supernatural. Then there's the size—like the Trojan horse the Greeks left as a tribute to ensure a safe passage home (see Chapman). The one "that was then stuffed full of armed knights," as Cervantes wrote. And that's what terrified me. Perhaps the number of men hidden in its interior was only known by a woman (to the chagrin of every male, especially T. S. Eliot), a woman called Laura Riding.

13.44. Stuck like remoras to its muddy flanks were water lilies, Victoria Regia, and scraps of posters—some with political captions, others by the CONACULTA with old ringing slogans like *Put the Garbage in the Trashcan . . .*

It looked way-worn; you could tell this was its second time out. A crowded boat with a mariachi band approached it, strumming their guitarrons, striking their marimba, and whining tiresomely. At my side, Aída began singing the Argentine National Anthem, which she knew by heart (she'd learned it at a private school, a multilingual college where she was made to memorize the anthems of many countries. But of all the anthems in the world, for some strange reason— not an intellectual one—the Argentine was her favorite).

13.50. That was quite painful. We vented our distress using appropriate exclamations in various languages, the last of which was:

13.51. *Good grief!* And I was reminded of (Terry Southern's and Cathy Berberian's) *Candy. Oh, yes*: as any spectacle or show, the manifestation required either an entrance into or exit from a body. To enter through the ass as Perelman's brother-in-law described in *The Dream Life of Balso Snell*. Our natural acquiescence to the rhythm of the spectacle seemed to indicate our weariness of flesh, our general malaise with all the rituals we perform to gratify it, with the institutions established in its name (including adultery). *Dung & Death.* And the voice of Aída, a firm contralto, at my side: ." . . digníisimo abrieeeron, / La*h*s provincia*h* sunida*h* del Sur."

13.55. *Y los libres del mundo responden.* Eroticism of the heart, of the gut. Naïve eroticism. Vargas was the first to capture this in his pioneering *Playboy* pinups. An intellection of adolescence and youth, *The playmate as fine art.* Rita Renoir, Balthus, Meret Oppenheim (those tight-fitting bridal shoes!).

In my country, zit-faced teens were given official sanction to go exploring in landfills and garbage dumps for their moral principles. So they gathered around a horrible toadstool covered in blemishes and eschars, for these made it look a fitting exemplar, or perhaps it was more a leprous garden gnome, who carried his personal tragedy with him everywhere he went, and because of his dual nationality, bumped into us more often than not. And overwhelmed by the lack of conversation . . . My first *sensei* used to say: "Leave it to Eiralis."

14.01. Slow liturgical return of the great canine of Xochimilco to his dwelling in the dark episcopal depths where he sleeps on a midden of his own making. Just before disappearing altogether, a wild yodeling voice suddenly rose above the mariachis whines and Aída's rousing song, a voice like a gringo's, a cowboy's, like Jimmy Rodgers'. I wanted to believe it was His voice speaking to Me. No, not to Me: I lost that majuscule some time ago.

Aída transferred the contents of her glass to Luini's. The act was appreciated. There was mention of the coyotes' encounter with the great dog we just saw. Hernán said it was idle gossip spread by Coyocoán intellectuals in order to secure their grants. As if they needed them. In the meantime, these intellectuals had moved to some godforsaken place far away which, after some years, became for them the true Coyocoán. There, Aída kept a garden of carnivorous plants cultivated in volcanic soil. *Carbonic anhydrase toxicity.*

14.08. He, however—Hernán Descortés—had failed to secure even a penny for the Lowry de Cuernevaca Museum, the posthumous writings of Sigbjørn Wilderness. "Sestina in a Cantina." Evelyn Waugh had written a book about Mexico (he promised he'd send it to us). Waugh was staying at the Ritz in the Zócalo: my first impression of Xochimilco eleven years ago. We offered up Christopher Isherwood's complementary: *The Condor and the Cows.* I had an abridged edition in Italian.

I commend Hernán's essay on Henry Green (we assumed it was the first authoritative one in Spanish). Of course, Luini confused Henry Green for Hugh Greene, so he spent quite a while blabbering on about *The Spy's Bedside Book*.

14.12. Aída said she thought the second coming of the Great Dog of Xochimilco was truly extraordinary. "Fairly extraordinary," said Zi, "taking into account . . ." "Fairly extraordinary": a form of meiosis intended to suggest the dullness of the thesis and make nonsense of its hierophanies. "And that's exactly what I was trying to explain," explained Aída. "What, a thesis or hierophany?" asked Luini. In reality, the great jackal of Xochimilco had only once pronounced against any kind of prophecy, she said. It was: February 31, 1965, the occasion of Mircea Eliade's visit. Yes, in the presence of the great Romanian interpreter of religious experience, the accursed fucking dog came out of his dwelling with a voracity that was memorable, romantic. Witnesses said they'd never seen anything like it. The impeccable bareness of its glabrous skin resolved in a mound of astrakhan on its head, like a bridal bun. The cynical dog stood on its hind legs, like one of those therapods children admire and know much more about than us. He peered towards the shoreline, towards the tufted jungle canopies, and beyond them, to the foothills on the horizon, and produced a howl or a roar so loud, it could be heard in Mixcoac and Sonora, Aída recounted. Now, at the feet of the great religious scholar—and pessimistic novelist—lay the hot-blooded jaguar. With rhythmic cuts, he removed the yellow ocellated skin from the elemental skull, carving a trophy made of bone as a tribute to the Great Dog of Xochimilco, who approached Mircea as if summoned by a familiar voice. He sniffed at it. Mircea offered it up. He opened wide its monstrous jaws and gave Mircea his olfactory reward (the smell of shit was reserved as a consolation prize). "Why didn't he record any of this in his diary?" cried the skeptical Luini . . .

14.12. Luini wouldn't shut up. He was trying to argue that all of the above was complete bullshit. He began listing his arguments one by one, almost shouting himself hoarse, and we were all ashamed, embarrassed by his toe-curling effusion. Luini, with his sympathy for all things abstruse, and his kind of erudition—derived from his prolific readings of blurbs and the inside flaps of books—was one of those literary aberrations the ministerial mother country sought to include at every convention: another Waldo Frank (Scott Fitzgerald believed WF was some homonymous agency determined to appear at every literary congress in the world), a diplomat, a municipal poet whose name . . .

[Almost] surreptitiously, Hernán tried to fix a drink with the last drop from the last bottle (of vodka?) to shut him up.

14.18. Then a few vagrants in a type of canoe or pirogue appeared. They offered us heroin (and trepidation—another sac of powder [kettle of fish?]), pulverulent cure for melancholy, raw material for the immediate construction of Kublai Khan's pleasure dome. From beneath the cloak of the Nahuatl tongue, microscopic daggers were flung at us. Silverfish, hagfish, mute wildlife, photophobic (no xylophagous insects, *please*) Xanadu in Xochimilco! One hundred and seventy-four Scrabble points!

14.21. But then somebody arrived from Porlock.

So I told them, the pornographer.

14.23? Zi said, tongue-in-cheek, that: "We travelled on an Argentinian airline surrounded by a troupe of robust Chilean virgins who were members of The Eucharistic Youth Movement. They made their graduate trip to Cancún singing hurrahs and vomiting at leisure . . . It's not easy traveling such distances at cruising speed with the spiritual and physical weight of virginity weighing on the soul, or, moreover, with such a sensitive peritoneum. He, from the Yucatan, yucateco. She, from Guadalajara, tapatía."

14.26. And when our shock and disbelief had already run its course, an obliging shadow, but not of a cloud, darkened the sky from north to south, while at the same time, a burgundy colored mist slowly extended from east to west. At their intersection was a yellow light, runny, like the yolk of uncooked egg, which then gradually appeared to solidify, the color changing to a [hard, boiled] strong, calcareous orange, as if the white and the yolk melted into one another, crackling, hissing. "I'd say we're lucky to be inside," said Aída. Hernán smiled and proposed another toast.

The great hummingbird of Xochimilco was, in reality, miniscule; the same size, in fact, as a hummingbird. (I imagined something as big as Coleridge's albatross.)

We couldn't see it from where we were, said Hernán. A tiny emerald amulet suspended in the air, the fluttering of whose wings would take us—Hernán moved Luini's glass aside and did the calculation on the table—fifty-two years, seven months, three weeks, two days, fourteen hours, fifty-two minutes, and forty-nine seconds to register. We swore to be reunited on the boat the day of Xochimilco's aurora borealis.

[But we also promised one another that, after receiving the Guggenheim Fellowship, we'd meet again on the boat, or if not, somewhere close by, to celebrate the foundation's error and gross overestimation . . .]

14.32. When everything seemed to be wrapping up, I heard a voice with an Argentinian accent address me directly. It was a soft voice, muffled somewhat, and a little hesitant, like that of Amelia Mevedev, who spoke as if she was rationing her oxygen supply.

"What are you doing here?" it asked. And I answered, or started to answer, that I was using this picnic, this excursion, to gather notes in a notebook, a journal, which I showed it, was showing it, and that I intended, was intending to use them to write my very first travel book. Before it moved off, I realized it was indeed Amelia Mevedev who imparted to me this scanty, Eucharistic puff of breath . . . The winde bloweth where it listeth!

Suspense

14.37. Hernán asked Aída who it was I'd been speaking to. She saw me leaning on the gunnel, gesturing to an invisible presence. As I saw no reason to keep it a secret, I told Aída all about Amelia Mevedev. I told her about my reservations, my suspicions, adding: "Amelia Mevedev was one of the people we alluded to, probably without realizing, when we were discussing the literary supplements earlier. A renowned critic, who grows old alongside one of the giants of our literature, *unless*, that is, this giant of our lit . . ." And Aída, who was barely paying attention, whispered: "Then you know who the second one was?" But before I could respond to her question, which she asked in a tone that implied she knew the answer already, she said: "You know Doctor Lafora who treated Jorge Cuesta? His daughter."

14.38. And Zi, overhearing our exchange, interrupted: "And what about the third?" At which point Aída responded defensively: "[Ah,] If you don't know that then . . ."

14.39. For God's sake!

14.41. After much badgering and pleading while blessing ourselves, some members of this self-styled navy crew finally acceded to grant our wish . . .

14.48. In a few instances, there were fits of hesitancy, distraction. Too much baggage, too much world. (*Cadaver full of the World*, that was the name of the book Zi loaned me. It belonged to his friend . . . Aguilar Mora? And the title's a quotation from . . . Vallejo? And *If I die far from you*? What was the other book by Aguilar Mora or that other Vallejo quotation?) "The seventies," Aída intoned, "how young I was!" She sounded as if she was delivering a quotation. "I'm younger than you are," said Luini, "and I hated the seventies. I was forced to do military service. But nevertheless, after I was drafted, I joined a group of political leftists. That was 1977." He didn't sound very convincing, but we nodded credulously. "But it kept me alive, being wedged between the two—accommodated," he stressed, as if to applaud his choice of phrasing. "But I spent the worst fourteen months of my life serving a sentence for a crime I hadn't committed."

Ah, the seventies.

"The Ethical Dative," said Zi, sagely. "I'm reminded of a poem by a now forgotten Mexican poet you'll probably never again see in print." Hernán looked at him as if he were about to betray himself a member of a secret brotherhood. Then Zi recited:

The ethical dative moved you. You disappoint me.

It's the same with almost every woman your age

(And age is what counts, almost all that counts).

True, we shouldn't be indifferent with the time,

But it's wrong to note the chime of every hour. We must

Do away with superstition, the tender bruise

Around our wrist, the thumb pressed on our veins.

But noting the passage of hours is what you do best:

You disappoint me. Noting the chime of every hour

is what women who know me better than you,

do their utmost to forget.

You have made me as true as a commandment or debt.

What a pity. I will do my best to ensure you forget me,

I will do my utmost to ensure I forget about you . . .

It was a crazy gathering of people, the consecration of memory, the forgetting about paradise, *the loss of a kingdom that was only for me.* The rhythm of the day must have consulted the laughter of a century's close to beguile me with such extravagance, such opulence, behind my back.

The Princess of Faucigny Lucinge was introduced to me by Amelia Mevedev, who, aspiring for proustian éclat, said: "you will have spoken to or seen her on more than one occasion, which is, I suppose, the same thing." Of course not. She was a mummy whose bandages reeked with the myrrh of premonition, leaving me with a sickening, cloying feeling. Vertigo, gooseflesh, a feeling of resonance with Chateaubriand. It was a supernatural resonance, hardly an aroma.

The entourage didn't halt as they passed, and I forced myself to salute a chattering of incumbents who kept tabs on the senescence and senility of their soon-to-be retired forebears. "A pleasure, Mr. Espeche."

Outside, with no sense of the time. Hilarión Curtis, a handsome man wearing a handsome amount of makeup (full crimson lips, eyes darkened with kohl), recited to me a sonnet by Salvador Novo about starched entrails or viscera or something, and after asking me for the time and politely requesting a kiss—and after I said that my watch had stopped—he recommended I read Novo's diaries from the period of the poem's composition. "Son, look at how much trouble I went through to be reborn."

Some chandelier crystals began to fall (from the canopy, the baldachin). And when everything seemed about to extinguish, recede, die out, when each of those crystal drops or tears had fallen, someone who resembled Onofre Borneo, with an accent less Chilean than drunken, began insisting, confusedly, confounding me with someone else—Luini?—that I give him back all his originals. How many were there?

The countess Merlin, disguised as Mother Hogarth, couldn't disguise her airs, so she left the group before she was detected. And Constantina Mevedev, like Harry Houdini, introduced Federico Prosan, who'd traveled clandestinely, as Nicolás Mancera—who was also present (I saw him walking away or ducking out of the meeting)—in a magic trunk, decorated with an old-fashioned sailor's compass. While the father of Lupanal—most recent proctological descendant—and newly invented biographer of Hilarión: Russ Tamblyn disguised as Tom Thumb.

"After my cursory glance at Nebrija's grammar . . ." I said, "I maintain that Nurlihrt doesn't write as badly as Elena . . ."

A squat, ill-mannered Mexican wearing an ugly jacket with a pistol barely concealed at his waist made his way towards us. He was Bernabé Jurado, the shyster lawyer who'd secured the acquittal of W. S. Burroughs for his uxoricide. I wondered what Yturri Ipuche would think.

. . . And in that sweet carnivalesque apotheosis,

That playful, Bakhtinian,

subversive, subjunctive

Hebraic,

literary apotheosis,

I extended a hand, like a blind man or woman who's remained at a pier,

Alone in the silence and spray

The conticent hour

when the gondola's left for [a] neighboring dark,

as in the film I saw [in the company of others]

long, long ago

(and those who were with me were

Corpses or wives, as Swinburne wrote,

And all I recall about the film

is it was inspired by a book,

Du Maurier's *Don't Look Now*), and a warning:

Be cautious, be alert . . .

On the contrary. Be heedless, unprepared in every situation . . .

And although I believed finishing a book, even a narrative like this, required a long and emphatic peroration, a prolonged and ecstatic yawp or agonizing howl, a grinding of the teeth and beating of the breast, I realized that for this ending—which really is the last one—I could dispense with an ecstatic or plangent finale, smother all feeling, suppress all effusion, and end my narrative with a whimper. And thus lowering my voice, lowering it below the register of a whisper, I told Zi, Zinaida Gippius, Zi Benno, Zeno Cosini:

"How costly and pointless it all turned out to be."

They looked at me blankly, vacantly, vacuously. Finally [their eyes] one of the two conveyed, repeated:

—And what's worse, it looks set to continue, very near to me, but apparently speaking from the other side.

And from the other side—from West Berlin—Zi and I saw the slow, uncreditable development of the showbiz aspect of the contemporary novel.

And then we saw a young, historical, couple running away, going into hiding. They took refuge in one of the izbas that are found dotted on the outskirts of Xochimilco's teeming suburbs.

We saw them or I saw them while Xochimilco's golden dawn was passing.

A hideous pariah dog followed them in.

And I retreated back until I *found myself*, three years or three millennia before, in the Ritz Hotel. When I lowered my eyes, I saw the same [oafish, unclaimed] error: tortillas mistaken for "tostadas." The sun was setting. I began to regret my perpetual error when we disembarked from the vessel

Common ending: St. Mawr / Xochimilk

In the airport, shortly before departure, I consulted [I consult] my watch, alive and ticking again: *while respiring in that little case, what [the hell] does the time be thinking?*

We may be the products of that anguish, narrowness, asphyxia.

The issue of the first and last erection of a god, dangling from a gallows that we built.

The heart of standing is not to fly. Empson, "Aubade."

Larkin.

. . . if we told that the surrounding aristocracy was accompanied by a serviture of ghosts, that . . . so as not to make it laughable (Cf. *The Barefoot Contessa*), their number should be doubled . . . ,

. . . there were an insufficient [odd] number of offices where we worked (headquarters of the impossibly-named business: Beehaitchhaitch), [above all because] one of the three was the boss. How old was the boss? Same age as I am now. How old was I back then? Same age as my buddy, Gustavo. We'd left military service the year before: eighteen, nineteen, twenty. The days when we stayed up until late, until ten, eleven, or even later if one of the employees lost track of the time. When we left, we used to stop the machines—an Olivetti 24, and an old Remington typewriter with a wide-carriage for doing the dirty work—a habit the consul's wife disapproved of, who, one morning or afternoon, passed a comment about her seeing them do the same thing in police stations.

We were living in the worst of times. The consul's wife was having an affair with one of our superiors. Our superiors—Blamires, Haedo, and Haines—were more accomplices than associates. Haedo worked with us in our office. Blamires was the one who said we should always return the machines to their natural state of repose. Haines had his lover in his office, or perhaps it's better to say, he made sure she was working with him in the same office. Molly was the one who took all the important phone calls, and addressed all five of us using the same submissive vocative: "my king." Once, Gustavo asked her to call him "viceroy." She was quite a curvaceous missionary, her hair dyed blond from raven black [I mean that without being funny].

We had three journals: one on cinema, one on music, and the other on rugby. At that time, I believed I knew a lot about the first two subjects and bragged about knowing nothing about the third. This was a cause of much hilarity for Haines, the one responsible for the rugby journal, just as Haines's lover was, in turn, a cause of much hilarity for the "viceroy." The journals didn't produce any revenue. The trick was to deceive the advertisers about the distribution and prints runs, an art Blamires and Haedo were particularly adept at, while Haines did all the talking.

The product that really *kept us afloat*—and brought lucre to the publishers—was a book we had translated: *Venus Cascabel*. It was quite a small edition, twee. Felix, the layout designer, did his best to make them attractive, copying the original designs that were based on *pulp fiction* illustrations of the fifties. Felix's skill was both a consequence of his extreme static perfectionism and his inability to draw

143

dynamically (perhaps the two are one), which stood out in the first edition, but was enhanced with a vengeance after the success of the following three. Felix couldn't have children, he always confused lemurs with [for] lemmings—thanks to which I won a bet: he had to buy us (Gustavo and me) a meal—[and he looked on with wistful resignation at the women's butts, like one who is to be ordained to an abstinent office. NO]

The first volumes of *Venus Rattlesnake* were on a shelf next to Gustavo's writing desk, each one with its corresponding translation. Gustavo was very organized. He read every copy in advance before sending them off to be translated. And he was a huge fan of Venus Rattlesnake, of Venus Cascabel . . .

Venus Rattlesnake—Venus Cascabel in the Spanish translation—an elegant woman and dedicated socialite, soon became the most important character in the everyday life of "the publishers."

Under cover of daylight she was called Prunella Crane. She had a husband, two children, and a lapdog, Toon (Chasco, according to the local version). She was affiliated with many charitable organizations. She used to consult the tarot as well as dabbling in many other kinds of sortilege. She ran a small and exclusive cosmetics company, *Liliata Rutilantium*. The names of her husband—Adam Hapwood—and of her children—Silvia and Bruno—were irrelevant, [at the end of the day], but not Chasco's, because, at the end of the day—literally, after nightfall—Chasco became Rascal (Rapáz, in our Spanish editions), and he ceased to be a mere lapdog, becoming instead a ferocious bandog, guarding her—Prunella, who at nightfall became Venus Cascabel—during her secret meetings at which someone's execution was discussed, among other things; or accompanying her and her henchmen in taking part in "sanguinary orgies," to quote our blurbs (the originals in English were anemic and overly descriptive). I transcribe the metaphorical enthusiasm of the early days: "As if it had been the sea, an orgy of sarcasm from which spawned two fish of human aspect."

The first two episodes, *Massacre in Hoboken* and *The Bullet in the Footprint*, introduced Prunella's ally and occasional enemy: the private detective, Tecumseh Talbot. Bearish and sullen in disposition, a womanizer by predilection, he was of Sioux or Shawnee extraction, and was plagued by odontological and intestinal problems. The masterful description of a toothache compares with that of the battle of the "serendips" ["sapajous" in the original] in *The Clashing of Penknives in Brooklyn Heights*, in which the Cascabel's business affairs led to her arbitrating a dispute between gang members.

From the sixth or seventh issue, it was evident Venus had lost a lot of ground to Tecumseh. In the eight, *Chicano Cocktail*, a new character was introduced, Silveyra (thereafter called, without explanation, Silvero), who dominates most of the action in this most over-the-top and remiss of the novelettes. For this reason, it is said, Venus came to respect Silvero. Tecumseh, on the other hand, despised him "because he'd murdered two of the best." In *Orange Juice for One*, my favorite, we discover that Venus's apparent misgivings about Silvero were only a show. She'd been completely and unambiguously in love with him, "a gentleman of some fifty years, white-haired and elegant, a silver fox whose boundless gentility had been a flue for his criminal impulses."

The original North American edition was published by Dout, a short-lived eighties version of Dell publishers (the eighties, decade of ephemera). Gustavo, editor of the local Spanish edition, had read the original English with gusto. But he noted one irregularity: The English series stops at issue sixteen, whereas our Spanish one keeps going, now with the garrulous tongue unrestrained. When I began working at Beehaitchhaitch, we were about to print issue twenty-one.

Sad Skin of the Universe:

I can't use Tecumseh (whom I cribbed from Wilson's *Patriotic Gore*), because Rex Stout (whom I know through Nero Wolfe) has a second investigator by the name of Tecumseh Fox. But the coincidence is worth the trouble, I so loved Nero.

And if the investigator was English? What would an Englishman be doing there? It is characteristic of the English, as Stevenson notes, to always be there. *Verisimilitude* (Brother Gerundio, Brother Gozne,

Brother Alpe) . . .

Antagonist of the last chapter: Regina Constrictor.

On considering these variants: Prosan's point of view, that of a woman who was in love with Nurlihrt (Prosan seems to have had the [good] fortune to know her), and from the point of view expressed by Nurlihrt himself—whom the woman in question, while seated in a canvas chair [taking in the sun], had interviewed the day before. From what I could gather, Lester wasn't very impressed. But Prosan's enthusiasm didn't need encouraging. I recall meeting Nurlihrt about three months afterwards (the second-last time I saw him), before he'd closed down his office. He rejected the story, telling Lester it was "an incredibly banal version of Rashomon," and invited the "wheedler" (Lester) to try dissuading the author, who was obsequiously willing to rewrite the whole thing. Although I can attest to Prosan's scrupulous literality, it's obvious he hadn't detected in the writer's monologue the same superabundant, highfalutin prose, the same tautologies, the same gimmicky hallmarks the senile founder of *Agraphia* exhibited to a journalist he was one day going to marry. There are so many errors, anachronisms, and stylistic defects in this bathetic rubbish, but I vow to shut up as long as it's not included in the volume. It would save us having to waste the whole budget in bowing to your request for a "thorough edit and correction of the volume."

People so complacent they haven't prepared their spouses for the prospect of abandonment. Predominance of cruelty. Predominance of self-reproach.

The Myope's Nightlife

In compensation for his lack of vigilance, the Myope's nightlife should be exclusively oneiric. We grant that nightmares are members of that genus, but we must frequently remind ourselves that this is the case.

Discard Tecumseh and the imitation of James since the publication of Lodge and Tóibín books. Horrible incursion of reality when trying to write and organize a novel. O therapy.

Post Scriptum 2004 (summary)

NO to "Occupation" after Lodge and Tóibín. Penalty for taking so long. No to the title, too many people dislike it. They believe the word games are taken exclusively from titles published by *Página / 12*. I don't like giving or receiving orders, but I'm no bastion of common sense, so I'll acquiesce. Look for other titles then. No to "The Cult of St. Mawr," which I wrote more quickly because I attributed it to the fake author, Eduardo Manjares, in an anthology of stories about London. No to the Tecumseh because there's already a series of books by Rex Stout (which I haven't read) with a protagonist called Tecumseh Fox. Change "The Old Bachelor" to "The Referent." Exclude prologue and epistolary. Try telling the contextual story—the history of *Agraphia*—another way. *Agraphia* or *Alusiva*?

Great shipwreck.

Look for a sequence.

List of edits based on lexical and syntactical habits of Eiralis, who, as news spreads about him throughout *Agraphia / Alusiva*, will be known as the most exacting, the most forceful of redactors.

64 interventions / fragments in total. 41 before the anthology, 23 after.

41 fragments

8 stories Early / The Soup / The Bachelor / St. Mawr / The Visit / Semblance / Replicas / Xochimilco

23 fragments

Or no: 32 and 32 (*Goldberg Variations*) If the general title was "News from Agraphia," replace News with Crossings

Departure and return

Preparations

1 Precisions

2 News

3 Ceremonies

4 Issues

5 Concealments

6 Emphasis

7 Farewells

8 Repetitions

Pushkiniana suite dispersa
(scan and recite aloud)

It wasn't good to know or to discover
(or to deceive ourselves into believing)
that yesterday's most notable act
happened in our infancy (which I now evoke):
the Kirkcaldy tinkers kidnapped
Adam Smith, Adam Smith, Adam Smith
(a name that resonates with the dessert, Balcarce).

The Kirkcaldy tinkers (cry, little boy, cry)
(whose only currency were golden ballads
hid in romanes scrips) kidnapped him. In those
hours stiff
from seizure and delay
you will have experienced, dear beagle,
beloved storyteller
working fulltime

(not a moment of which you spend
fretting over the prodigal Icarus)
A ventriloqual distaste
(yours and/or mine)
for that source
Of wealth
That falls from the master's table:*
a scattering of syllables (yours and/or mine).
It is a virtuous economy, so to speak.

*(Avaricious Scotsmen,
Oídos sordos; far-off militiamen,
sóngoro cosongo)

1 news

2 emphasis / anecdotes

3 liturgies

4 concealments / calumnies

5 precisions

6 issues / lots

7 preparations

8 farewells / positions

1 news

2 preparations

3 precisions

4 issues

5 emphasis

6 concealments

7 liturgies

8 farewells

1 precisions	farewells
2 emphasis	preparations
3 liturgies	calumnies
4 concealments	issues
5 issues	concealments
6 calumnies	liturgies
7 preparations	emphasis
8 farewells	precisions

sestina sequence [[x6]] reproduce scheme and simplify

precisions

emphasis

liturgies

concealments

issues

calumnies

early

specular soup

semblance

replicas

xochimilco

thunbergias

Sestina takes round trips between fictional and factual references to *Agraphia*

6 x 8 48 NO 6 x 9 54. 54 parts of six chapters each

Books from which the fragments that appear under the title "News from *Agraphia / Alusiva*" are taken

Hilarión Curtis: *Bannerless Days, The Two Nations*

Nicasio Urlihrt: *A Nightcap with Death, The X-Positions,* work in progress, *far from complete*

Elena Siesta: *Final Drafts, The Place of Apparitions, Unedited Letters, Dead Aunt's Diary*

Oliverio Lester: *Unimportant Details, Plan for a Plagiarism, Plan for a Preface*

Felipe Luini: *Diary of the Surrounding Area*

Federico Prosan: *Out of a Greek Gift, Mexican Journal*

César Quaglia: *Reflections from Afar, on the Effects of Distance*

Emilio Duluoz: *The Office Next Door*

Eduardo Javier Manjares: *Postcard from the Inquisitor, Burdensome Book, Maghrebi Agenda*

Zi Benno: *The Epsilom*

Lalo Sabatani: *The Mass in Tongues*

Cristóbal Niaras: Agraphia: *A Chance Laboratory*

Eloy Armesto: *Zero Vowel, A Round Number*

Remo Scacchi: *Age*

Delfín Heredia: *Touched by Evil Days (A Fictional Biography of Doctor Yturri Ipuche)*

The Sycophant's Soliloquy

Lord Swindon: *A Bachelor in Bedlam*

Adam Pause

Make sure the titles accord with the kinds of events narrated. Insert the fragment of St. Mawr which corresponds to the initiation ceremony.

32

36

32

100

I adore italics, don't you? A. R. Firbank

"News from *Agraphia / Alusiva*"

#1 PRECISIONS

1.

Agraphia / Alusiva, a journal founded by Nicasio Urlihrt [(Emilio Teischer)] and his wife, Amanda Corelli Estrugamou [(Elena Siesta)], intended to be entirely anonymous. It was to publish only the best literature, at least according to the couple's criteria. Their taste for pseudonyms, a legitimate reflection of their era's zeitgeist (and the cause of wildfire gossip once word got out), yields to serious critical scrutiny today. The contributors were known for—or ignored thanks to—the heresy they'd committed, and of which they took every opportunity to boast, even calling themselves "the writers without stories." They went around publishing books espousing the theory that it's better to simply write stories than to write about the writing of stories, and to illustrate this, they simply wrote stories. Few readers remember those stories today, but many recall the anecdotes associated with [relating to?] them. [Such that] Forgetting is not so serious an affront as long as we remember what it is we've forgotten. If it were [it was?] ever to become necessary to exonerate [the coterie, the conspirators], Nurlihrt would just publish a series of [unsigned] editorials to adduce a controversial synthesis of two seemingly incompatible theses, and at the same time, [to] proclaim that generation and corruption are one and the same. From the middle of the last

century to the beginning of this, *Agraphia / Alusiva* was the evangelizing force behind this and many other naïve generalizations.

Oliverio Lester, *Plan for a Preface / / [without assistance] for a Plagiarism, draft agreement*

2.

Four days after the crime, Lalo arrived at the office on Basavilbaso
Street, where Elena and Nicasio were waiting for him. He told them
he'd spent the last four days not knowing what to do. On Tuesday,
he shaved, called Elena and Nicasio from a public phone, and had a
chance meeting with Belisario on the street. An hour later, he was at
Elena and Nicasio's place. What else could he do? Elena went to the
kitchen to get some scones. Lalo said he had an argument with Spiro
the previous Thursday. Spiro left, slamming the door behind him,
but then came back the next day acting as if nothing had happened.
They got into bed, spending some time in silence, looking out the
window, watching the lights of a neighbor's Christmas tree flashing
intermittently. Eventually, said Lalo to the couple, Spiro got up to
retrieve a pack of cigarettes but, when he returned, he had a knife
in his hands. He exhibited, saying it was a trophy he stole from his
brother's house, although it was a house they both shared. But you're
not interested in knives, said Lalo to Spiro, you've never been interested in them, so why the hell are you showing off something you're
not interested in? Apparently it belonged to his father. Lalo went to
the chair to heap his clothes and retrieve a cutthroat razor. Spiro said
that that too once belonged to his father. He'd decided to bring these
objects to Lalo's house where they might prove more useful than in
the house he shares with his brother. Lalo said—gesturing politely to
refuse Elena's offer of a scone—that he later learned Spiro was never
quite right in the head, but that between the time he left and the
time he came back, he seemed to have lost yet another marble. The
whole time Lalo was speaking, Nicasio scrutinized him with a look of
disgust, although he'd later say, in more distinguished company, that
"Lalo never ceased to disgust me."

3.

Agraphia began publishing in the late fifties. The journal lasted until the mid-nineties. The content seems to suggest that every page was set aside for "a word-pimp's larding-on of obscurities and contradictions, the better to obfuscate the plagiarism—and written in light tone to sugar over the gravity of the crime." Inspired by the sequence of plagiarisms ("Misery of a Realist," the novel *Dreadmist*, and the omitted story by Birt), one could either pursue the conventional path of reading by beginning with the prelims, or start with the appendices and work backwards.

Founded by Nicasio Urlihrt (Emilio Teischer) and his wife, Elena Siesta (*née* Cora Beatriz Estrugamou), *Agraphia* set a premium on anonymity and uniqueness of style. The plague of names that issued, interacting and contaminating one another in the journal, attest to the project's total failure. In the years just after its foundation, Nicasio—in his early forties—had published (beginning in 1958) two books of poems and a book of short stories. He was a model of the elegant porteño—which became almost extinct by the following decade, all those peculiarities of habit and dress swept away like footprints in desert sand. Nicasio's way of saying "hey"—very *rioplatense* to any educated ear in any of the districts on either side of the river—resounded in the memory of both his admirers and detractors. Elena Siesta was the author of *A Night is the Lifetime of Stars*, a title that, according to Urlihrt, incorporates her two main obsessions—stardom and aging—both of them entwined. Nicasio Urlihrt would often say that Elena was a little too Renaissant for a presbyobe, and a little too Pre-Raphaelite for a myope. And as for her nose, on a rounder face it might have looked aquiline, on a more angular face, it might have looked retroussé, but thanks to her ambiguous features, her nose had the better qualities of both. Nonetheless, men tended to fall in love with Elena's back and nape so as not to commit the error of loving her face. Nicasio indiscriminately circulated his opinion of these paradoxical qualities: "Our first and only love is a vulgar woman," he used to say, without finishing the quotation: "whose chastity is a myth, and that myth is our life." Myth and biography never ceased their prolific interbreeding in the whole pitiful history of *Agraphia / Alusiva*.

6.

—yours isn't serious

but it is [an] illness.

It's called kleptolalia

and it has more or less

the same symptomatology

and prognosis as gout,

although it hasn't got

the stamp of aristocracy.

The reception for Nicasio Urlihrt's journal, *Agraphia*, was held in office "A." We were in the office next door, which Urlihrt leased to his nephew and associates at *Agraphia*. His nephew was called Alfredo Haedo. His associates: Sergio Blamires and Benjamin Haines: Bee-haitchhaitch. And one of the three was the boss. How old was the boss? Same age as I am now. How old was I back then? Same age as my buddy, Gustavo. We'd left military service the year before: eighteen, nineteen. The days when we stayed up until ten, eleven, or even later if one of the employees lost track of the time. When we left, we used to turn off the machines—an Olivetti 24, and an old Remington typewriter with a wide-carriage for the dirty work—a habit the consul's wife disapproved of, who, one morning or afternoon, passed a comment about her seeing them do the same thing [for those martinets] in police stations.

The consul's wife was having an affair with one of our superiors. Our superiors were more accomplices than associates. Haedo worked with us in our office. Blamires was the one who said we should always return the machines to their natural state of repose. Haines had his lover in his office, or perhaps it's better to say, he made sure she was working with him in the same office. Molly—a curvaceous missionary with her hair dyed blond from raven black—was the one who took all the important phone calls, and who addressed all five of us using the same submissive vocative: "my king." Once, Gustavo asked her to call him "viceroy."

The translation of *Venus Cascabel* was done out of house by one of the editors of the three journals, specifically, the one we never met. And we more or less avoided the other one. Gustavo had more luck in this than I. But on one of the occasions we bumped into him, he said:

—Look, we [my partner and I] aren't exactly lacking in insight, we understand that you, like ourselves, are only galley slaves working in a trireme that masquerades as a company, Beehaitchhaitch. Still, despite the tight shackles and endless drudgery, despite the difficulty in dealing with all this, how should I say, journalistic prose—for that's what it is: lifeless, banausic drivel that rushes like a torrent and lacks all color and rhythm, except that it seems to come in waves, but you could at least pace yourselves by contending with these waves one at a time, consider only the number of strokes to be made between each strike of the clock, instead of dwelling on the calendar. The problem is, guys, we [my partner and I] have noticed the same two tendencies in all of you. Primordial tendencies, unforgivable, although at least correctable. Their names don't matter. Let's just call them A and B. Every time the strict numbering tightens its mummy bandages round the body of the text [[without yielding any reward]], A, in desperation, lavishes commas, rococo curlicues, resting points for idle intellects, to ease some of the strain, and if the bands are still too tight, it sprinkles needless "buts" and "thoughs," like gaudy rubrics packing every page. B, on the other hand, specializes in either avoiding the continuous present tense, or abusing it whenever it's employed, and worse, doing so in a mawkishly Gallic fashion. Blessed be friar Feijóo and friar Isla, and even William the Conqueror, that you guys forgot about one of them. One of the two. They were renamed by one of us [two] Coma Ocioso and Gerundio Galicado.

Emilio Duluoz, *The Office Next Door*,

[move to Calumnies?]

The Scacchi brothers played the part of the Goncourt brothers during an overlong literary soirée. The evening was organized by Elena, but Belisario was the one who invited the two brothers. Nicasio lost all interest in them after he discovered the real reason for their pig-headedness. It was the subject of Lester's longest story, which, indeed, took him the longest time to finish. "One of the two," said Manjares, "has to have talent, but I can't decide which." They're both painstaking artists—Remo an engraver, Enea a draftsman—and they do pretty well in managing the printing press they inherited from their father, Lino Augieri, a painter of majestic scenes that purport to disclose the secrets of the Dalencourt school. After his death, however, the brothers took their mother's maiden name, boasting that it was a tactful decision—they were both fond of chess. They've since earned a reputation as braggarts. In the early days, when they were wandering up and down the country [very á la Goncourt], creating sketches for works they never completed, provoking both the admiration and suspicion of Répide (the only art critic to whom Urlihrt confided about them), they divided their responsibilities between them, although scrupulously taking into account their respective individual needs. Incidentally, it was during this time that the earliest draft emerged of a story for which Eloísa and Nicasio would use the title "The Imitation of an Ounce" (later versions of which would be given the title, "Specular Soup").

[[Remo ended his days as an editor of horoscopes and other bric-a-brac for an obscure newspaper. Enea, although now obsessed with numerology, is still living. Lester depicted them—like Gilbert & George—as a pair of lovers (combining some of their qualities with those of Richard and Charly, friends of Inés) in "Too Late." As a tribute to them (or an epitaph prepense), Luini copied [translated] a few lines by Augusto dos Anjos:

Harried by misfortune, it is my fate

To live my life fastened to that wing

As an ember always rooted in the ash

As a Goncourt brother, a Siamese twin]]

It's not unusual, representative examples of the "brushstroke I didn't see."

The lack of completeness. The final draft.

7.

At that time, in response to an ad, a timid ingénue, Inés Maspero, joined the editorial team at *Agraphia*. She told Ingrid, Urlihrt's secretary, that she was an art critic. She contributed to the magazines *Expert*, *The Night Watch*, and *The Court of Apelles*, all of them insignificant. She said she'd begun working at fourteen, sorting out court records. Despite Inés claiming to be a specialist at something that didn't exist in the country, Ingrid and I were moved [sic] by her former Galdosian trade, so we hired her without further quibble. Inés arrived the following day with a letter of recommendation from Belisario. [Elena, who spent her lunch breaks in the office next door, noted that] she was chewing her nails, she was a nail-biter. The second person who came in the door was the first who fell in love with her.

Elena Siesta, *Dead Aunt's Diary*

8.

I went to Cambridge in 1992 at the behest of my friend (and, in time, my editor), Henrietta [Bonham-Carter / Hornsby-Gore], to follow up on two investigations I'd started on in Barcelona. The first concerned the musician, Bruce Montgomery, who was known for writing a series of crime novels—utter *tosh* he'd written under the pseudonym, Edmund Crispin. Secondly, I had to meet up with a scholar, who was giving me a copy of his thesis on an Argentine literary group, a cenacle of unequivocal and "magical" influence, which functioned almost as a sect. But both investigations were interrupted. The first, because a magistrate of the High Church intervened (I remember the series of gestures—three—with which Henrietta took for granted my discretion and obedience. In English, *primado* and *primate* are both subsumed in the latter word).The second, tragically, because the scholar was found dead in his Cambridge dorm. It isn't known whether the cause of death was suicide or misadventure. We assisted the youth's father in arranging the funeral service. He was a jobbing actor based in London, who was forced to get by—as many were in the decade following the one of excess—mainly on welfare. The next day, there began a series of events that would bring us from Cambridge to London, which I tried to adapt in a work of fiction—my oft-repeated "St. Mawr."

Eduardo Manjares, *Postcard from the Inquisitor*

#2 EMPHASIS

1.

One doesn't write well when not writing, one doesn't write ill when writing well. The writer doesn't really want to write, he wants to be; and in order to truly be, he must face up to the difficult challenge of not writing at all—not even a single line—of not theorizing, of not lifting a finger. I took the precaution of becoming deaf. There are whole days that go by when I don't hear a single word, when not a single thought obtrudes upon my thoughtlessness. It doesn't matter if there are voices around me, speaking, so long as I cannot hear the words they say. Everything I know or have learned to do well, I don't know how to teach. Everything I could know or learn how to teach, I cannot do well. Our age is too pessimistic to allow us to pass comment on complex matters, or even simple matters, without recrimination. After all, didn't you know our age is a tribunal? A tribunal of vultures. The kind of chopped up verse you only disregard, I regard with utter contempt (as I do poets who'd make firewood of King Arthur's table): verse without measure, without form, ephemeral, ill-fated. The time goes by so slowly, and slow is the memory that reckons the delay: I was almost twice as old as this age is old when I realized this for the first time. The poets whose recitals I attend are therefore twice as old as you. The world never changes, only the cast of players. Yet, the work doesn't seem to improve. [He lifted his head to see if *we were taking* note of what he was saying.] Apart from plagiarism, the only natural cure I know for this particular kind of drunkenness is inspiration, but in our age, sobriety is inimical to inspiration . . . Or maybe we should give up the plagiarism. Remember what Sterne did with Burton.*

"Memory is the least attractive of the muses. And although she always changes her appearance, I only ever remember the least appealing. But why should this be if imagination dresses herself like a bawd in her rouge and seamed stockings—surely gaudiness is worse than ugliness . . .? It had been some years since my divorce from memory, but only a few months ago, there was a reconciliation." (. . .) "There's no better example of this than Dámaso Alonso, a man capable of discerning the significance of every syllable in a poem, and yet incapable of writing a poem with a single discerning syllable . . ." And he repeated Barnet Newman's maxim, "Aesthetic is to the artist as ornithology is to the bird." But he thought he was quoting Wallace Stevens.

Nicasio Urlihrt, A Toast with Death at Night / Nocturnal Toast with . . .

Cheers, [Cheerio]

'The plagiarist laboratory is absolutely beyond the scope of the word-for-word copyist drudging away at his desk. Let's not forget about Mallarmé, who, according to Valéry, restored syntax to its proper place on the summit of mount Helicon. And so we all continue to aspire—as Duchamp, as Leonardo—to achieve the draft, the final draft.

2.

Elena Siesta was obstinate; Nicasio Urlihrt a pedant, who brayed solemnly about succession and inheritance. Lester was, and then he was no more. Felipe Luini never was: although he tried to be. Belisario Tregua faded away years before he died. The Scacchi brothers faded away before they could even be. Inés Maspero, alias Eloísa Betelgeuse, killed herself; many others tried the same, without consummating the act. Because of love, despair. (The key year 1979?)

#3 LITURGIES

Annick Bérrichon was one of the most prestigious literary critics; (which is the only reason why) Nicasio had been greatly interested in her. Besides this, she was also a professor of Balkan literature, although no one knew how she obtained the title or to what institution she was affiliated. But this last mystery is what piqued Belisario's interest. Annick's friendship with Elena soon led to her being introduced to the most prominent committee members of *Agraphia*, including Nicasio. One afternoon in June, almost seven months after Eloísa's death, they met with a medium in the house on calle de las Posadas (*not* the one on calle de las Piedras).

Miss Bérczely's face was a grotesquery of warts and other excrescences, an especially nasty case of what Elena termed—post-laforgian, post-lugonian—"lunarism." She spoke with what sounded like an imitation German accent with a hint of French in the guttural. Everyone pretended to understand what she was saying.

Those present were Dos, Oliverio Lester, and someone else who came with them; Elena had dragged along her best friend, Sofía Sarracén, who was even more superstitious than she—a pianist with certain mediumistic talents, who brought along her fiancé [Eloy Armesto: Lupanal . . .]—a student of Bérrichon's—to introduce him to the rest of the group.

At last, Nicasio arrived. His system of responses resembled those adopted by Elena to translate Blevgad: quibbling, nibbling, double negatives—disagreeable in any language—delivered in the passive, *reflexive*, voice . . .

As it was a commemorative date—June 23, launch of *Oxyrhynchus*—the committee was hoping Hilarión Curtis would attend (who not only owed the journal but also his fellow Argentine citizens answers).

According to the more or less reliable testimony of those present—particularly Sofía's fiancé—the first to induce a fit of histrionics and table tapping was a confused little girl who was communicating with the medium on the subject of writing. Suddenly, the medium began coughing and choking, perhaps because there was a change of . . . "visitant," or because someone had taken off their shoes . . . [???] A high pitched voice then spoke in impeccable Castilian: "I am Zelda Bove, grandmother of Benkes, and the legitimate proprietor of his falsehoods . . ."

Annick Bérrichon's spiritual ancestry has been discussed in an essay by Lupanal. Suffice it to say the literary critic's grandfather—whose *nom de plume*, Belén Mathiessen, is better known to the uninitiated—[was a partner] of Dunglas Home, who had duped many nineteenth century positivists. Today, we can conclude that Annick Bérrichon and all her pseudonyms—so suited to *Agraphia*—was born, as Blevgad prophesied, to unpack this piece of history, although her activities would succeed only in blurring the chronology. Her grandfather died in a pitiful way, although not as Luini described—nobody will ever know if her account precedes his—in both "Lemurids, Cheiroptera, et Cie" and *Sherbet Aria*.

2.

Hilarión Curtis—illustrious ancestor of Nicasio Urlihrt—took a seat in the second row. From there, he could espy, without anyone noticing, everything that was happening backstage. The theater had little to offer. Managed by a board and a consortium, it received financial contributions from Doctor Yturri Ipuche and Hilarión himself, although their efforts would cost them dearly. All to bring culture to those [so-called] forgotten lands.

The function began with a recitation by Iris Oratoria of a work of Doctor Yturri Ipuche's // [an adaptation of Andrés Bello's then out-of-print "Silva a la Agricultura de la Zona Tórrida"]. Afterwards, what looked like a bunch of school kids enacted part of Juan de Miramontos y Zuazola's *Armas Antárcticas*. Then Culcuchina and Curycollor appeared, two Inca princes.

Finally, Atanor Lupino was on the stage, a porteño actor with a yellow beard who performed musical improvisations and imitations of other artists. He sang a ballad in denigration of Washington Barbot. After this, he said that, with the exception of imitations of anyone present, he was going to do his "classics." He started with Don Julián Acosta . . .

With his imitation of Don Lucio Mansilla, the act became a farce, because some poor mulattos and a midget were playing the part of Ranquel Indians, wriggling in obeisance on the ground, while the plump and pompous Don was running up and down the stage with his prop sword hanging from his belt.

[*Exaggerated scene from the* Junk Museum]

Then, twirling his moustache and raising his eyebrows high, an affected Frenchman no one knew took to the stage. He started giving orders left and right, which the extras obeyed by halves, because by the time he'd finished barking one command, it was already superseded by another more urgent one.

This is the River Plate, said Hilarión to himself, *that everyone around ridicules.*

Midway through the interval. A dozen people, mostly ladies, approach him to say hello. Hilarión gets the impression some of them—the more serious-looking ones, the more astute ones—were approaching to apologize. How odd, he thinks, as if there were something [in this] that offended him. Doctor Yturri Ipuche [a one-time foundling] had arrived late. He rushed to take his seat next to Hilarión. The effort to do so made him breathless. But he had enough left in the tank to say the tribunal believed everything he said was true. The lights dimmed and some very terrestrial [[pedestrian, territorial]] acrobats came onto the stage, dragging their feet behind them. A woman was singing the national anthems of various countries, while it seemed Iris Oratoria was free to do whatever she wanted. After this, Atanor Lupino made another appearance. He made the appropriate apologies, in case the public had been put out [troubled, confused] by the presence of so many figures onstage . . .

The most eminent and imposing was . . . And, without saying the name, he proceeded to imitate the features and gestures of a doctor who is at the point of a great discovery. Darwin confronted by the missing link. Stroking his beard, he assumed the air of a bald [glabrous] skeptic, his doubt, his silence, suspending the public's literal function as an audience—hearing—and thereby keeping them all guessing.

Many years later, Hilarión Curtis and his stepdaughter went to watch a silent film in a crowded room on Corriente Street specifically to recapture the outrageous, uncanny effect of that performance.

The rabbits of Malambo, the frogs of Aristophanes

The fighting cocks

Bad Times, fictional biography by Hilarión Curtis, Delfín Heredia Kleiber, Cisplatina publishers, 1960.

Reading Mackay (*Popular Delusions*) is like reading an over-edited, systematized Pynchon.

3.

#21 Giordano Bruno, John Florio, Philip Sidney

Sir Valdemar Hilarión Curtis, who are your physicians?

They are:

Dr. Phibes. Dr. Génessier (*Les yeux sans visage*).

Dr. Angelicus. Dr. Sublime. Dr. Sardonicus. Dr. Zhivago. Dr. Atl. Dr. Scholl. Doctor No.

The Mass in tongues by Remo Sabatani

Quote Poe, Ivor Winters

—Is this a tribunal?

—Don't get your hopes up, friend: it's only a social gathering.

—The Pole told us it's Sircular Cymmetry—said Mardurga. It was recorded as such in the Club Maguncia logbook.

—Sircular Cymmetry expelled us.

—Nefelibata—someone sneered.

—Tungsteno—sneered another.

—Tusitala.

—Barbelognostic.

—Sircular Cymmetry.

—Sircular Cymmetry is the way for expats to die far away from here, too far to make their way back home. Sircular Cymmetry is nature's way of distributing ash in the cartographical game of chance. Hazard. Azure.

—You must have seen it—interrupted the Basque—but if you haven't, here's the test. Place the remains of a loved one on a stable, uniform surface—smooth and flat, like language. Not a carpet or rug, please. They're not in the same category ["stable"]. They tend to move, travel: from Tripoli to Beirut, from Baghdad to Missolonghi, from Algeciras to Istanbul. Then, in this rapacious situation, force yourself to a helping of the divine air so small its inhalation doesn't add to your cultural malaise, or its exhalation blow a single annoying diptera away. The [vegetal] rustle of a pubic hair, [or] the baritone bellow of an irregular verb.

Hell came freely through the narrow doorway of the monastery. All doorways lead to Rome [which is precisely where you won't find it (La Haya)] . . .

The world is purely rhyme, conjecture. He enters dressed as a gallows-bird, a maimed cowboy in spurs who walks with the mien of a prince consort in front of the gardener and makeup artist, who take turns as his manservant. For the Spaniard, at least he does the favor of treading loudly.

Mock-Tudor house in Kenwood, in the abbey of exorcism, far from the first instance of excess—or abuse?—that didn't even come close to leading us to the palace of wisdom. Or would it be a basilica? It makes the ship stink to high heaven. The Angels have reached the foothills crawling on their knees. The smoke, swamp fumes. Moreover. Cloister without threshold, shadow of an ash cloud. From here his beloved left, and his circumflexed spirit, and from there it will depart. Repeat undirected. Repeat undriven.

And later it left for good, departed. And gone was the interval between departure and return.

[Everything seemed better.] Help us, Urbain Grandier.

But no. Once experienced, the sea air up in arms or an orbit around Saturn, *the rest goes back to the black caviar cave of the inevitable return*. Or the inevitable path. For the unshod. For the odd ones. Now nothing preoccupies us. Now we've seen that justice will collapse through abuse of hendiadys. The critic of art through calumny, the white wisdom of her bones, the brush of a fly. Capellane. Toe cap. And next, an epigenetic phenomenon, the *retinto* ally of both. And the Episcopalian Italian, incidentally, gasping for breath. And all multiple forms: the snail, the Holy Bible, the landing strip . . .

A son of Aberdeen of two Hereford males.

—*I can't leave*—said the starling.

—Sircular Cymmetry, yes. The inversion was the tangential formula—continued Madurga. That's to say, the tangents of his religion, the thurifers, the censers [none other than the progenitors of the epsilom]. And there were even secret tangents, well-rounded symmetries. The tiger he spoke of was Sumatran, which, I'm not sure if any of you noticed, has a crazier aspect than any other tiger. It was said he was to come bearing justice. He was surely something like what Blake saw between the bars of his art before writing of that "fearful symmetry."

—Yes, yes . . . —said Seregni who, for the first time, seemed interested.

—The tiger belongs to a narrative tradition we've ignored. Gobeluncz knew this, although he was as ignorant as we in every other respect. We had to accept the blame—he said—never the punishment. The incorrigible God, he said. The collector of prepuces.

Gobeluncz knew things we didn't know by his cold nose, his borrowed nose, because he was a European, because of his extensive reading, and because, unlike us, he didn't work in an office. The preputial bridle. He invented a type, a category—many ways to classify us. Those who came on Thursdays—which included our group, for we came to this very place to play billiards—he called Jovellanos. Those who came on Wednesdays, a group none of us had ever met or even seen, he called barbelognosticos. But rest assured, there's no need to fret, I've already made inquiries. I never encountered any of them but I did discover this much: it seems, the barbelognostics were a Christian sect whose members—at the end of their ceremonies, their rites— . . . drank . . . semen. It wasn't thought unchristian, but something divine, a mandate or commandment. *Thy statutes will be my songs.*

—The whimsical heifer used me so the rebellion would go unnoticed. The nuptial colloquy above leaves me more eager than before. Not because we competed [by the whim of the heifer] but because we won. The proof is in this scapular. The sestina and chalk drawing thrown in for good measure.

—Where did you make your inquiries? asked Seregni, firmly.

—Not far from here. There's a subsidiary nearby . . . a branch, I suppose you can say.

—You mean a parish. I'm a member. And now all of you . . .

—To pretend you were born earlier, you use a monocle and take snuff . . . —said Madurga, erroneously.

—No sir, no gentlemen. I'm Gobeluncz—said he who sought to remove Seregni's mask—. But don't deny me—he continued—the punishment I deserve.

Lie. Like a good Christian, like a modern, a good Pollack, he preferred punishment to guilt. He'd rather die with his eyes open. He'd rather die. Genteel petit bourgeoisie.

To please him, Angus and two others pounced on Seregni. One of the two was he of the nasal passages [giant nostrils]. With the effort of the three, he was, as they say, subdued. And although it wasn't a fair fight, the result wasn't exactly a foregone conclusion. The fray resembled a certain hand game that consists of putting one hand atop another, the other hand atop that one, and so on successively. But the lack of manual parity between the two teams made it a fiasco. Moreover, the game isn't suited for a lot of players because the number of bodies gets in the way of all the hands. Another failure imputed to the lack of bilateral symmetry among featherless bipeds.

Gesu Bindo was the last to throw himself upon the body of Giordano Bruno Seregni, after Angus had already exhibited the mask in triumph. In that moment when he was thinking (when Madurgo and I, when I thought) the worst—that we weren't going to be able to make it happen, make the seregnate follow the gobeluznate, vicars of power, exemplary dictators—we heard the overtures of morning. Muffled overtures.

Peal of bells. Treat yourself at the close with a brief [zealous] beat.

The feral beasts—by reputation for truthfulness or a slavery to thirst—are often wary of discarded rotting flesh, flesh they themselves discard, flesh that is generally discarded. Some, schooled by boredom and disgust, even shun [it] (although it's been often witnessed that they crave it: odd parity of the times). This is also called (in another world, another circumstance, another latitude) Sircular Cymmetry. Cymmetrical like *surgery*, sircular like *seismic*. Gobeluncz said everyone on Earth is at fault for having a limited vocabulary. How quickly they putrefied in that strip of garden, the zen Serengi and the basque Egozcue!

It wasn't easy negotiating the entrance to the library, which seemed impassable as a Schliemann obsession. The feral beasts had swallowed the custodian almost without chewing and continued onwards. Their subjects, however, halted long enough to lick her makeup. The beauty of these posthumous acts derives from the skin that's marked with a sacred rubric, as that arbiter of taste, Osberg, once divined. Streaks, ocellations, grooves. The martial monotony of death is always distant, always behind.

Everything went well, as the feline [feral], ferocious troop advanced, as the regiment invaded the temple, the workplace, the factory, as the accursed, white giant's gastric requirements were sought. As they made their way upright. As they asked for the whereabouts of the principal equine body.

Such are the factious fictions, the apocryphal affiliations. Such are feral beasts.

But for the sake of symmetry, we will stop here.

Lalo Sabatani, *The Debut* or *The Mass in Tongues*

(unexplained in *Lycergical Glossary*)

#21 Again: Giordano Bruno, John Florio, Philip Sydney

Shortly before getting out of bed, Annick Bérrichon perceived that the animals that smile in the dark were absent from room 103 of the Maria Cristina hotel in Mexico City. If it was true, then she must've been somewhere other than the Maria Cristina Hotel in Mexico City, because, though they were invisible, she sensed they were very near her. How strange! She hadn't been afraid of the dark before, while she was very afraid of the animals, but now those fears were reversed. She tried calming down by thinking that it was only a result of her being in a strange place . . . but what place, since she wasn't certain where she was?

Dark is the way, light is a place. Who'd said that? Which of her poets? Or had it been uttered in seventeenth century Spanish by one of the creatures in her room, a room that may or may not be in the Maria Cristina Hotel in Mexico City?

She extended an arm. Instead of finding the switch, her fingers brushed against the wing of one of the creatures hanging from the ceiling (they weren't all of one species, but she had to somehow identify them), which caused a disturbance that from initial stirrings led to shrill and raucous protestations [that infected the others] and, in effect, multiplied the noise into a clamor, a general uproar [although fleeting and retractable] that, in effect, multiplied her fear. They seemed to flicker in and out of view, their eyes blinking, searching in the darkness. Their laughter illuminated them. Her memory must have failed her to not find some justification for this nightmare.

A.B. had recklessly abandoned her studies of Balkan literature . . . And besides, this horror has been going on the past two days! The interminable journey, her proud and condescending peers always near her: a nightmare on terra firma. It's not that she [Annick Bérrichon] lacks the courage to insult them and be free of them. She doesn't do so because they're her "colleagues," and together they form a single body, so that any insult would only bleed [spread] like a lacerated organ; indeed, any repudiation, calumniation, would only redound on her, lacerate her, multiply her fear. They didn't matter to her personally, individually (although they're all her "colleagues," they each belong to different species), it was the group that mattered, the corp. The historical fact. It was the collapse of its reputation she feared.

That the creature hanging near her left shoulder (she recognized the general design and principle parts of its corporal vesture) was a female, she was in no doubt. She'd learned from Sister Juana's *First Dream* that bats are birds without feathers. Of all the obscurities to unveil, [for God's sake]! Incubus / Succubus: *taenia saginata.* She was well acquainted with the delay, the docility, the asthenia: for whole semesters she'd been afflicted by self-reminders of her corporate guilt. Orphaned girls in rags, scribblers of theses and dissertations, of papers and *ponencias*, like the ones she read on campus, safe offerings, inspiring clumsy harmonic and acoustic reverberations by others, avoiding all the risks she herself had taken. Behind mirrors. Behind the mirror of the stand-in poet's indrawn conceitedness, of the cheiroptera's tremulous [trembling] voice that whispers near her shoulder (on which she believed it was now perched) a soft interjection that through impatience would grow into a peremptory demand. And this will be the last straw, provoking her, Annick Bérrichon, to an angry boast about having never been corrupt, about having never stooped to be a quadruped, about having acquired as much knowledge as she needed. For she knew everything. And yes, she was female.

And how strange [it was] to be [so] exposed, so visible! At her age! [During the course of her long life,] she continually shed her coquettish vestures although she continued to make them the butt of her jokes. Even now, with her wrinkles, her involuntary whistles, her sudden outbursts, her habit of praying, and her occasional lapses of memory, she's managed to retain her peculiar style.

How long it took to impose it on the others! Almost as long as it took her to adopt it herself. An ugly old crone who became well known for her wit and wisdom. What seminal moments in her life [or her biography] vindicate this reputation? None. They were foisted on her all at once, as if she'd lived her whole life in a daze until, one day, when she was ugly and old, she awoke and found herself famous for being witty and sage.

Lie. She'd been ugly from birth, and only became intelligent long afterwards. Ugly as sin. As she discovered when she looked in the mirror and saw her distorted features and lamented the fact they were immutable as stone, and afterwards, sought the intervention of these animistic powers that now beleaguer her, imploring them to make her literary hobby a cosmetic and prosthetic veil—to make a covenant, a pact with her: that they allow her, at least in part, to be someone else, to be their half-sister (they didn't have a sister, but she suspected there would be a temporary easement of parental divisions). Her ugliness had moreover two aspects, one distinctive, the other alarming: together, they aroused sympathy in no one except herself. It wasn't the consecratory effect of the whole that made others recoil, but a meticulous examination of each part. For example, her eyes, her nose and her mouth had each been considered ugly *per se*: one had to get used to seeing them in combination to appreciate the coherency of the whole.

So it was perfectly understandable why the animals approached her, [then and now,] curious about something that wasn't very different from themselves. Unseen, timid, ignorant . . . without a theory!

Another of the friendly, filthy zoomorphs had landed on her left shoulder, biting her [corresponding] ear. It didn't hurt very much: a mere pinching sensation incident to the mechanics of mastication. A sensation that bordered on pleasure, an act that seemed to solicit from her a [reciprocation] reciprocating gesture. Something she was unaware of because of her age—78 years—as she was of many things except the things she already knew. Her vast knowledge of Balkan literature, for example, brought her great renown. But, in compensation, Annick Bérrichon knew nothing about Malagasy fauna. In compensation, indeed, because, in that ultimate or penultimate hour, all her experiences seemed to vanish, evanesce before all those snouts and muzzles, the beaks and claws surrounding her—the sudden intervention of a gifted imagination, or the chance effect of light on the surrounding scenery. What a pity! Otherwise, she'd have known the imperfectly penitent occupant of her sinister shoulder was actually an aye-aye.

Atrius Umber (pseudonym of Belisario Tregua), "The Dreadmist."

"The Dreadmist"

And Moses drew near unto the thick darkness where God was.
Exodus XX, 21

God was, and Annick Bérrichon also was. They weren't speaking. Madame Scardinelli was searching in the dark for those diurnal creatures that a long night's digestion had caused her to imagine. Madame Obstreperous had learned to cross herself far from the mirror. She did so that no one but God would notice. And the preponderant maki on Annick Bérrichon's left shoulder, which unlike the owl that hung upside down, could not see the future, but both cried in unison: "We can't get out."

Side discussion with Cornelius Sacrapant (Wynthrope-Smyth)

—I could hear them on your shoulder—said Cornelius Sacrapant— although it just struck me that they speak with great authority about something they know little about.

—You mean about the mysteries of the sects and French songwriters?—I asked.

—No, no, about English Literature.

—Do you think you know more than we are ignorant of?

—The question isn't well phrased. You are ignorant of far more things than I happen to know. Don't take it the wrong way: You ignore without knowing you do so.

—Then please give me an example.

—If I take yours and your Argentine friend's taste for naturalism seriously, I'd have to point out the fact that, of all the practitioners of the genre, you omit the only names that are actually worth mentioning—said Sacrapant [smugly, pointedly].

—I don't believe we mentioned any names, but how about . . .—so I ventured—Ford Madox Hueffer, also known as Ford Madox Ford?

—Nonsense—dismissed Sacrapant—. That's [logically] the one name I'd expect one of you to say. An outstanding exponent of international modernism, his reputation's been challenged a thousand times over, but he never seems to go away. A kind of walrus carcass, long since emptied of its innards, which the ingenious hidalgos of cultural journalism float to the surface every now and then. So eminent is he, that they suppose him—not that I'm changing the subject here—the "discoverer" of D. H. Lawrence. (You can imagine that "discovering" Lorenzaccio wasn't the most difficult thing in the world, true?) No, not Ford Madox Hueffer, nor his cognate.

—Then who?—I asked in mock reverence to conceal my dudgeon.

—Hubert Crackanthorpe, for example, a matrilineal ancestor of mine, or George Egerton. I know erudition is misleading in every language, and the sea in every language is deaf, but have you heard or read anything about them?

Without saying a word, I admitted no. But [I must say in my defense that] the gesture of admitting denial isn't an easy [simple] one.

—Well, I won't be too hard on you; after all, your cases aren't exactly unique. Many things were obliterated in the Great War [as, for example, proper instruction on methods of reproach], but I have to find at least one book on which I can speak with the same authority.

—What about this Terry Eagleton fellow? Do you think you'll be able to get a copy of his book in Cambridge?

—Eagleton is just plain Terry, whom I sure you've already met. Egerton, like the other George—Eliot, Mary Evans, as you'll recall—is a lady: Mrs. Golding Bright. As in my case, remember the dash [between the two surnames].

—I see, I see . . .—I said, nodding.

—As regards your Argentine friend's favorite subject, the metrical arrangement of Spenser's *Mutability Cantos*, it wouldn't hurt to consult T. S. Omond . . .

—He consults it regularly—I said, trying at least to preserve his honor.

—The Oxford edition or the mutilated new edition?

—I don't know—I huffed—I wasn't paying attention . . .

—How odd, you being an editor and all . . .

It was impossible. I'd read somewhere that the number of English surnames with a hyphen was seven, and, after a day, I'd already found three in my notebook.

Zi Benno (and his collected series of novellas that can be read as one very long novel) and Edgar Alan Meaulnes (and his very long novel that can be read as a garbage heap of literary scraps, both his own and those of others) persuade me. NO

Eiralis?

Writing a masterpiece isn't something anyone can do, only he who heeds blindly the prediction concerning his fate to be alone on a tiny stage or in a cramped laboratory, an exclusive space where exclusive work is done, has any hope of writing one.

Mirceau Eliade's unease at the proselytizing propaganda of Jim Joyce. Scruples of the artist corrected by the superstition of impersonality—never of anonymity—that lends to his art a link / vehicle that's functional, inconsequential, invidious, equinoctial, marketinero.

I think I copied this way of writing from Girri. Marketinero, NO.

[In preparation]

And don't dare enlighten them; it's best if they continue as they are, in pursuance of something we're not sure we know ourselves, something we may ourselves be ignorant of; if we do in fact know it, we haven't been told what good it will do to communicate it to others; if we're ignorant of it, then perhaps one day, your Excellency, we will come to know it. Nevertheless, let us prepare ourselves since they do not: when the truth overtakes them, memory and volition will give way, melt into one another and evaporate, and the [luminous] day and [certain] night will also cease to be. I'm here to tell you that it's better if, in this world, they remain in obscurity and confusion; I'm here to tell all of you that it would benefit the pack if the light of civilization never dawned on them.

Francisco Aldecoa Inauda, from the letter to Saavedra Fajardo

(original epigraph of "The Imitation of an Ounce")

As the editor-in-chief and publisher of [responsible for] the irresponsible literature we produce at *Agraphia*, it's left to me to apologize [rhet. *Captatio benevolentiæ*]. It was difficult converting the anesthetic [set of] abstractions they believed [was] to be literature into something readable. Although I tried my best, it suffices to read "The Mass in Tongues" and "Lycergical Glossary," both of which were printed in those forgettable notebooks, to see I did not succeed. The collaboration with Victor Eiralis added very little: he was a jealous and inexorable defender of the same [abstruse and elusive] esthetic. I often say that whoever's responsible for a literary journal has two jobs: keeping up appearances and bridging gaps—tasks more worthy of a [suicidal] theologian or [inhibited] geometer than a publisher. As to "keeping up appearances," this basically demands that the one responsible uses his moral scruples to present to the reader a coherent [and consistent] intellectual pattern in the publications; and for "bridging gaps," that risks must be taken with every literary adaptation, accepting that there can be no fixed model or approach for doing this, or if there is, it must be unintelligible. Of course, I was far from perfect in executing these tasks, but I am grateful for the interest, goodwill, and counsel of those individuals who helped me to exhibit the results.

César Quaglia, *On the Effects of Delay, Reflections on Distance*
[*Reflections from Afar, on the Effects of Delay* [*Distance*]]

Time suspended in the real-time of "Diary of Xochimilk"

#10 [in Liturgies]

It was the moment for which all other moments are either altered or bartered. It was my turn to answer. "Was it true about Nicasio and Elena in Spain?" It was true, insofar as they refused—or didn't bother—to deny it, though they were all too familiar with the *enemy rumor*. Yes, she was pregnant by another—the late fifties, it was—and yes, it was because she had taken a *risqué* stroll to the bohemian corner that beckoned them with promises.

Adventure of the sun [Gastr del Sol], revenge of the solstice. A ray suddenly—I suddenly exclaimed—fretted Aída's divine [marmoreal] thigh and magenta shorts . . . And was it true what they said about us, that no one paid attention to us, that no one—to put it bluntly— "gave a damn" about us? That we were the writers without a legend or story, that all we ever did was read? Lies, Lies. Not entirely. It so happens that the books arrived—our books arrived—in the editorial hands of someone who wanted, in short, to take his revenge. Some-one, a bigwig in the editorial department, whose wife had cheated on him with Nicasio or Remo—or perhaps it was both—a good man, a gentleman, the boss of the supplement, who said to his employee, an unpaid employee, an intern: "Look, I want you to fuck this book up. And don't worry about the consequences. The author's an imbecile. I don't know if you've ever met him. He used to go to all the cocktail parties. Morally, he's retarded; but intellectually, he's a survivor, and of nothing resembling a battle or a tragedy . . ." And I heard all of this first hand, because I'm practically invisible.

Another source?

I saw, from a great height, the tiny dot of our boat, and I prayed to return to myself. I prayed to return to the group. But the supplica-tion was to no avail, [the] my prayer was quenched in the utterance. The jungle was stretching in the distance, water lapping the shore-line. Old gray god. Capybaras in the pampas transformed into [a herd of] neutrinos. And afterwards, from the same height, still pres-byopic, I squinted at a little bark where four people were tirelessly rehearsing sham civilities, and the fifth, forcing himself to cooperate in the farce *in situ*—a dissimulation that would be obvious to anyone [else] (especially to someone remote [like me])—which would seem less ridiculous with repeated exercises in loyalty. [Then,] once again, I was peering at the telltale oval of my watch before once again try-ing to rejoin the [lost, niggardly] conversation. It was sixteen after twelve: a prosaic piece of information that makes one forget about the adverbs of time, as I used to say in my palefaced infancy.

The specular soup [vision] *is the saline solution of the imitation of an ounce.*

As a result of an involuntary sacrifice, the effects of the drug that only one of us had consumed—nothing less than the specular soup—we were floating on high, manning the wicker basket of a hot-air balloon. We? So I thought, at first, but none of my companions were actually with me. "Come on, Phileas dear, tell the truth, tell me about that friend of yours, Nicasio Urlihrt, you so often mentioned in conversation . . . What did he do, what did he create?" It was my late Chilean friend, Onofre Borneo, a ghost summoned out of death, out of absence, out of a change of custom. "Urlihrt was a difficult man," I said, "very difficult." We flew to a cruising altitude of at least two-and-a-half thousand feet above sea level. It was late, very late. "In the final days, he left Elena Urlihrt all on her own, and she was dead before he died afterwards. But she started doing the same after she met Bindo Altoviti—standing him up on dates—and he was dead not long before she died on her own. And she was doing the same earlier when it was Remo Sabatani, not Bindo Altoviti, who frequented her place."

Subtraction after subtraction, I remained in the wicker basket. I thought my disappearance—sorry, my absence—would make them miss me down below. Make them feel relieved, I immediately thought. I was reminded of *Tom Sawyer Abroad*, when the Negro, Jim, believes he sees Virginia because he once saw it colored pink on a map. While traveling by balloon. Then time dissolved, and I saw the map of my past, in monochrome at first, until a few colors began appearing here and there. And I saw myself arriving at the first meeting of *Agraphia*—me, still wearing glasses—when Remo Sabatani was still at the journal. And nearby, in a kind of rhombus of ochre hue, another scene, the famous black mass at the house on Giordano Bruno Street. And then a mad rush to the present, to Hilarión Curtis's wake at the house on Piedras Street, Eloísa's house in Avellaneda. And, symmetry goes, symmetry comes,

Semblance [A Russian Tale]

There are people who wait for us and those who disappoint us. They come to us without us having to go to them [reciprocity], as if these encounters happen for the sake of only one of us, as if they'd been randomly or deliberately [premeditatedly] set in motion to range across the world searching for the one among us, the only one in the world, who is equipped to tell their story. Or maybe not, maybe these are in fact the most predictable of encounters, and we, although we'll never fully accept it, are perhaps for them as shadowy a group as they appear to us. As long as we cling to our consciousness [conscience], I suspect we'll never know [[if any of them talk of reciprocity.]] They are difficult people to keep inside the head, beings whose lives are only imaginable because they reside in the suburbs of our memory: imaginable but obscure, because these suburbs skirt the frontiers of oblivion—that which cannot be imagined—so that they're only capable of being recalled, evoked, by a formula that sometimes works, but more often does not. If it does work, then the story begins to emerge, although the character, the protagonist, remains shadowy. So it was in the case of Velemir Dimitrovich Pachin. It matters not that we came to learn about him during our wanders in exile. It matters not that the unwavering dark forces of the imagination enveloped him until someone came along and announced—or shouted, rather—*Attempt*. Suire's [Sartre's] work was the password that unlocked it, and the pretext for telling the following tale. So although the premiere was so long censored, confirmation of the rumored plot was leaked by both major and minor actors alike, and Velemir Dimitrovich finally became a part of the permanent cast of characters in the shadowy opera buffa of memory.

Velemir Dimitrovich Pachin didn't attend the meeting at Elena Fiodorovna's home because his coat was frayed. For years he'd treated it with neglect: an old-fashioned serge doublet with beaver skin lapels that his uncle on one occasion had brought him from Oslo or Helsinki. [[On one occasion, he forgot it . . . and managed to retrieve it a year later. But that's another story.]]

Velemir Dimitrovich had no virtues to speak of, but neither had he any vices, unless his proneness for distraction could be considered a vice, or his neutral stance concerning all things good and evil, complemented by an expressionless face—somewhat comic, adorned with one of those Russian noses that provoke teasing in childhood but, in adulthood, becomes a harmless, unflagging instrument—accorded him the virtue of being a good actor, a consummate actor. Yes, although his nose had been a cause of much affront and inconvenience to others, he, Velemir Dimitrovich, was completely lacking in that quality which, in the vaguest terms, is called intuition. When Olga Fiodorovna invited him to stay one October afternoon in the gazebo beside the train station, Pachin said yes, he would go. The winters in Berlin are less bitter than those in St. Petersburg, although the bitter unhappiness of temporary exile would make the sojourn bittersweet.

Two days afterwards, three before the reunion, he was sitting on the bunk in his quarters at Frau Heise's boarding house, wondering what the devil to wear to the party, complementing the rumination by quoting gravely, aloud, some of the more dramatic speeches from Suire's opus. (He'd read the work in haste, as was his wont, but thanks to his prodigious memory, he was able to quote all his character's speeches and interjections, as well as those of others.)

Now then, he thought, none of his friend's coats ever came close to fitting him, so he couldn't entertain the notion of squeezing into any one. Night was falling. Pachin heard a droplet fall from one of Frau Heise's taps, all firmly shut the night before by the silentious Giuseppe, [who always got back after ten]. Darkness flowed over the enemy city, a city in which no one had a spare coat for him. He heard the fretful stridulations of the tram as his eyes rested on the partial images drawn on the glass of a car on which someone (himself, the night before) had scrawled a word now almost erased. "Perebredev," he spelled out. "Perebredev," he then said, pronouncing it properly. He'd encountered him the week before in the market. Luckily, providentially, he hadn't escaped his notice.

Perebredev was the least trustworthy person in the world. His reputation as a conman spread well beyond the frontiers of St. Petersburg. His misdeeds, his contagious lack of discretion, once transmitted through the ear, infected the mouths of all. To make matters worse, Pachin had rehearsed with him a sketch of one of Perebredev's misdeeds, hoping Nemerov's company would perform it. All the same, Perebredev had a magnificent trenchcoat, and his smile was as welcoming in Berlin as it was in St. Petersburg. So he wouldn't have a problem loaning his trenchcoat, because Perebredev was at once proud, amiable, and affirmative in attitude, always ignoring— as everyone knew—the deflationary "no." He was born to say yes, born to allow his curiosity [proboscis] probe every nook and cranny of other people's goodwill and confidence. Perebredev was [[a man]] as tall as Pachin, perhaps a little taller. Pachin had scribbled [[the fantasmal, fleeting]] Perebredev's address and kept it in the only pocket of his only coat, the one from Oslo or Helsinki, [[the one he retrieved after once forgetting it]]. Pachin's coat was hanging on the only chair he had in his room. So it wasn't difficult, even for Pachin, to retrieve.

No core narrative in these short stories, more like referential, allusive, flashes of information. And this won't make for an easy novel. Moreover, I can't simplify it (without altering its nature).

As for me, life below always seemed to me excessively laborious. All that editorial drudgery [and muckraking], that urge to do something worthwhile, something significant, and all those egos so different from my own. I like being up here, which is to say, deep down within me; although, I'd like to be higher, of course, and without the aid of a balloon or wicker basket. *My splendid art, my sad profession.* My swarthy self, morocho, always full to rupture with either darkness or splendor.

We all tried speaking differently and we all spoke the same. To write differently and we all wrote the same. Broken logic: we all started differently and ended up the same. No, it wasn't about stylistic exercises, as some believed. Literature isn't done by mechanically arranging syntactical and grammatical clusters, it must achieve buoyancy, drift on the air like music. And there is someone down there who understands this. Who elects, who chooses to hear this. It would be better if he listened.

Zi Benno, *The Epsilom*

Federico Prosan, *Xochimilco Diary*

Mexican Journal

Music. Pessoa. Contra Verlaine, contra Mallarmé:

"For vague sentiments that resist definition, there is an art, music, whose end is to suggest without explicitly stating. For those sentiments that are perfectly defined, so that it is difficult for emotion to reside in them, there is prose. And for sentiments that are fluid and harmonious, there is poetry. In a healthy and robust age, a Verlaine or Mallarmé will always emerge to write the music they were born to write. They would never be tempted to try and utter in words what words will not suffer them to say. I asked the most enthusiastic among French symbolists if Mallarmé's ability to move them was no better than that of a vulgar melody, or if Verlaine's want of true expression sometimes reached the same want of true expression we hear in a simple waltz. They said no, and to this end, they meant they preferred Verlaine or Mallarmé's poetry to plain music, which is to say, they preferred literature as music to plain music. But in so saying, they're telling me something that has no meaning outside the meaning it has for them."

(Fernando Pessoa, 1916?)

"As we strolled home, Iris complained she would never learn to cloud a glass of tea with a spoonful of cloying raspberry jam. I said I was ready to put up with her deliberate insularity but implored her to cease announcing *á la ronde*: "Please, don't mind me: I love the sound of Russian." *That* was an insult, like telling an author his book was unreadable but beautifully printed."

V.N. *Look at the Harlequins!* 1974

The quote that justifies the laziness of the author (Revol, Cortázar)

The burden of publication

Sharing a defeat is one of those human weaknesses this book intends to lambaste; I therefore share the triumph of this failure with my companions of the ear: Duncan Browne, Emitt Rhodes, Fred Neil, and Tim Buckley.

For the characters' getting together in order to die: the *Alegretto* from Beethoven's Seventh.

Adrogué, June 23, was thinking of *Oxyrrinco*, Hilarión Curtis's journal

Don Julio:

I was in the busiest bar (say the local newspapers) in Androgué with my niece (and goddaughter) and that friend of hers I told you about, the one that showed up at Quaglia's place (Quaglia, who's a local). The friend reminds me a little of Sofía Sarracén, because she has an outstanding [thick] mole or beauty spot on her thigh. Speaking of thighs, she spends a lot of her spare time on my brother-in-law's, imagine! Among other things, I told her there are no holidays without love. We could barely understand each other. That's what's tragic about getting old, believing we're interesting when we're just another group of foreigners. She barely understood what the words meant, I mean words in general. I won't bother giving examples.

She answered me no. She, who didn't want to know what the words meant—but why didn't she want to know?

What a shock, Don Julio. My niece's friend performed a horrible gesture, a gesture replete with that very substance, disdain: she raised her hand to her face, as if it was a telephone, with her thumb as the receiver, her pinky the transmitter, and her remaining fingers clenched between. And, with her other hand, she tweaks the air with quotation marks, a gesture I already explained to you. She must have picked it up from some nocturnal instructor when socializing. Then she says "no," sounding the space between the quotes.

Nonetheless, I have to admit that [my niece's friend—her second-best friend] is a good-natured girl. I'd almost forgotten my intention to invite her to the warehouse [the hangar / warehouse discussion]

on the night of my sister's twentieth wedding anniversary. The happy couple decided to celebrate it at a restaurant in the center of town—alone (I don't want to make myself seem important, but the reason was probably me). Lorena was at her best friend's house; her second-best friend wasn't to know. In the stories published by [the journal] *Agraphia*, of which I was the editor-in-chief for twenty years, both blemishes and beauty spots abounded. Women with moles. The moles were arranged [with rare beauty] around a shoulder that resembled an isthmus, or upon a long continuous esplanade of flesh (*the white giant's thigh*). Nurlihrt swore by this anatomico-geographical convention of mythmaking—his dictum, everything lasts that becomes legend—until he himself realized the damage.

Luz—she's called Luz—has another mole in the lumbar declivity of her alluring, provocative back. A stunning back, the star to a footnote no one could ever fill. [That consequently would be filled with evidence of wrath and frustration—detritus, old-fashioned words, isoglosses, deltas of Venus, making us lose our footing; that molehill that continues to grow when expressed in her language, the second-best friend's, her English, outdated, worn. All the rest is secret, darkness, delight. Hidden in nooks and crannies.] Although she said even the tungos (the boys who hang around the markets here) were lavish with their praise. Not that any of these ruffians could do her back any justice. Luz described what one of them said as a miracle of efficacy, exaggeration, devotion, lechery, among other words, of course. My goddaughter's second-best friend didn't ask me for explanations, until—exhausted—I myself seemed to request that she ask me. She turned around with elegant curiosity (because the dorsal session had persisted for some time, without variation) and said:

—Isn't that the way men your age like it?

—Men in general—I said, defensively.

—Why?

—I don't know *why*, exactly—I said. Unlike in written prose, in spoken prose, I was able to avail of more adverbs, [I grant my fallacy of arguing from my own authority]. With determination, she thought me the variants "toboggan" and "stake," and I didn't object to them as variants. When we'd both then moved from our respective

183

positions, Luz was close enough to breathe on my chin through her nose. I kissed her. My thin, firm lips, acquainted with lies but not repentance, an answer to those thick, full surgical lips (kisses in the penultimate dark). She said she had a good time. She said, for the sake of my goddaughter—who was Luz's best friend—we should try to avoid such situations in the future.

With all this waste of expletive, digression, circumlocution, bombilation, *niaiserie*, redundancy, stupidity—Ah!—that characterize Eiralis's letters, we can't see the supposedly attic narrative scheme underneath.

#16 [in Preparation?]

1 Hyde Park: Serpentine, Rotten Road (*i.e.* "Route du Roi"), Pall Mall, Green Park, Science and Technology Museum, Victoria and Albert, Courtauld Institute;

2 Tate Gallery, National Gallery, Leicester Square (*hic sunt leones* . . .);

3 Butcher's in Harrods

4 Places I like to say I "checked off," (Dickens's house, Johnson's) without overlooking graves and cenotaphs (Blake, Bunyan, Hardy);

5 To Hampton Court by double-decker and return by commuter boat

6 Long walk: Buckingham Palace, Westminster Abbey, Parliament buildings, Whitehall, 10 Downing Street, Haymarket, Fleet Street to St. Paul's Cathedral, Bank of England;

7 Belgravia, National Embassy (Argentine);

8 Oxford Street and Fitzrovia, Soho: bohemian pubs of the forties. Tambimuttu, Dylan Thomas, Henrietta Moraes, Bacon, Maclaren-Ross, Nina Hamnet ("the laughing torso," the best tits in Europe, according to Modi[gliani]);

9 South Bank Cultural Complex (Purcell Room and other concrete eyesores);

10 Charing Cross, a full day trying not to belittle the most miserable

bookstores, dedicating special attention to my bookseller friends, Larry Grosvenor Letham and Brian Boole, to see if I can get my hands on an impossible Shiel or a Sexton Blake by Flann O' Brien;

11 Savile Row, to determine the amount of damage done to proverbial elegance by The Beatles;

12 Abbey Road, to determine how much they did to repair it;

13 Battersea, to investigate a hunch: that Giles Gilbert Scott's constructive genius—like the musical genius of Elgar—can't solely be attributed to raw talent, like some of his contemporaries (for instance: Le Corbusier, Mies, Wright, Schoenberg, Berg, Stravinsky) but seems to emanate with the help of the fabled city itself, *London . . .*

List of places in London I should've seen during my first visit and their order (according to my guide, Enrique Villa Veralobos, alias Harry Woolfstoncraft Shady, alias Eduardo Manjares, alias Basilio Aspid, in 1992):

Gabriel Donovan / Sebastian Birt to Eduardo Manjares

Bertorelli's

#18

(. . .) they were the over-sensitive clingers on, the ones who couldn't spend a moment away from Elena, the ones who copied everything she did to the letter. They followed her everywhere, entertained her infidelities, sat down to have tea with her in her little room, or worse, on her mat. In the little room: through a high window one could see the train passing. Many years later, I discovered that through the former dentist's office window, I saw the same train passing, leaving; the same train that we (Elena, Remo, Felipe, Dos, and I) saw that first time through Elena's window . . .

Victor Eiralis, private letters to Julio Clausás

#19

See Ibiza Trip

They postponed their return so Teodelina could be born in

London—despite their deciding to christen her Teodelina. The discussion, which was briefer than the one about the naming of the journal—Elena wanted to call the girl Ema—ended when Nicasio said: "don't sentence the girl to a lifetime of misery for the sake of a ceremony."

[Ivan Salerno Scacchi], *Out of a Greek Gift*

For a time, they fantasized about [entertained the illusion of] spending the rest of their lives in Cuevacaviar, the hidden island [cave, fortress] off Bañalbufar. For Nicasio, it seemed the most desirable of destinations: where he could distance himself [definitively] from Eloísa, continue paying little attention to Elena, and educate Teode far from the madding crowd. For Elena, it was pretty much the same: a place where she could distance herself from Remo (from Lalo, from everyone), continue to reciprocate Nicasio's indifference, and personally educate Teodelina . . .

Eduardo Manjares, *Postcard from the Inquisitor*

Ingrid gave Inés the job of sorting the archive, of dealing with the public "behind the screen,"

A portrait of Elena by Lino Scacchi [in sanguine chalk, the same instrument she used to correct his original] was hanging in the office where Elena was working, a Trompe-l'œil to compensate for the small number of people working on the floor of clients and contractors at *Zigurrat* and of collaborators and collectors at *Agraphia*.

Screen. Description.

Urlihrt's writing desk was behind that screen. Once, unexpectedly, Oliverio and Dos opened the door without knocking and saw something they'd rather not have seen or, afterwards, described, because all that was visible was carnage, evidence of a recently-committed act of *violence* left abandoned on his desk; a spectacle others might confuse for mere disorder, mere chaos, a mere simulacrum. So that one might be tempted to say there was only a belt and a plate on his writing desk, a plate with a single fried egg and a cigarette extinguished in the yoke.

Something else Urlihrt must have heard and later seen.

Opus. The style. Prescriptions for its propagation.

Warn the reader that the emphasis placed "in those days" on the evangelical formula wasn't a way to pass off [disguise] style as inspiration, but a way of establishing a simulacrum, essential when the lack of dates sanctioned our commitment to vagueness, [to discredit and even despair.]

Years later, when Eduardo Manjares paid them a visit, he described Nicasio Urlihrt's curiosity in women as "proboscidal" [using the adjective, "proboscidal," apt for a man with a large nose, corpulent frame, premature wrinkles, and a clumsy gait]. This should be of concern to us because Manjares, who was passing through Buenos Aires, was guilty of an attempt at courteous dissuasion, citing Proust: "Let us leave the beautiful women to men of no imagination." Urlihrt, who was good with a riposte, and imaginative (or perhaps just in love), twice emended the citation with the intention of improving it, first saying: "Let us leave the imagination to men undistracted by pretty women"; and then: "Let us leave pathetic theories to men of tragic nature." Oliverio, Felipe, and someone else were also present *with us*.

[*The X-Positions*, novel under preparation] [NO]

The gloss of a diptera's wings to the triumphal shadow of a soaring falcon

NO

#20

He was a typical Galician, Don Julio, just as you're a typical Catalan. (No, I mean, that's just from our point of view of course, I mean my point of view: and I'm from Valencia. Or from Valladolid?) But younger, with certain pretentions. He brought back to Buenos Aires an overcoat he acquired in Paris, along with a silk scarf and an attitude of modest abandon. And he deceived us all. He came with so bad a reputation, half the Buenos Aires intelligentsia was after him, following the piratical inktrail he left after translating Bataille and Benjamin without paying royalties. And he translated them badly too. If it was said there was a skirt-lifting flaneur walking the streets of Recoleta whose name was Walter! I'm sure you, Nurlihrt, Luini, and Lester immediately brought him into the fold, and Luini and Nurl introduced him to me in The Giralda (where the two rogues will have begun the process of transforming him into a local legend), *thinking* (I know it's inconceivable, but in this case, the verb can apply to them) "that they're doing me a favor." I was without a job, without burden. Urlihrt and Luini read one of my fawning pieces and the Galician then immediately filed it away. My diffidence must have been an artisanal requirement. He invited me to dine at La Guillotina, the restaurant in which you and I met for the end of year parties and which, today, is but another cathedral submerged in memory, foreign. And this is was what convinced me. I was only one of his *nègres*.

Perhaps *The History of the Secret* the narrator mentions is an allusion to *Brief Decoding of the Mystery*, the book I wrote for him and for which I was never paid . . .

Despite the occasional nonsense, Manjares's short story is quite good—the best in this court of blind men. Gullibly, one of the cretins felt obliged to justify the publication of such a strange a story (although all of them were strange), doing so in the worst possible manner—praising it until he was hoarse, trumpeting about it being full of "secret codes" that allude to the works of D. H. Lawrence and F. R. Leavis—as if these trifling concerns of university cloisterers would interest anyone.

The adulteries in parallel: Lalo Sabatani / Elena Siesta. Nicasio / Inés Maspero

Inés said [to him], "he was afraid of something" (referring to his evasive attitude with regard to his interaction with Belisario in his study, where he slept the day before). Nicasio was brazenly impudent: he became engaged to a beautiful woman as a token of defiance.

Lorenzo (Lalo) Sabatani used to perform his magic tricks (and he only had a few) in some of the crowded cafebars on Corrientes Street. He examined their pulses ("between the wrist and the thigh, diction and metastasis," he'd say), read their palms, and again examined the pulses of those he called "lacanian monjitas," and when he wanted to, he'd choose one of them to sleep with, and go back to her apartment. His preference for married women, though, meant he often ended up sleeping alone. [[He had a preference for married women; he frequently slept alone]]

Elena never went to those bars. She arrived one afternoon with an air of alarm and "irrepressible" indignation (exaggerated Lalo, who kept boasting until late, very late in the night, about his conquest) . . .

#20

It hurts to recall the journal's degree of semantic instability during those years. As Urlihrt argued: it oscillated between epileptic absence and rigorous malapropism. The work Luini had to present as evidence before a tribunal, like the one in the stories (*go-betweeners, feticheurs*, etc), was, according to Luini, a plagiarism larded with quotations, proportioned (although disproportionately) by Lalo Sabatani, *Agraphia*'s warlock of black magic par excellence.

CEREMONIES / LITURGIES

On Elena's way of cutting the uncut pages of a book

On Nicasio's means of quitting smoking

On Eloísa's way of opening a pack of cigarettes

On the state in which Nicasio leaves his writing desk

On Elena's way of tucking away a keepsake

A few words on Elena's way of underscoring.

In more than one sense, Elena's underscores are perfect. First, there is the sense of their being painstakingly worked over—abusing at least two meanings of the Spanish word *prolijidad*—and there is their sense of harmless, innocent accomplishment. They concealed [conceal] both her general temperament and her mood in the [moment, act of] reading while, at the same time, they showed [show / exhibited / exhibit] her infallibility in distinguishing what's important from what's trivial, accessory, and most of all [most often], obvious. The method was unique. Inés employed it with neither violence nor moderation in every book of every genre she read—drama, poetry, narrative, essay—in the three languages she'd understood—English, French, Spanish—an exercise, which, at first glance, may have seemed evidence of a strict upbringing, a rhetorical tribute or stipend to her harsh [hard-going, traumatic] orphanhood.

Perusing her underscores leaves the reader in no doubt as to the expectations, intentions, or interests of the young poet, nor, incidentally, of her desire to become cultured—understandable in someone in pursuit of independent judgment—accumulating [accordingly] hints, indications, suggestions, and *ritornelli* for the enrichment of her conversation.

Monitoring the behavior of these designs on the page could lead us either to an alleyway or into an ocean in the manner they evince the capacity or skill of distributing patterns and concealing them, discouraging any search for symmetry—every indication of it being interrupted with astonishing frequency and irregularity by so many irrelevant, extraneous, and self-indulgent diversions.

#22

The trip was supposed to end in Athens, [but for some unknown reason] it ended in Treviso . . . *With a bang, a whimper.* Topics suggested [are]: an untimely confession, a lovers' bedroom spat, not in view of the whole world [[Frost poem in Yvor Winters refers to Thoreau [in Blyth?], *an inseparable accident*]]. It was difficult, at that point, to give credence to Elena's love, [respond to that] affection or show of affection responsible for Nicasio's affection or show of affection. It is possible Elena contrived a scheme of indiscernible grudges and surprise attacks similar to those woven into the first sestina. The mutual disloyalties are an apotheosized exaggeration of error and inaccuracy. For Elena and Nicasio, who never collaborated on anything or even wrote in the same room together, this style was captivating.

Oliverio Lester, *The X-Positions*

#23

Sestina of Departure

The Self from others always shies away

To taste the bitter bread of solitude

Boasts of knowing what it means to live

But blurs the trail, adulterates the prints

On that crudely-executed map of fate [:]

Whose exploration amputates his shade.

(V. 1) The Sun at midday amputates our shade

I was gullible, inconstant as a shade.

Even what remains eventually goes away:

The farewell prose of destiny, of fate

The asymmetric rule of solitude,

The foot's unbroken contour in a print,

And the rival act of truly being alive

#5 ISSUES

[*The ages / Connection. Dos. Nicasio.*

Style á deux—*writing in collaboration*]

1.

The Two Illnesses

[[#17]]

The two illnesses and the theory of the three endings and the decision on the title of the story taken from the collection of stories rejected by Belisario / Basilio in accordance with the narrative version in the plagiarized book—Accents?

There was a trend, in *Agraphia*, for taxonomy, for purblind classification. The writers, collaborators, had to—*we* had to—get inside familiar types. We decided on Elena and Nicasio. This was the idea: I would try to commit suicide within the first hour, i.e. of Hilarión's departure, but would prove incompetent. Likewise, Nicasio. Not to mention Lino (Scacchi). But Lalo Sabatani referred to an earlier tradition, originating with Aldecoa Inauda, a poet of the Golden Age. Note: Gabriel Bocángel wrote of him: "Being acquainted with many styles / he imitated all." That is, he had an illimitable repertoire . . . and during the Golden Age too! Or maybe it was a joke, a *boutade* by Bocángel. Aldecoa was famous for his ability to adapt, for his skill in accommodating himself to the court (careerism, we now call it). The "being acquainted with many styles" could very well be a reference to this aptitude, instead of an encomium on his reputation as an imitator. But he, favored by nature with her gifts and the court with its endowments, did his imitating in the open; whereas we did it behind a screen, deviously, unscrupulously, copying and imitating, as if there was a chip in our brains directing us to plagiarize. For this first classification, there were [added] long-term consequences. For example: those of us who adapted to Hilarión Curtis's practice would have an easy life but a difficult death. Note that I have *sanpaku* eyes so I always believed I'd die by accident. Remo's death was what convinced us. Some of us would die of cryptodermia. They, the others, the better ones, they would live out the rest of their lives having adapted to kleptolalia.

Basilio U., an oral confidence

2.

Felipe has grown too much. He's become a lot like me. But I, on the other hand, have gotten younger, so I no longer look old enough to be his father: more like his older brother, according to Dos. So, [disregarding me] Dos gives the impression that Felipe only had a mother—despite his being fat enough to have been incorporated by several parents—and since Eiralis lacks both matter and memory, Felipe's father is conceived as a mismatch of body and soul, or vice-versa, the result being a kind of ghostly figure with an out-of-focus skeleton covered by a film of breath. As such, he talks like a ventriloquist. The most recent of such creations arrived without my noticing and without anyone telling me their ages at birth or how old they are now. It's all a matter of perspective, in the space where chronologies are made but time is indiscernible, eloquent, but also cruel. Oliverio seems to mock him to Luini, who must be the one who warns the character of the joke as he ages more and more to resemble me. But the small age gap between Lester and Prosan remains the same and only becomes nil at Elena's discretion. Hazlitt or Lamb spoke of the satellitic character of women; the kind who write the sort of servile, saturnine characters who in turn becomes the satellites of others.

Belisario confessed, smoothing his moustache, trying to be subtle but avoiding understatement, that I reminded him of a Hungarian consul in a movie by Molnar [Lubitsch]. He emphasized his resemblance to a small graceful animal whose tiny cage left him room enough to do little else than chew the bars and lick his claws. Belisario, who's still five or six years older than me, belongs to another generation. When I first met him, he was wearing a chambergo, so I thought he was more like a century older than me. Who knows what the kids think of me, the ones eighteen or twenty years younger? It's true that differences shrink between thirty and forty, and they shrink even more between forty and fifty. But sixty establishes its own law of gravity. And many fell away, like Belisario and me. While others continued *gravitating*: in the case of Lalo, without making much progress. I see him leaving, squeezing through Vidt's narrow doorway, like a bony-ass coward. It helps to be of an age where one can be irresponsible without being accountable [backed by the myth about youth, which covers any misstep or error with the lie of singularity and potential]. How many excuses are made for mediocrity in the young! They said he lives in the Balearics, perhaps in Banyalbufar—where Elena and I once planned to elope—living his life immersed in the company of others, in better company than ours.

Nicasio Urlihrt, *The X-Positions*

Eiralis: Nurlihrt via Empson: Nerrida

3.

The collaborative writing at *Agraphia* required at least two pleasant adherencies. At least two simultaneous missions and a lack of purpose encouraged (and attenuated) by the lack of evidence for the anonymity. The act of writing therefore required confinement, indulgence, speed. Conditions ideal for lovers. Writing together will be: Elena and Nicasio, Inés and Nicasio, Elena and Lalo, Inés and Elena. But not Nicasio and Lalo, due to the lack of proof (although there are suspicions "The Mass" came to be on that inexplicable [clandestine] night Nicasio and Lalo colluded together). In a publication made possible by a bevy of accomplices / adversaries, it was inevitable and went with the job. Now, according to *Agraphia*'s presocratic numerology, two was not a number. Like good primitives, they needed a figure that lacked the balance of two, the unity of one. From this came "*Agraphia*'s principle of adultery," which implies a number more than two, an interloper: a third wheel, an "*intruder in the dust.*"

The Cristóbal Niaras, Agraphia: *Chance Laboratory*

The three periods of *Agraphia / Allusive* can be classified before the conclusion. The predominance of Elena, with her luminous vocation of vanguard and error, her puerilities and idiolectal glossaries, (noninterventionism, *errancy*, contrerejet, *renegations*, *freakatives*, *inindicial*, inkhorn, *lepro and graphorrhea*, [naiserie], *malapropism, oliguria, umbilicapedia, panxiety, titubiosis, xelexion, zeuxidia*), her unyielding latticework [revision of final proofs from the editor, accounting for foreign words with a dictionary in hand] lasts until the first trip to Europe. Period of estrangement that led Sabatani to inaugurate a period of lapsing, the one corresponding with "Salon of Independents," known later as "Diet of Worms."

The period known as the Luiniad lasted as long as the Council of Trent (eighteen years), and according to Urlihrt, the period should've been called "Trent," but, because of a lack of foresight and planning, the result was less ferocious, less feracious. But such foresight and planning culminates "by its own means and fears, in the atrocities of the worst of Argentine dictatorships," alarumed Isabel [Teodelina] Teischer, "with remarkable boldness" in a literary pamphlet (Matilde Urbach publishers, s/f). Proof of this can be read in "Lycergical Glossary to Sircular Cymmetry," "Ysir," "The Dreadmist," "Out of a Greek Gift," and a great number of stories that aren't seen in canonical anthologies of Argentine literature." We can add every other anthology, including the lamest of those published in those lamest of years.

Eloy Armesto, *The Sycophant's Soliloquy*, in *Parts without Justification*, for the Symposium on Invisibility (included with modifications in *From Secret Zero to a Number Less. Biography of the Invisible*)

#4

Going against Occam's razor, the nominative entities of *Agraphia* are born to reproduce themselves, to proliferate, and after a short time, be discarded. Their life-cycle can be compared with that of the common cold virus. "Each syllable of their names, a germ, a potential pandemic." Categorical proliferation, diametrical. The names function as algebraic permutations [that make no difference to the final result]. They gestate, accumulate, are collected, arrayed, and then *spent* (in the double sense). The metastasis occurs where fame is hierarchically [unevenly] distributed. A sectarian argot of terms: first, the "paludinal [glandular] glitterati" in *Septic Midrash*. Then, the "phalansterian demographic" constructed to "contradict the anecdote." In the journal, "there is no hint of theory," except what makes you rich. Theory, they proclaimed, plagiarizing Proust, is the price tag on a gift. Oliverio Lester proclaimed that admission into *Agraphia* relies not so much on intellectual common ground, but on the postulant's mandatory baptism at the font. With regard to the oblivion of narrative, "no one who had anything to say dared to write [be a literary casualty]." It is Nicasio Urlihrt's motto and blazon.

Cristóbal Niaras, Agraphia: *Chance Laboratory*

#5

The Epsilom, called a "Treatise on Small Quantities," is a difficult novel to describe (and yet, I'll try, because I want to justify [my] our admiration [for Zi]). The protagonists, a gang of [perennially] homeless guys, all of them *enfants savants*, go wandering around making friends with the [common] people. According to the narrator, they have two serious flaws [one of diction and another of understanding]: stammering whenever they attempt to make a comparison, so that the second term never arrives [appears], or it is one the interlocutor / adversary can simply ignore, of a type "equivalent to Mezzaloth when . . ." The first adventure occurs in Patagonia. The epsilom, in this case, is . . . [Medellín the good], "The Imitation of an Ounce," "Xochimilk."

In order to begin late, and beginning for no particular reason, the epsilom live their lives in reverse: they're born as geriatrics in the future and live each day improving on that condition, rejuvenating, reaching full maturity at roughly ten years old. [However,] Due to time's reversibility, and a complementary mechanism of adaptability, for which Zi has an explanation I cannot remember (which saves me having to explain it), the events in their lives are mapped out and so anticipated [[as long as there is [intervened] was an accident]] by ordinary mortals who live their lives in the conventional way, and for whom the clocks run normally ["correctly," according to the dogmatic Urlihrt], an idea that accounts for [the now outdated admiration of] Zi's precocity.

It makes no difference whether one reaches today from yesterday or tomorrow: for both past and present meet at the crossroad of the present moment . . .

So the Zi Benno of "Xoch." still hasn't attained the remarkable maturity of a *wunderkind* and has to be around thirty years old. The Zi

Daisy Ashford wouldn't appear for another twenty years or so.

When I mentioned her, he didn't seem to remember her.

In the early eighties, Mario Levin invited me to write for his journal, *Cinegrafo*. For the first issue, I drew upon all my ignorance and pedantry to write a piece about cinematic rock. I reviled the genre, vindictively lambasted everything I'd seen, doing so, I believe, with juvenile zeal (although, at twenty-one, I wasn't that young), to make myself worthy of inclusion.

None of that exists today (I've seen many things that contradict my daring, "transgressive," claims), but a taste of the era still lingers in my mouth, and that's strong enough to vindicate all my mistakes . . . seen immediately.

The cover of that first issue—a tremulous Bogarde at the end of the Fassbinder film, *Despair*, screenplay by Stoppard, adapted from the novel by Nabokov—exhibited, according to Mario, our paranoia about concealing—reason enough to turn to the inside front cover: photo of Orson Welles in full armor playing his own Macbeth—our omnipotence. Included before without footnote.

Tears shed for the profession

Hilarión Curtis on the quantities and the disasters

6.

Urlihrt lived by his insomnia. The perfect work Nicasio had promised would be divided into two parts, each part in turn divided—like the *Goldberg Variations*—into thirty-two fragments. Now, the first sixteen chapters would proceed as if up and down eight steps, each step having its own peculiar signs that are met first on the way up, and again, but in reverse, on the way back down. Now, although the number of fragments left by Urlihrt far exceeded the stipulated quantity, no one—not even Lester, Luini, or Urlihrt's daughter—could make them [that accumulated heap] appear like an orderly collection

. . . The excesses of symmetry lead to the desert of boredom.

His diary ended: this has set its seal upon the age

The old bachelor pays a visit to the dead poet's library

Soon after publishing my first fictional piece in the journal, *Change* ("Misery of a Realist," first extract from *Finesse*), I was thought to have risen high enough in the disordered hierarchy of the literary world to be called upon to judge my first short story competition. I read more than a hundred; there seemed to be no end: none were displeasing, but all were unmemorable, except for one, which I remember because I particularly disliked it. It had a title something like, "Diphteria of a Cereal," and it was a perfect parody of my first piece. I felt the same way I did that time in fourth grade when I entered the classroom and caught L(eporello) imitating me. I never saw myself like that before, but now I saw myself perfectly as I was. There's something in an imitation, however foolish, that always supersedes the model: imitation is the only advantage left to the featherless biped whose evolution left him with a paltry handicap for racing against any of the quadrupeds. The progress of our steps is always backwards. Barefooted humiliation. Why we can't justify Bates's outrage *after* Maclaren-Ross; or comprehend the spit in the eye that so annoyed Carpentier and Lino Novás Calvo *after* Cabrera Infante (despite his stating explicitly "Parodio no por odio").

Look for Ivor Black in The H., V.N.)

Ravel

In defence of the stories, though, one can invoke an extraneous though irrelevant detail. When Oliverio Lester—who'd won various prizes by that time—was judging a short story competition for which he had to read "almost three hundred stories," he arrived at a curious and exasperating conclusion. All of the stories were populated by similar characters following neatly constructed arcs in neatly constructed fleeting unrealities. As if the contrivance were an instrument or toy for imaginations dominated and constrained by outdated modes, so the arts and trades, occupations and situations described in those three hundred stories Oliverio Lester had read were the same arts and trades, occupations and situations he'd read about in stories from the forties and fifties. The first mawkish scruples prevailed in the realistic narratives—gatekeeper grandfathers, office lovers, tenement suicides, miserable prostitutes with guilty consciences, miserable narrators with guilty consciences, and just plain misery by the bucketload. But even the fantasy tales—encounters with aliens more clever and civilized than ourselves, discoveries of old documents that have a modifying impact on the present time, predictable suspensions of reality for unwelcome forays into the oneiric—arrogantly flouted any implementation, insinuation, or hint of the modern.

So he was determined—roughly a decade ago—to publish a collection much like the one the reader will encounter here, but with a mere exemplary, didactical intention. But then other issues distracted him.

#6 CALUMNIES

Elena Siesta, "Sestina of Departure"

What did our detractors mean when they said "without stories" . . . ?

Nicasio Urlihrt, *letter ending on a semicolon*

Letter ending on its tippy-toes

What did they mean to say, Don Julio? They meant to say that no one understood what in the world they were talking about or writing. What do they mean to say? They mean to say that all of them, all are just gazing at their navels with the kind of smug self-satisfaction that others find repellant. See, for example, if anyone can understand a word of the discussion regarding *Agraphia*'s aporia in "The Mass in Tongues": there is so much understatement, so many baffling interpolations and obscure references, it would exhaust most normal readers' curiosity and patience. To know that Duchamp's nine malic molds correspond to the thirty-six family doctors, and that the number of ocular witnesses weren't in fact four but three: north and south; that 646416 was the magical cipher in the arcane numerology known to the initiated. One must become familiar with automatic formula for the anagrams and pseudonyms and use it to share ones devotion to cryptic books . . .

Victor Eiralis, idem

#24

Carelessly, I got used to the idea that paradoxes themselves were acceptable to everyone, and often mentioned them in passing, though I saw no signs of support or even sympathetic smiles around me. But, occasionally, when I was alone, I indulged my superstitious sense of self-importance. Thence, ready to begin my narrative about the cult, or the legion, I remembered that my two favorite stories in English are about sects or lodges: "False Dawn" by Kipling, and "The Primate of the Rose" by M. P. Shiel. But then I realized, after thinking a while about these stories and their themes, that I was wrong: neither of them have anything to do with sects or lodges. Sebastian Birt, *Lenten Diary (Diary to Elena)*

#8 Farewells

[#27]

Before closing the door on the previous day

[Shortly before Elena sneaked into the background with Bindo, quietly and deftly, so they wouldn't hear her speak about them, she left a note that was, in both style and substance, the very opposite of a suicide note.]

By doing it so badly, maintaining my distance and calm, and because Remo was there, and because his languid liquid stare made me nauseous. For this and because of my rough and narrow throat (almost all we ever did was smoke). For this and because I knew about Allegra Siri, all of those characters, so to speak, placed at yours and our mercy. Dos, Pimpernel, whoever. And I see I must carry away a flock of adjectives ("every ewe with its mate"). Except they're not ewes but lemmings. The edge of *Agraphia*'s fjord placed by you over there so we don't fall.

(. . .) All the stubbornness, the foolishness, the constant betrayal, and the pride—especially in his case. My constantly aching molar seems unjustly to be at his temperament's disposal. Without justice of divorce, you'll say. I don't deserve it when he's the one to blame. He'd like to be the next presbyobe, the one who pays no attention to the details—not I, the one who stays at home. *La plus cruelle absence est celle que l'on peut toucher avec le main.* Toulet, apt, isn't it, considering our arrangement? Remind her of it, whoever she is. The drafts are still there [in Vidt]. If, at some point, Teode wants them back, it's *your* duty N. to return them to her. Also, give her those books you merely hoard without bothering to read them. *It would help if you collected books instead of women*, they said to CC. I [on the other hand] feel incapable of doing either: I have no contempt for books or women, but I'm quite indifferent to collections of them. I only lately understood the impulse: collections, collections. *I'm an irregular verb.*

[There are things that surround us, that abound in great numbers, that slither or crawl, and yet, today, they don't matter. The monkeys are clamoring above our heads. I assert, I insist: *I'm an irregular verb.*]

Note of farewell by Elena Siesta / Laetitia Pilkinghorn

Shortly after the last throes of *Agraphia*, justified because of the password "after the first death, there is no other" [Dylan Thomas bromide], and after the latest babbling in search of a scheme or pattern ["Specular Soup," "Early"], the group had been reduced to a small circle of snobs with exclusive tastes and reverential airs, committed to a grim [sterile] formalism, that varied between free experimentation and idiotic *oulipienne* extremes, but which had the virtue—or defect—of not incorporating the audacity or stringent formalism of the latter, only the enthusiasm, effeminacy, and acedia [anesthesis] of its practitioners.

Emilio Duluoz, *Last Paid [Pure] Vacations*

On Hilarión's resurrection from the dead and the reburial

Luis Chitarroni

I live in communion with the dead [Quevedo]

One stormy night, Nicasio brought us to the house in the south where Hilarión's wake was being held. We gathered round him. He said: "there won't be many of us." Since there was no more coffee, they brought us mugs of milk. The smell of dead flowers was repulsive. "After three days, the body starts to reek," said Nicasio before adding: "these three are the cultural apostles of *the distant far away*." He was referring to a certain young man, an older man with the look of a lawyer about him, and Felipe Luini's girlfriend. [Dead?] The Fedora [of imitation felt] resting motionless on his chest, a recent Band-Aid on his ring finger, a copy of *The Barefoot Path*. Also, an umbrella dripping outside the narrow furrow of his march, a standing ashtray brimming with inhuman ash, and some empty mugs balancing on a coffee table. At certain times, in an adjoining room lit with tubes, the three were face-to-face with the ambassadors of the distant faraway, and the youth took the opportunity to air his relationship with a woman ten years his senior.

"I expect the worst: that she'll commit suicide. And that she'll make the decision while I'm away." The confession prompted a contest. The lawyer revealed he was in a relationship with a woman who was making his life impossible. Luini's girlfriend said her brother was running the risk of being assassinated by a group of vigilantes, and that no one knew how to convince him to flee the country. Back in front of HC's coffin, someone standing next to Lester said: "How strange it is." At which Nicasio explained: "Like a crustacean. The integrity of the corpse and the lack of smell are due to the illness. As it advances, it stops growth and corruption. We'll be attending a premature burial." Luini's girlfriend—the sister of the threatened man, whom we all wanted to save in that same hour—ventured to ask something we'd disregarded: "If it wasn't going to last more than a day, why have a wake?" Nicasio delayed in answering: "Don't know. A whim. It just had to be seen." And someone else puffed: "Was it really worth it?"

The following day, the dead of night seemed to reward them, but it was a false alarm, although it made the priest's youth sermon more tolerable, and for Luini's girlfriend, it made more tolerable the incessant

202

advances of the obsequious lawyer with the ridiculous name.

Before they sealed the coffin, one of the three apostles pointed at the ring finger of the deceased [enringed with a piece of tan paper], around which there was a piece of paper. He asked Nicasio if he could remove it. After a questioning glance at the lawyer, Nicasio approved. The lawyer seemed to be waiting for that moment the whole night. He nodded with a smile, adding: "Don't hesitate, do it immediately, but slowly: I also happen to be a notary public."

It was a piece of rag paper. On the side in contact with the skin, there was a printed inscription: *The illness has assumed the likeness of death that death, the same death you question! [sic] on the way out, will not deny.*

Nicasio was left with the rag paper piece, that is, one of the apostles.

["Thoroughness" extends in two directions because of the two senses of the word: comprehensiveness and meticulousness.]

It's difficult, and especially now, to find out in detail what he did for Inés, who was always wishing for someone to visit, but someone who didn't immediately become, or become by degrees for that matter, tiresome on visiting. She used to say, to claim, it was a result of her middle class, her bourgeois vulgarity. But there was something else.

[#26]

It's not easy writing a sad tale after a happy one. [Perhaps] Tolstoy had this in mind when he heard the first beating intimations of his Anna K. It may be hard to hear a beat in here. My family bedroom is host to every kind of noise.

Beginning of "Replicas"

Fantin-Latour. To block outline.

Blocked outline.

Anales diáfanos del viento. Góngora

Mourir

Although nothing prepares us for it, dying suddenly when young exempts us from having to go through the slow process of dying when old. Two ghosts have stood up [in unison]. They are the ghosts of old age and of sickness. [And] they stood up together and got ready to leave when we alerted them that we still hadn't died, that we hadn't died yet, that we are still standing, [that we will remain standing,] that we've begun walking. We caught up with them almost immediately. All our actions were mirrored in theirs, as if they were glued to our backs, beginning at the hip. Duelists, if we were, in truth, chronological caricatures. After they cross our path, we will not see them again, but we will hear them say, illegibly or inscrutably, through the semi-consciousness of awakening from sleep, that since they began expecting us (waiting for us, frightening us), the slow process of dying is no respecter of age. Dying and aging are very different things, as if one was written in verse, the other, in prose. Even now, when I think I'm beginning to understand them, I do not. And perhaps it's because "now" demands too much exercise of will, and "do," even more. And everything I had set out to describe here, before Basilio stopped me, is inaccurate, an implausible version of what really goes on. And what really goes on: birds decapitated over headless torsos. And this makes me think of D. H. Lawrence, and the precise way in which he ends *The Woman Who Rode Away* by dismissing what is loved and what is seen. But Lawrence himself isn't an example of what I mean. In him, the illness, the sickness, isn't a ghost, and old age is only an intruder insulted by his good looks. Not a ghost, but a beggar that follows him, circling round him, a dervish, spinning round him, transforming him with every turn, as Morgan Le Fey does to Prince Valiant in the first book I ever truly loved. That lets him see, through graying orbits, time spent, what the years ahead will bring. He will have the good sense not to fulfill them, but not so as to die suddenly when young, but to go through the slow process of dying . . . Yes,

free

with weariness of flesh when the dice that we spend our lives burnishing fall outside the precisesly measured circle of error that predicts the probability of a sudden accidental death and are blunted . . .

In *Precisions*

Chronology & Critique

Emma Steele (???) Cristóbal Niaras

The zero, a round number—*achievements and memorabilia of* Agraphia

A great puzzle whose answers are all out of place

It's easy to determine the system of belonging at *Agraphia* from a stylistic criterion, and despite what's said *above* or *below* [Niaras and Armesto were mere footnotes] about collaborative writing. "Specular Soup" and "Replicas," for example, are covered in the stylistic fingerprints of the *folie à deux* collaborations of Nicasio Urlihrt / Eloísa Betelgeuse and Oliverio Lester / Elena Siesta. In the first, the tendency to supply an aphoristic generalization followed by a narrative conclusion ("We know it takes time: Tashtego awaited the revelation two centuries after his departure from the Puerto de Palos of his invention, languishing on a Patagonian coastline") competes, paragraph after paragraph, prayer by prayer, with the transmission of useless technical terms to the reader (example, transcription) . . .

The correspondence of mythological ambiguities (with additional ones taken from Sebastien Birt's *Diary to Elena*) in the latter: "my male sister," etc. etc.

In contrast: the profusion of expletives in Eiralis's letters, not solely attributable to the epistolary tone, and their scarcity verging on dryness (not solely to be blamed on ambiguity of phrasing) in Felipe Luini's "The Office Next Door."

At the height of their dalliances and defiances

Lalo and Remo began moving as one, intrigued by the delectable matter offered them by their master. They snuffled with equal misgiving, with the same animal mistrust. Then they submitted unanimously, obeyed. While Elena's ability to respond to compliments, or pretend to respond, was strong, [well-known, profound, as her listlessness] her dry disinclination for returning them was characteristic: in the case of Lalo and Remo, a rejection of either one was to be taken as a rejection of both. A strange procedure indeed. She appreciated in [others and in] herself the capacity for contempt and invective, but not for passive flattery. For Lalo, her lack of response made her seem almost a widow, dead to love because of Urlihrt, because of condescending indifference. She, disposed [as was stated] to use up all her nine lives at once, was already familiar with those nuances of love as they are reckoned in the tribunal of a single glance.

#28

Basilio's briefcase [Charles Bovary's cap]

—Stop describing it, Basilio. I swear I didn't see it.

Francisco Xavier Aldecoa Inauda (1569–1616). Aldecoa recounts: "I was born under the aegis of the twins, heralded by a pageantry of signs. The first born, having already deprived my mother of her prime, and fifteen years of working life, I would be the son that, after a difficult labor, deprived her of her life. The place of my birth was the village of Yeste, at the house of the Inaudi, the which being my grandparents' home, in the distant far away, and I know not how my father came to traverse that distance for the conception. He was the court bailiff, and was never at home. That I grew up beset by poverty, but in the tender care of one of my mother's sisters, was the will of the omnipotent and simpleminded Lord. In my works, by contrast, the reader will discover in the disarray that life is not disposed as verse or prose, and for a man to persist in trying to arrange it thus, makes him vain, obstinate, and deficient in skill, in reason, and in memory." Those works include the sonnets and *décimas* from *La semana horizontal*, which was dedicated the duke of Osuna, and is often compared with the *Devotions* of Donne (1573–1631), since the Spaniard's work was also the product of a lengthy convalescence; the comedy in verse, *La ceñida visitada*; the long meditative work, *Ejercicio malogrado en homenaje a la vista*, which, between 1608 and 1611, was translated and exported all the way to America (where it was used by certain schools of thought for matutinal instruction), and sometimes known by the title *Lengua de pájaros*, after one of its longest chapters: it was his most frequently printed book. A victim of mild insanity—the Spirochaete way—Inauda inaugurated a mode of free expression that belongs more to the twentieth century, which is the reason why he's been variously celebrated as a precursor. Much of Inauda's oeuvre remains secreted and unpublished by his estate, which is kept by a fanatically religious descendant who prevents "their being known to a wider public, which is neither here nor there, since the works themselves aren't aware of being read, or that they risk my soul's place by the side of the righteous."

Eloy Armesto made his critical debut for *Hendiadys* and was afterwards encouraged to write for less boring journals by Cristóbal Niaris and, above all, Annick Bérrichon. Author of valuable works of fiction: (*The Prince of Modesty, Tatami, Sensei, Progress [[Vienna while in Prague]]*) (novels). *Pretérito anterior* (Past Perfect) collects all his critical works to date.

The Meaulnes, Edgar Alain: the journal's first exegete and faithful apologist. Berna, while in Riga.

Biruté Aurigón: the first lady to penetrate the virile cloister of *Agraphia*—patterned after a confessional—was this Cuban exile living in Buenos Aires. She was married to Virgilio Anscombe Melián, who held a diplomatic post at the (. . .) embassy. In the early fifties she was officially Urlihrt's lover. All her books, which anticipate magic realism, merit republication. They are: *Sepúlveda and us, The Tales of Jeremiah* (children's), *The Dazzling Kingdom, The Bone and the Salt, She Recovered at Home* (Casa de las Américas Prize), *Beyond Them were All, The Fruit of Yesterdays, Spring of Ashes, The Statuette Prince* (children's), *Migraines and other Private Weaknesses, George Gershwin* (illustrated biography).

Zi Benno: *nom de plume* of the author of a gigantic work entitled, *The Epsilom (or My Scruples)*, a cycle of almost four hundred novels (among them, *The Surface of Venus, The Sirius Point of View,*

The Anecdotal Father, The Times, A Small Wonder, The Spartan Minutes, The Ionian Spy, The Gay Physicist, For a Terrible Theatre, Without Sensing that they Call Me, The Chance Encounter of V[irgilio] P[iñera] and T[ennessee] W[illiams] at the Poolside Surrounded by Guests, The Ankles of Memory, Mexican Journal, High Jump, Embroidered with Cadmium Thread, Mortuga, The Snail, The Winding, By the Grace of Terence, Fossil Chamber, The Unfortunate, An Adaptation, The Patrol, Ghetto Bosses, Age of Fractals, The Intellectual Hoard, In Search of Madame Tussaud, Tabitha Salieri, The Bearcat's Search, The Mongoose's Pagoda, Titanium Thigh, etc.)

Shortly after his death (September 11, 2003), when the identity of this prolific and well-regarded (though still poor) writer was revealed, those who didn't know the man by his real name—a few close friends—were astonished: César Quaglia.

Constantin Beret (1899–1966). "For all exiled Russian writers, the German word *Zeitgeist* is a fairy with no counterpart," wrote Beret, christened Constantin by his fantasist mother, who was an admirer of his homonymous precursor, Balmont. He even wrote a work in Russian, French, and English in which he homelized on this maxim throughout, although it had failed to conquer his imagination, an environment inimical to fairies. He dedicated himself to showcasing his style, which tended more to the playful and suggestive than the polemical and invective, in his first collection of short stories, *Broken Mirror* (from which "Semblance" is taken), which remains the best place to encounter at once his elusive heroines, his borrowed moneylenders, his transgressions, and predictable use of candelabra. He also wrote a tedious biography of Lermontov (translated into Spanish with the title, *El héroe sin tiempo*), which cemented his reputation in France. The translation of "Semblance" was attributed to Belasario Tregua, with multiple emendations by Urlihrt, Luini, and someone else. Of Beret's many works, the *Agraphia* committee used always to recommend three titles: *Rhapsody in Pink, Symmetry and the Diabologhs, Hotel Abîme.*

Annick Bérrichon (1888–2000)

Eloísa Betelgeuse (1950–1979) *a.k.a.* Eliza Beetlejuice (*née* Consuelo Inés Maspero), author of *The Chysalid Initiation, Perspective in Botteghe, Catalogue of the Annunciation.* Committed suicide on November 22, 1974, in Buenos Aires. Publication in French [?] and English earned her a universal reputation for . . . A sequence of posthumous poems, edited and published in 1980 with the title, *Gris gris. Tango Elegies.* The author of this note first encountered her famous sestina in 1997, and it was [almost immediately] translated into French by . . . Bettina Agutter.

Deborah Dubois Verdoux

Letter to Artemisia Gentileschi

Hilarión Curtis Ertebehere: A writer, dead almost six decades. *Agraphia*'s most assiduous contributor and its Canterville ghost. Indeed, he was more than just a contributor to Nicasio Urlihrt, who said he was "the legend I'd wanted to be" . . . To his other descendants, Curtis was just another Argentine writer, but according to another exegete, Federico Prosan, he was "The most extraordinary Latin American writer you can imagine: typical and, at the same time, completely atypical." Although none of Urlihrt's forefathers had his surname, it is certain he's Curtis's direct descendent, his grandson. (See also "The Seychelles.")

Urlihrt was a German from Bavaria: proof in the Almanach de Gotha

Eccles, Ciaran: wrote under countless pseudonyms, including Lord Swimmingpool, Eliseo Arias, Sabás Salazar, Sal Simpson.

Oliverio Lester: (see Liborio Treles).

Cora Beatriz Estrugamou. Primary studies at the Mallincrodt College then, immediately afterwards, lottery of cards, escoba de 15, truco, canasta, card routines. Backgammon. Chess. Go, Mahjong and Tarot, luck and anarchy. Never learns to draw. First happy book: *Unfavorable feast*. Later: *We Visited, Sleep of Night, Original Sins*.

Her poetical works. Her versatility. The little that's known about her. The pseudonyms.

A Night is the Lifetime Stars (Calderón), *Biography of the Imagination, Original Sins . . .*

The Place of Apparitions, her unfinished novel and a smattering of short stories, and *The Times*, which collects all her theatrical works (*Kropotkin's Closet*, etc), published under the pseudonyms, Clara Gazul, Elena Sombra. There are some legendary stories about Elena, some disseminated by her ex-husband, but it is certainly untrue that she resurfaced in Italy as the interior designer of the Gnu house (which her ex-husband, by then senile and reduced to a state of infancy, thought a belated tribute) (*Principles of the Imagination on the Other Side of Sleep*, translated into Spanish in the early seventies, in Chile).

Lord Swindon: see Museum, *Sherbet Aria*.

Felipe Luini (Buenos Aires, 1938). His first book, *Misery of a Realist*, won the [national award for unpublished literature] critics award. This was followed by *Stepping into the Dubious Daylight, Someone Else's Dream, Foolish Verses*, and *Reckonings of the Possible* (poetry). In 1992, the novel *Noisy Deaf*, which chronicles the adventures of a few Buenos Aires teachers during a vaccination campaign, won the municipal prize. In 1997, he was touted to be awarded for *The Redskins*, an atrabilious collection of short stories that didn't seem to have any endings, or which actually didn't have endings (since, according to the author, there was a secret unity that renders the collection a single novel), and which was therefore thought innovative, or reproductive of what was once innovative. The theme of the extermination of the local Indian populace counterpointed the extermination in the seventies of all talented primary school children. In the early 2000s, during his self-imposed exile in Barcelona, the author's last three works—the titles of which are all proper nouns—attracted both popular and critical attention. But [alas] we cannot recall the titles. It was the director of the adapted movie who used the title *Noisy Deaf* (movie title),

In the letters Eiralis refers to plagiarism

Irene Inauda: the journal's most recent [decent (a misprint)] contributor is a figure of widespread, even international, notoriety with a multifaceted profile [what the heck's a multifaceted profile?] that this brief annotation could hardly limn [or do justice to]. Born to a good Argentine family of the patrician class, she had early—one could even say immediate—access to the world of haute couture, of high society, and as she grew, so did her admiration for this world and the people in it so that, remarkably, when she was barely out of adolescence, she was already a seasoned socialite. Her parents and grandparents were and continue to be prominent cultural and political figures in Buenos Aires. In the early sixties, there wasn't an exhibition, parade, or other significant "happening" they didn't attend. And although her father, a prominent lawyer, used to undermine—as a patient does to his therapist—all these past ticker tape events and the part their family played in them, saying that the best thing about the era [decade] was the stuff that came out of the printing presses, she always felt she was a precocious [and privileged] witness of that era, and afterwards, a victim of the one that followed.

Eduardo Javier Manjares. Spanish writer and editor, born in Russia in 1939. After writing his first Catalan volume and an essay on the English translation of the poet Bernart de Ventadorn, Manjares founded—in more than one continent—quite a number of publishing houses with the honorable aim of reviving that exquisite though forgotten trade of literary piracy. Within Spain's piratical publication industry, his collections, Caliban, Etiquette, Distance, and—the most frequently discussed—Estrambote were unequaled. In 1975, he published *The Last Days of Ernest Fenollosa*, an imaginary chronicle about the sufferings of the man who made Ezra Pound believe he could translate Chinese poetry. Then, in 1978, there was *Southeast Postal*, a major collection of masterworks—half of them cryptic, half

211

touristical, the latter composed in melodic hendecasyllables—was inspired by a trip to various places in China and India. In one story, there's an Asturian living in Albi; in another, a Manchegan living in Laos; and in yet another, a Valencian in Cambridge and London. Such geographical versatility or promiscuity was perhaps the most appealing aspect of the collection, whose title is taken from one of the stories. The author himself believes this to be the case. Later, he began manifesting a double incapacity—as author and publisher—to the latest literary trends. His final publication (under the pseudonym: Andrés Zubillaga), *Concise Dictionary of Detectives*, was prompted by his passion for the kind of data that's correct, exact, the kind that makes a man seem wise. His hatred of progress, of technology, the Internet, made him a pariah. "I've been using an Underwood typewriter since I was twelve. The only literature I understand and admire is the acoustic kind: inspiration without style, *reality and typing*. But now that there's a fashion for imprecision, gracelessness, and such a paucity of great literary role models, and now that the Internet whips up the masses in an atavistic frenzy, I've become in my antiquity an ogre under a bridge, or less dramatically, a footnote.

Note: In 1956 in Buenos Aires and 1962 in Gerona (postmarked Bilbao), respectively, Nicasio Urlihrt and Javier Manjares published similar works under the same pseudonym, Macabru (See Macabru). The reason being that both Nicasio and Javier liked to be called Macabru in their respective cities. Macabru, an exotic, vaguely oriental appellation.

Cristóbal Niaras: expounding on the work and reputation of a critic of Niaras's eminence would exceed by far the space designated for these merely informative outlines, but because this rector's professional competence has been brought under continual scrutiny ever since his journal put that special issue in circulation . . .

Amadeo Arancibia Loayza (Buenos Aires, 1940—Buenos Aires, 1999). Discreet, fantasmal, and very prolific, Amadeo was known by the members or inductees at *Agraphia* as "Dos de Nosotros" or "Two of Us." [because] He was fat, victim of a hereditary obesity that caused him much professional inconvenience, in spite of his exquisite Spanish. "A translator of disarming honesty and a writer of such reticence" according to NU, "he deserved an honorary box in the River Plate theatre of neglect . . ." Only a single collection of poems: *Vereda de los impares.*

Neville Orpington: See Museum, *Sherbet Aria.* Along with Hector Hugh Monro (Saki) and Arthur Ronald Annesly Firbank, Neville Orpington was a cynosure among the group of English eccentrics that emerged at the beginning of the twentieth century. He came from a wealthy family, proud of its distinguished lineage and the fact their rustic roots remained firmly planted in the English countryside, despite the deracinating effects of the industrial revolution. The way he managed his fortune, squandering it in London in little over a decade, was what set him apart from his predecessors. This young dreamer disposed of his inheritance with Mediterranean, epicurean conviction, a treasure that took at least five generations of parsimonious Protestants to hoard. His only literary associate was the misanthropic Barbellion, who wrote *The Journal of a Disappointed Man*, who had a passion for entomology that accorded with Orpington's mania for collecting bric-a-brac. Orpington dedicated his last collection of short stories to him. More than merely a snob or an exhibitionist, Orpington's vanity and egocentrism were so great he would not deign to perform in public, which led to a paradox: private exhibitionism.

The complete list of Orpington's works is brief: *After Euphues, Nissus in Brobdignag, Maybe I'm Amazing, Svelte Lavendar and her Slender Sisters.* "Pimlico," which he wrote under a heteronym [Beauclerk], was the only story he took the trouble to rewrite thirty-three times: he called them his "Diabelli Variations."

Remo Sabatani [born in Gualeguaychú, Entre Ríos, from thence, it's all just myth]: once touted to be the world's greatest writer, he dashed that promise by only delivering at the end of his life what he called his "demora en tinto" or "belated ink," a wondrous achievement of arrogant display and inanity. The most mysterious of *Agraphia's* contributors, he was the model of the secluded writer for many of the stories in the anthology. According to his relatives, he is currently living in Davos. [[He'd be roughly the same age as Urlihrt, 73 or 74.]] Like other contributors, he had an evangelical enthusiasm for founding magazines and journals, above all throwaways: *The Manchurian Candidate, Gaucho Marx, Brother Marx* . . .

Sabatani, Remo: *Stepping into the Dubious Daylight, Plan for a Plagiarism, He who Counts the Syllables, Sonnets and Falsonnets, Notebook in Extremis, Novel with Three Endings and Seven Beginnings, The X-Positions.*

Bruno Scacchi: sizes and excesses (always either too big, too small, too much, too little) . . .

Lino Scacchi: a shy and reticent author of works Urlihrt valued for their "laconic richness." An illustrator and caricaturist (in pen and pencil), he was overshadowed by his overrated younger brother, Bruno. *Nondescriptions* [1972], *Idiomaties* [1979], and *Nondescriptions and Idiomaties* [1986].

Elena Siesta: see Cora Beatriz Estrugamou

Federico Prosan: FP's career really only begins, happily for him, around the time *Agraphia* begins its decline. Or as he boasted: Too young to be around, too old to be expelled . . . FP had therefore been "without acquaintance, without welcome, without farewell." Nevertheless, it was he who played the greatest role in disseminating most of the journal's "secrets" and those of the group behind it. Although Lester later denied it, Prosan, due to his remarkable academic delectation, thought himself a disciple. FP's books have achieved recognition in central Europe, Spain, even England and the United States. *Instead* and *Otherwise*, two collections of alternative versions of stories he'd already written, achieved—perhaps because the originals had been ignored—enormous success, both critically and commercially. Furthermore, he [also] compiled an anthology of the mistaken story, which was based on his hypothesis that every good collection contains "one incorrigable or irredeemable error."

César Quaglia Quiroge Valdés, see Zi Benno

Elijah Levi Sapirstein; see Lord Swindon, in Museum

Sal Simpson (see apocryphal biography in *Sherbet Aria*): pseudonym of Ciaran MacDuff, who was born in Ystradgynlais, Wales, in 1929, and died in Topanga Valley, California, in 1992, where he founded, twenty years before, the influential Tantrum Press, a publishing house that dedicated itself, from the very beginning, almost exclusively to indignation, a mission that today has spread to the world wide web via *The Internail*, a business run by his wife's adopted son, Yusuf Ystrad. After writing many serious novels that garnered little attention, he wrote a series of nine novels introducing a new character— Priscilla Grayce, alias Venus Constrictor—a kind of femme fatale, whose popularity guaranteed him not only prosperity, but exile and death, the latter preceded only two months by his companion, Memsahib Banian.

Una Traherne (better known as Arnu Popish Lemniscate): *Brief Biography of Imagination, Principles of Uncertainty Beyond the Dream, Theory and Practice of Jeopardy in Wales, Jaundice, From Anagnorisis to Delirium Tremens.* [[Another of Eiralis's errors, attributing Una's works to Eliphas.]]

Born in Wuthering Heights, Una was educated by an indulgent Presbyterian instructor and thought discipline by the preacher of a provincial vicarage. The great prestige of her treatise, *Visions of Imagination Beyond the Dream*, may be the result of its being attributed to her mortal enemy, Eliphas Morph . . .

Belisario Tregua: [is] known—insofar as an artisan can be known— for his translations that, over the course of nearly three decades, led to the homogenization of all mystical literature published in Buenos Aires. *The Dreadmist*, a magisterial tome of disenchantment, describes all the liturgy and bacchanalia that typified Argentina's dark ages. His only publication, *13 Attempts to Abolish the Present*, is, despite its ingenious premise, one of the worst books to read in the Argentine literary canon.

After his book of poems, *Prosodia*, went unnoticed, he began writing briefs for current affairs magazines. Shortly afterwards, he published a book, *False Steps*, a collection of short stories, remarkable for their sober style, precision, liveliness, in which—whether by conscious effort or an impulse resulting from a combination of the dream life and the encyclopedia of anxiety—each word seems to be in the wrong place . . . The journal *Scalp*. In 1989, OL moved to Italy, where he launched the publication, *Popolo Norte*. His *Eyelet for a Pendulum* collects together all his journals, diaries, and musical criticism: the ostentatious volume that X, the skeptic, who was a lot closer to Z of "All your nerves" compiled for Tintagel, publishing house of Eduardo Javier Manjares's . . . from page to friar, and onwards from there
In 1997, Faber & Faber published Instead—*The B Side of the World Book of Lies . . . Instead Alternate Takes* [in America], Tantrum Press *Otherwise & Instead: Both Sides Now. Alternate Takes of America*

Nicasio Urlihrt (pseudonym of Mario Arrón Teischer) (Nurlihrt, Septimo Mir, Uter Pegasus, Upper Lippius, Aspargus, Hesper Vegetalis, Everlasting Koba) The one who counts the beats and syllables, indisputable representative of the greats of obscure literature, Nicasio originally wanted to be among their detractors and antagonists. It's no surprise he produced an excessively refined and corrected volume of poetry with the title, *Between Clearings, 1958–1991*, from which he excluded all the "social poetry" he'd written in the last four years. He wrote at my side . . .

Pushkiniana (III?)

Stanza operated on (as they say)
Be reasonable,
Luini: Agraphia reposes.
(luckily their projects are all
Barratries of prose.)
But the Stanza will prevail,
The arpeggio that addresses
The slighted submission you bore
To that blindest of publishers.

Parasites of prestige
They keep yours well hidden
It seems (to your great disadvantage).
So the lineage led to litigation
—Kleptolalia, Cryptogamia—.
That perfidious defamatory game.

#29

Delayed *relief* in the story of Rebatet's music:

"Boulez—who was not yet thirty—provided an example, which fitted well with the accounts of his countless enemies, especially the 'classical' dodecaphonists, of those sessions he devoted to vomiting out diatribes: 'Let's leave them to surrender themselves, alone or in groups, to frenetic, arrhythmic masturbations. They don't ask more of us: they know only how to count to twelve, and then in multiples of twelve. Nothing even remotely interesting may remain.'" (Compare with Oliverio Lester's preface.)

Final. All in: *The Legend of the Writers without Stories*
(in the reproaches of the title, Joseph Roth (*Holy Drinker*). Not

wholly feasible)

Certitude not yet reached

24. Ekaterinodar, April 23, 1899 [sic]

While the revolution (if one can call it that) was progressing, Ouspensky—before meeting Gurdjuieff, and before he was Ouspensky—lived in Ekaterinodar, "the cheapest place in Russia," he wrote, a place where it was possible to indulge one's tastes, to luxuriate, a city where he dedicated himself to observation, so that he could note how it contrasted with the ferocious cost of living, for example, and consequent spiritual enervation that typified the rest of mother Russia. Such is life. That wasn't Europe. Or was it? And did it really matter? Ouspensky, the greatest economist of the twentieth century, whom everyone in that great wasteland nonetheless denigrated—everyone in that Grand Hotel Abîme, property of Lukács and Houdini—was at least famous in Moscow, his native city, famous and respected and referred to by his given name—perro pila—by the police—manto negro—because . . . Because, when drunk, instead of provoking fights, he'd endeavor to stop them.

In the roguish and puerile kingdom of speculation and despection.

Please, don't tell me about the translations. I don't want to know. To be informed of the disastrous oversight of writing without an agent or publisher. I don't care if Prosan is translating it for both Gallimard and Faber & Faber. In fact, I don't even consider the news to be bad. I have none of the dermatological symptoms of envy. I was born and raised—what a disappointment—having never experienced an outbreak. Nothing, nada, zilch. The definitive proof of the decline is, after all, the dodecaphony of the fault: *The loss of the kingdom that was only for me.*

One time, we were the last ones left, waiting for a performance of I know not what. Tango bar. Eduardo Rovira. Café Concert. Gustavo Kerestezachi. A swap, some tickets in exchange for a notice (an ad, placed, in case I ever became famous in Spain). It was a Friday. The "we" were Nurlihrt, Luini, and me. We were the last ones there, waiting for who knows what. *Friday nights*, said Luini, *bring promises of naked shoulders and champagne, and that's what we like.* Let's say Viamonte and Reconquista. We went down quite a few steps, staggering, tarrying, reeling, because we decided to go drunk, so even those few steps we managed to negotiate without a hitch, seemed like many. A scene within touching distance. An upright piano. We took our seats and asked for the most expensive. A woman took care of it, a lady who was surely famous and whom we treated as if we knew she was famous. Then the waiter came, whom we treated as if we were the ones who were famous.

An adult male was singing. He had striking eyes and a hippopotamus's gaze. He was holding a glossy bag for some reason, and was wearing a horrible violet and beige cravat. We'd seen him before on occasion. He'd grown so fat in the last few months, he was struggling to sing, whether standing or sitting. Grizzled and rotund, with two lateral streaks of dandruff on the collar, he tried to appear relaxed speaking English, although he mispronounced almost every consonant and distorted all the vowels. Like Charlie Parker, he was lacking a canine, which lack its base metal replacement threw into relief. There I met my tenant, my landlady here: Chiquita Zucco Lezcano, whom the reader—although I don't provide a key—will recognize as being better known by the name, Ilaria Prior.

DON'T BOTHER ME ANYMORE WITH YOUR DOUBTS AND JUST PAY THEM FOR THE TRIP. IF YOU DID IT WITH THE MAGNANIMOUS AND SPECU-LATIVE IGNORANCE OF AN INVOLUNTARY PARIAH, LEAVE IT TO THEM TO DO THE WORK OF TRULY APPRECIATING IT. BLESSED BE THE LAST PAYCHECK.

26. Colony. December 15, 1958 (sic)

Serendipity. I am going: to Sarandipti del Yi. Island.

Arrecife. Castling (no traveling to the North Pole on a tricycle: (??!) To Sri Lanka in a skiff like back in the days of yore. I dressed in manly robes. Horripilated. Arundel. From here. Dying of pain, since they don't keep out the cold. Hither: Ekaterinodar, the paradise (which is ever the cheapest principality, thanks to speculative business dealings, and hence, the wealthiest in Europe, but the condominium still managed between the Alpine and Uralic authorities still isn't mine: I [who] inherited nothing. Adir. Nadir. (Note *adir* is a verb and *nadir* not.) Abur. So long. No more the old oversight of Juvenal's satire. I want to stay asleep. Sleep the siesta. To love. To fear. Elena systole, Elena diastole. Rítmo hesicástico. Suddenly I noticed—yes sir, pray tell—that it's a matter of conversion (that no, that he hasn't seen) the light of implacable Zion, having seen the abyss, the serrated cesura, sitzfleisch, he waits to see his friend to hand him the handsaw (toothed. The stammering fern.) Gather the diminishing desire to finish! At this time of night, this Edomitish night, in the Washington Barbot, político colorado, I welcome you to my *Bar Mitzvah*. Ruined by the sight of this chain of hotels—of which the one that now shadows me isn't even famous—I give up. Cualunque. On embarking, on taking a leap, I'd like to make my way gropingly when—as I already said—I head for Sri Lanka. Back in Serendipity del Yi. In a skiff. A rolling skiff or gunboat, the means of escape, and to some—some followers—the means of giving up. Followers like a supporting cast. I who once had asthma. Asthma and Family, book of a graduate friend I once had, who, once in a while, did corrections for me. Corinaldesi, proceeds from the neglected friend. Grébano! But who will have done—I now wonder—the technical revision (as we said before)? What neglect! *Which reminds me*, the appointment I made—to please the others— for a medical checkup is still pending, although it's still some time away. My art doesn't stop for checkups. It doesn't leave footprints. Not a single lively idea lies in its wake. How marvelous! It finishes them off without having to kill them.

1997–2003

Luis Chitarroni was born in Buenos Aires in 1958. He is a writer, critic, and editor, and has to date published two novels and two collections of nonfiction and critical writing.

Darren Koolman is a poet and literary translator from Spanish, French, and Dutch.

SELECTED DALKEY ARCHIVE TITLES

MICHAL AJVAZ, *The Golden Age.*
    The Other City.
PIERRE ALBERT-BIROT, *Grabinoulor.*
YUZ ALESHKOVSKY, *Kangaroo.*
FELIPE ALFAU, *Chromos.*
    Locos.
IVAN ÂNGELO, *The Celebration.*
    The Tower of Glass.
ANTÓNIO LOBO ANTUNES, *Knowledge of Hell.*
    The Splendor of Portugal.
ALAIN ARIAS-MISSON, *Theatre of Incest.*
JOHN ASHBERY AND JAMES SCHUYLER,
    A Nest of Ninnies.
ROBERT ASHLEY, *Perfect Lives.*
GABRIELA AVIGUR-ROTEM, *Heatwave*
    and Crazy Birds.
DJUNA BARNES, *Ladies Almanack.*
    Ryder.
JOHN BARTH, *LETTERS.*
    Sabbatical.
DONALD BARTHELME, *The King.*
    Paradise.
SVETISLAV BASARA, *Chinese Letter.*
MIQUEL BAUÇÀ, *The Siege in the Room.*
RENÉ BELLETTO, *Dying.*
MAREK BIEŃCZYK, *Transparency.*
ANDREI BITOV, *Pushkin House.*
ANDREJ BLATNIK, *You Do Understand.*
LOUIS PAUL BOON, *Chapel Road.*
    My Little War.
    Summer in Termuren.
ROGER BOYLAN, *Killoyle.*
IGNÁCIO DE LOYOLA BRANDÃO,
    Anonymous Celebrity.
    Zero.
BONNIE BREMSER, *Troia: Mexican Memoirs.*
CHRISTINE BROOKE-ROSE, *Amalgamemnon.*
BRIGID BROPHY, *In Transit.*
GERALD L. BRUNS, *Modern Poetry and*
    the Idea of Language.
GABRIELLE BURTON, *Heartbreak Hotel.*
MICHEL BUTOR, *Degrees.*
    Mobile.
G. CABRERA INFANTE, *Infante's Inferno.*
    Three Trapped Tigers.
JULIETA CAMPOS,
    The Fear of Losing Eurydice.
ANNE CARSON, *Eros the Bittersweet.*
ORLY CASTEL-BLOOM, *Dolly City.*
LOUIS-FERDINAND CÉLINE, *Castle to Castle.*
    Conversations with Professor Y.
    London Bridge.
    Normance.
    North.
    Rigadoon.
MARIE CHAIX, *The Laurels of Lake Constance.*
HUGO CHARTERIS, *The Tide Is Right.*
ERIC CHEVILLARD, *Demolishing Nisard.*
MARC CHOLODENKO, *Mordechai Schamz.*
JOSHUA COHEN, *Witz.*
EMILY HOLMES COLEMAN, *The Shutter*
    of Snow.
ROBERT COOVER, *A Night at the Movies.*
STANLEY CRAWFORD, *Log of the S.S. The*
    Mrs Unguentine.
    Some Instructions to My Wife.
RENÉ CREVEL, *Putting My Foot in It.*
RALPH CUSACK, *Cadenza.*
NICHOLAS DELBANCO, *The Count of Concord.*
    Sherbrookes.
NIGEL DENNIS, *Cards of Identity.*

PETER DIMOCK, *A Short Rhetoric for*
    Leaving the Family.
ARIEL DORFMAN, *Konfidenz.*
COLEMAN DOWELL,
    Island People.
    Too Much Flesh and Jabez.
ARKADII DRAGOMOSHCHENKO, *Dust.*
RIKKI DUCORNET, *The Complete*
    Butcher's Tales.
    The Fountains of Neptune.
    The Jade Cabinet.
    Phosphor in Dreamland.
WILLIAM EASTLAKE, *The Bamboo Bed.*
    Castle Keep.
    Lyric of the Circle Heart.
JEAN ECHENOZ, *Chopin's Move.*
STANLEY ELKIN, *A Bad Man.*
    Criers and Kibitzers, Kibitzers
    and Criers.
    The Dick Gibson Show.
    The Franchiser.
    The Living End.
    Mrs. Ted Bliss.
FRANÇOIS EMMANUEL, *Invitation to a*
    Voyage.
SALVADOR ESPRIU, *Ariadne in the*
    Grotesque Labyrinth.
LESLIE A. FIEDLER, *Love and Death in*
    the American Novel.
JUAN FILLOY, *Op Oloop.*
ANDY FITCH, *Pop Poetics.*
GUSTAVE FLAUBERT, *Bouvard and Pécuchet.*
KASS FLEISHER, *Talking out of School.*
FORD MADOX FORD,
    The March of Literature.
JON FOSSE, *Aliss at the Fire.*
    Melancholy.
MAX FRISCH, *I'm Not Stiller.*
    Man in the Holocene.
CARLOS FUENTES, *Christopher Unborn.*
    Distant Relations.
    Terra Nostra.
    Where the Air Is Clear.
TAKEHIKO FUKUNAGA, *Flowers of Grass.*
WILLIAM GADDIS, *J R.*
    The Recognitions.
JANICE GALLOWAY, *Foreign Parts.*
    The Trick Is to Keep Breathing.
WILLIAM H. GASS, *Cartesian Sonata*
    and Other Novellas.
    Finding a Form.
    A Temple of Texts.
    The Tunnel.
    Willie Masters' Lonesome Wife.
GÉRARD GAVARRY, *Hoppla! 1 2 3.*
ETIENNE GILSON,
    The Arts of the Beautiful.
    Forms and Substances in the Arts.
C. S. GISCOMBE, *Giscome Road.*
    Here.
DOUGLAS GLOVER, *Bad News of the Heart.*
WITOLD GOMBROWICZ,
    A Kind of Testament.
PAULO EMÍLIO SALES GOMES, *P's Three*
    Women.
GEORGI GOSPODINOV, *Natural Novel.*
JUAN GOYTISOLO, *Count Julian.*
    Juan the Landless.
    Makbara.
    Marks of Identity.

FOR A FULL LIST OF PUBLICATIONS, VISIT:
www.dalkeyarchive.com

SELECTED DALKEY ARCHIVE TITLES

HENRY GREEN, *Back.*
Blindness.
Concluding.
Doting.
Nothing.
JACK GREEN, *Fire the Bastards!*
JIŘÍ GRUŠA, *The Questionnaire.*
MELA HARTWIG, *Am I a Redundant*
Human Being?
JOHN HAWKES, *The Passion Artist.*
Whistlejacket.
ELIZABETH HEIGHWAY, ED., *Contemporary*
Georgian Fiction.
ALEKSANDAR HEMON, ED.,
Best European Fiction.
AIDAN HIGGINS, *Balcony of Europe.*
Blind Man's Bluff
Bornholm Night-Ferry.
Flotsam and Jetsam.
Langrishe, Go Down.
Scenes from a Receding Past.
KEIZO HINO, *Isle of Dreams.*
KAZUSHI HOSAKA, *Plainsong.*
ALDOUS HUXLEY, *Antic Hay.*
Crome Yellow.
Point Counter Point.
Those Barren Leaves.
Time Must Have a Stop.
NAOYUKI II, *The Shadow of a Blue Cat.*
GERT JONKE, *The Distant Sound.*
Geometric Regional Novel.
Homage to Czerny.
The System of Vienna.
JACQUES JOUET, *Mountain R.*
Savage.
Upstaged.
MIEKO KANAI, *The Word Book.*
YORAM KANIUK, *Life on Sandpaper.*
HUGH KENNER, *Flaubert.*
Joyce and Beckett: The Stoic Comedians.
Joyce's Voices.
DANILO KIŠ, *The Attic.*
Garden, Ashes.
The Lute and the Scars
Psalm 44.
A Tomb for Boris Davidovich.
ANITA KONKKA, *A Fool's Paradise.*
GEORGE KONRÁD, *The City Builder.*
TADEUSZ KONWICKI, *A Minor Apocalypse.*
The Polish Complex.
MENIS KOUMANDAREAS, *Koula.*
ELAINE KRAF, *The Princess of 72nd Street.*
JIM KRUSOE, *Iceland.*
AYŞE KULIN, *Farewell: A Mansion in*
Occupied Istanbul.
EMILIO LASCANO TEGUI, *On Elegance*
While Sleeping.
ERIC LAURRENT, *Do Not Touch.*
VIOLETTE LEDUC, *La Bâtarde.*
EDOUARD LEVÉ, *Autoportrait.*
Suicide.
MARIO LEVI, *Istanbul Was a Fairy Tale.*
DEBORAH LEVY, *Billy and Girl.*
JOSÉ LEZAMA LIMA, *Paradiso.*
ROSA LIKSOM, *Dark Paradise.*
OSMAN LINS, *Avalovara.*
The Queen of the Prisons of Greece.
ALF MAC LOCHLAINN,
The Corpus in the Library.
Out of Focus.
RON LOEWINSOHN, *Magnetic Field(s).*
MINA LOY, *Stories and Essays of Mina Loy.*

D. KEITH MANO, *Take Five.*
MICHELINE AHARONIAN MARCOM,
The Mirror in the Well.
BEN MARCUS,
The Age of Wire and String.
WALLACE MARKFIELD,
Teitlebaum's Window.
To an Early Grave.
DAVID MARKSON, *Reader's Block.*
Wittgenstein's Mistress.
CAROLE MASO, *AVA.*
LADISLAV MATEJKA AND KRYSTYNA
POMORSKA, EDS.,
Readings in Russian Poetics:
Formalist and Structuralist Views.
HARRY MATHEWS, *Cigarettes.*
The Conversions.
The Human Country: New and
Collected Stories.
The Journalist.
My Life in CIA.
Singular Pleasures.
The Sinking of the Odradek
Stadium.
Tlooth.
JOSEPH MCELROY,
Night Soul and Other Stories.
ABDELWAHAB MEDDEB, *Talismano.*
GERHARD MEIER, *Isle of the Dead.*
HERMAN MELVILLE, *The Confidence-Man.*
AMANDA MICHALOPOULOU, *I'd Like.*
STEVEN MILLHAUSER, *The Barnum Museum.*
In the Penny Arcade.
RALPH J. MILLS, JR., *Essays on Poetry.*
MOMUS, *The Book of Jokes.*
CHRISTINE MONTALBETTI, *The Origin of Man.*
Western.
OLIVE MOORE, *Spleen.*
NICHOLAS MOSLEY, *Accident.*
Assassins.
Catastrophe Practice.
Experience and Religion.
A Garden of Trees.
Hopeful Monsters.
Imago Bird.
Impossible Object.
Inventing God.
Judith.
Look at the Dark.
Natalie Natalia.
Serpent.
Time at War.
WARREN MOTTE,
Fables of the Novel: French Fiction
since 1990.
Fiction Now: The French Novel in
the 21st Century.
Oulipo: A Primer of Potential
Literature.
GERALD MURNANE, *Barley Patch.*
Inland.
YVES NAVARRE, *Our Share of Time.*
Sweet Tooth.
DOROTHY NELSON, *In Night's City.*
Tar and Feathers.
ESHKOL NEVO, *Homesick.*
WILFRIDO D. NOLLEDO, *But for the Lovers.*
FLANN O'BRIEN, *At Swim-Two-Birds.*
The Best of Myles.
The Dalkey Archive.
The Hard Life.
The Poor Mouth.

FOR A FULL LIST OF PUBLICATIONS, VISIT:
www.dalkeyarchive.com

SELECTED DALKEY ARCHIVE TITLES

The Third Policeman.
CLAUDE OLLIER, *The Mise-en-Scène.*
Wert and the Life Without End.
GIOVANNI ORELLI, *Walaschek's Dream.*
PATRIK OUŘEDNÍK, *Europeana.*
The Opportune Moment, 1855.
BORIS PAHOR, *Necropolis.*
FERNANDO DEL PASO, *News from the Empire.*
Palinuro of Mexico.
ROBERT PINGET, *The Inquisitory.*
Mahu or The Material.
Trio.
MANUEL PUIG, *Betrayed by Rita Hayworth.*
The Buenos Aires Affair.
Heartbreak Tango.
RAYMOND QUENEAU, *The Last Days.*
Odile.
Pierrot Mon Ami.
Saint Glinglin.
ANN QUIN, *Berg.*
Passages.
Three.
Tripticks.
ISHMAEL REED, *The Free-Lance Pallbearers.*
The Last Days of Louisiana Red.
Ishmael Reed: The Plays.
Juice!
Reckless Eyeballing.
The Terrible Threes.
The Terrible Twos.
Yellow Back Radio Broke-Down.
JASIA REICHARDT, *15 Journeys Warsaw
to London.*
NOËLLE REVAZ, *With the Animals.*
JOÃO UBALDO RIBEIRO, *House of the
Fortunate Buddhas.*
JEAN RICARDOU, *Place Names.*
RAINER MARIA RILKE, *The Notebooks of
Malte Laurids Brigge.*
JULIÁN RÍOS, *The House of Ulysses.*
Larva: A Midsummer Night's Babel.
Poundemonium.
Procession of Shadows.
AUGUSTO ROA BASTOS, *I the Supreme.*
DANIËL ROBBERECHTS, *Arriving in Avignon.*
JEAN ROLIN, *The Explosion of the
Radiator Hose.*
OLIVIER ROLIN, *Hotel Crystal.*
ALIX CLEO ROUBAUD, *Alix's Journal.*
JACQUES ROUBAUD, *The Form of a
City Changes Faster, Alas, Than
the Human Heart.*
The Great Fire of London.
Hortense in Exile.
Hortense Is Abducted.
The Loop.
Mathematics:
The Plurality of Worlds of Lewis.
The Princess Hoppy.
Some Thing Black.
RAYMOND ROUSSEL, *Impressions of Africa.*
VEDRANA RUDAN, *Night.*
STIG SÆTERBAKKEN, *Siamese.*
Self Control.
LYDIE SALVAYRE, *The Company of Ghosts.*
The Lecture.
The Power of Flies.
LUIS RAFAEL SÁNCHEZ,
Macho Camacho's Beat.
SEVERO SARDUY, *Cobra & Maitreya.*

NATHALIE SARRAUTE,
Do You Hear Them?
Martereau.
The Planetarium.
ARNO SCHMIDT, *Collected Novellas.*
Collected Stories.
Nobodaddy's Children.
Two Novels.
ASAF SCHURR, *Motti.*
GAIL SCOTT, *My Paris.*
DAMION SEARLS, *What We Were Doing
and Where We Were Going.*
JUNE AKERS SEESE,
Is This What Other Women Feel Too?
What Waiting Really Means.
BERNARD SHARE, *Inish.*
Transit.
VIKTOR SHKLOVSKY, *Bowstring.*
Knight's Move.
*A Sentimental Journey:
Memoirs 1917–1922.*
Energy of Delusion: A Book on Plot.
Literature and Cinematography.
Theory of Prose.
Third Factory.
Zoo, or Letters Not about Love.
PIERRE SINIAC, *The Collaborators.*
KJERSTI A. SKOMSVOLD, *The Faster I Walk,
the Smaller I Am.*
JOSEF ŠKVORECKÝ, *The Engineer of
Human Souls.*
GILBERT SORRENTINO,
Aberration of Starlight.
Blue Pastoral.
Crystal Vision.
*Imaginative Qualities of Actual
Things.*
Mulligan Stew.
Pack of Lies.
Red the Fiend.
The Sky Changes.
Something Said.
Splendide-Hôtel.
Steelwork.
Under the Shadow.
W. M. SPACKMAN, *The Complete Fiction.*
ANDRZEJ STASIUK, *Dukla.*
Fado.
GERTRUDE STEIN, *The Making of Americans.*
A Novel of Thank You.
LARS SVENDSEN, *A Philosophy of Evil.*
PIOTR SZEWC, *Annihilation.*
GONÇALO M. TAVARES, *Jerusalem.*
Joseph Walser's Machine.
*Learning to Pray in the Age of
Technique.*
LUCIAN DAN TEODOROVICI,
Our Circus Presents . . .
NIKANOR TERATOLOGEN, *Assisted Living.*
STEFAN THEMERSON, *Hobson's Island.*
The Mystery of the Sardine.
Tom Harris.
TAEKO TOMIOKA, *Building Waves.*
JOHN TOOMEY, *Sleepwalker.*
JEAN-PHILIPPE TOUSSAINT, *The Bathroom.*
Camera.
Monsieur.
Reticence.
Running Away.
Self-Portrait Abroad.
Television.
The Truth about Marie.

FOR A FULL LIST OF PUBLICATIONS, VISIT:
www.dalkeyarchive.com

DUMITRU TSEPENEAG, *Hotel Europa.*
The Necessary Marriage.
Pigeon Post.
Vain Art of the Fugue.
ESTHER TUSQUETS, *Stranded.*
DUBRAVKA UGRESIC, *Lend Me Your Character.*
Thank You for Not Reading.
TOR ULVEN, *Replacement.*
MATI UNT, *Brecht at Night.*
Diary of a Blood Donor.
Things in the Night.
ÁLVARO URIBE AND OLIVIA SEARS, EDS.,
Best of Contemporary Mexican Fiction.
ELOY URROZ, *Friction.*
The Obstacles.
LUISA VALENZUELA, *Dark Desires and
the Others.*
He Who Searches.
PAUL VERHAEGHEN, *Omega Minor.*
AGLAJA VETERANYI, *Why the Child Is
Cooking in the Polenta.*
BORIS VIAN, *Heartsnatcher.*
LLORENÇ VILLALONGA, *The Dolls' Room.*
TOOMAS VINT, *An Unending Landscape.*
ORNELA VORPSI, *The Country Where No
One Ever Dies.*
AUSTRYN WAINHOUSE, *Hedyphagetica.*
CURTIS WHITE, *America's Magic Mountain.*
The Idea of Home.
Memories of My Father Watching TV.
Requiem.

DIANE WILLIAMS, *Excitability:
Selected Stories.*
Romancer Erector.
DOUGLAS WOOLF, *Wall to Wall.*
Ya! & John-Juan.
JAY WRIGHT, *Polynomials and Pollen.*
*The Presentable Art of Reading
Absence.*
PHILIP WYLIE, *Generation of Vipers.*
MARGUERITE YOUNG, *Angel in the Forest.*
Miss MacIntosh, My Darling.
REYOUNG, *Unbabbling.*
VLADO ŽABOT, *The Succubus.*
ZORAN ŽIVKOVIĆ, *Hidden Camera.*
LOUIS ZUKOFSKY, *Collected Fiction.*
VITOMIL ZUPAN, *Minuet for Guitar.*
SCOTT ZWIREN, *God Head.*